DATE DUE

TH...
S...

THE DARK STORM

Kris Greene

St. Martin's Paperbacks

This is a work of fiction. All of the characters, organizations, and events portrayed in this novel are either products of the author's imagination or are used fictitiously.

THE DARK STORM

Copyright © 2010 by Kris Greene.
Excerpt from *The Demon Hunt* copyright © 2010 by Kris Greene.

For information address St. Martin's Press, 175 Fifth Avenue, New York, NY 10010.

ISBN: 978-0-312-94422-3

Printed in the United States of America

St. Martin's Paperbacks edition / February 2010

St. Martin's Paperbacks are published by St. Martin's Press, 175 Fifth Avenue, New York, NY 10010.

10 9 8 7 6 5 4 3 2 1

THE SEVEN-DAY SEIGE

In the seventeenth century a supernatural anomaly swept across Europe, leaving chaos and death in its wake. The anomaly finally settled in Naples, Italy, where it manifested itself as a storm that would blot out the very sun. The locals called it the Dark Storm.

So powerful was this Storm's fury that it created a rip in the dimensional barrier between the realms of men and demons and loosed the forces of hell on earth. The demons wrought havoc and destruction in an attempt to secure a hold in the realm of men.

Leaders from the surrounding provinces dispatched troops of men to battle these new foes only to have them slaughtered or bent to the wills of the dark things that had come through the rift. With most of their forces being decimated, the leaders of the great nations decided that it would take more than ordinary soldiers to combat the threat. Emissaries from all the lands touched by the demons assembled in Vatican City to petition an audience with the good and wise Pope Alexander X.

The pope was a pillar when it came to his devotion to his faith, but even he understood that it would take more than prayers to repel the invasion. It would take steel along with the word of God to drive their foes out. Pope Alexander dispatched his twelve most trusted cardinals to the farthest corners of the world to gather warriors who were pure of heart, unwavering in their faith and touched by the hand of their lord to stand against the threat. These twelve men each took a vow of secrecy and complete loyalty to the church and became the Order of the Knights of Christ. In addition to their God-given talents they were entrusted with one of the Vatican's most closely guarded secrets, the weapons of the First Guard.

The First Guard had been composed of twelve Roman soldiers who empathized with Jesus and his mission, so they secretly protected him up until the time when they were discovered and executed for their crimes. The weapons were the things they held dearest to them, and so said to carry the strength of their faith within them. Armed with these items the Knights had become the ultimate weapon of the church, but it was from the thirteenth that they drew their strength.

Bishop Michael Francisco. The Bishop was the favorite amongst Alexander's initiates within the church and one of his most skilled captains on the battlefield. The Bishop was whispered to be a bloodthirsty fanatic who employed unsavory methods in his insane quest to spread the word of his pope, but because of Alexander's fondness for him none dared challenge him. It was he who was chosen to lead the Knights of Christ and wield one of the church's greatest treasures, the Nimrod, a jeweled trident of untold power.

There were many stories about the Nimrod, but the most common and closest to the truth was that it was forged by saints and cooled in the tears of angels. It was a gift to Neptune, the true king of storms and guardian of the seas. Neptune held the trident for nearly a millennium, drawing the attention and animosity of the death god Thanos.

The jealous god recruited a young Egyptian warlock named Ezrah and his pirate crew, the Sheut, to wrest the trident from Neptune. Ezrah was able to successfully steal the trident but was captured by the Templar knights before he could deliver his parcel. The Egyptian was made to watch as his crew were locked belowdecks on their ship, the *Jihad*, and burned alive. When the massive boat was reduced to little more than a smoldering frame, the Templar bound Ezrah's hands and feet and cast him back to the very seas he'd plundered for so long. The Templar had left Ezrah to drown, but what they didn't know was that the death god also had an agenda.

All the slaves who had been rescued from the *Jihad* had been put to death to cover the story of the murders, save for the defiant young boy, who amused the Templar captain. The boy was taken back to Vatican City and brought to stand before Alexander, who held the office of cardinal back then. The cardinal too was intrigued by the boy's defiance and decided to take him on as a student. Alexander gave him the Christian name Michael Francisco and began him on the path of Christ.

Under Alexander, Michael proved himself to be a worthy Catholic and devout in his newfound faith, soon rising to the rank of Bishop. Though he was one of the quickest and most accomplished studies in Alexander's charges, this was only part of the reason Michael was chosen to lead the Knights. Like Neptune, Michael had been a child of the sea, and just as the cardinals had hoped, the sleeping weapon came to life in Michael's hands. Blessed by his holy father and armed with anointed weapons, the Bishop led his Knights into the eye of the storm.

The battle that followed was a historical one, but never recorded in the books of men. For seven days and six nights, the two sides clashed, neither yielding nor gaining ground. But on the seventh night, the Knights turned the tide and the demons' strength began to waver. Victory was finally in sight.

Though one of the most devoted of the pope's follow-ers, the Bishop was also human and subject to flaw. His captain and closest friend, Titus, arranged a secret meet-ing between the Bishop and the demon lord Belthon. Belthon promised to bestow upon the Bishop the power of the gods in exchange for an unholy alliance that would drive the other demons out and allow Belthon a small path of the world for himself. The Bishop reasoned that it would be a small sacrifice when measured against the millions of souls he would be able to cleanse with his new power. He accepted the demon's offer, which proved to be his own undoing.

Being loyal to the Bishop, the Knights followed him blindly, never knowing of the bargain between him and the dark lord. When the demons had been vanquished down to a few hordes, Titus decided to change the terms of the agreement. Belthon would have his small victory, but it was Titus who would become the god. Under the cover of darkness, Titus took up the Nimrod and struck down the Bishop.

As the Bishop lay bleeding out onto the cold and rain-soaked earth, he had some parting words for his one-time friend. "Hear me and hear me well, for these words shall haunt you till the end of your days. You've set out to steal my weapon and my power, but that which is one can never be parted," the Bishop sneered. The closer he got to death, the more violent the storm became. "I curse you, Titus, murderer of your brother." The Bishop crawled to Titus' feet. Both Knights and demons recoiled, but Titus stood firm. Even when the Bishop was standing eye level with him, Titus never budged. "So you have stricken me down with the Nimrod," the Bishop continued. "Know that its same unforgiving points shall also know the taste of your blood. And when the day comes, it shall be me staring into your eyes as you take your last breaths." The light faded from the Bishop's eyes and he crumbled in a heap at Titus' feet.

With a knowing smile Belthon called forth the Sheut to imprison the soul of the Bishop to place with the others they had already captured during the siege. The life forces of the holy men would be ferried to the dead lands to serve King Morbius' dark designs. But when the wraiths tried to collect the Bishop's soul a most unexpected thing occurred: the Nimrod flared to life. As it turned out, the weapon wasn't quite ready to part with its wielder. Both Knights and demons watched in shock as the spirit of the Bishop was sucked into the trident.

A Knight called Redfeather, who represented the buffalo hunters, took up the trident and was immediately consumed by its power. Hearing the whispers of the Bishop from the great beyond, Redfeather turned the weapon on the betrayer. Redfeather's strike rang true, sinking deep into Titus' chest, but the blow was an untrained one and the center point broke off in the chest of the betrayer and the magic went wild, slaying both friend and foe. Only when the Bishop's thirst was sated did the trident go still, taking the storm with it and closing the rift. Most of the demons were destroyed or sucked back through the rift. The few who managed to escape retreated to the farthest corners of the world, where they would regroup and prepare for the day when they would again seek to take control of the world of men. Nearly four hundred years later, their time is at hand.

CHAPTER ONE

Run, the thought exploded so loud in her head that her temples ached. She turned to shout a warning to her cousin Michal, but his rib bones had pierced the soft flesh of his stomach. The second shot separated his shoulder from his collarbone. Michal fell over, lifeless eyes staring up at his cousin. Her heart cried for him to get up, but she knew that he was too weak in the blood to heal the wound.

The sirens in the distance snapped her head around. She could see the flashing lights in the distance, but there would be no salvation from the law. Another bullet shattered the window of the car she was standing next to, causing her to drop. Her back rested against the car with her package hugged tightly to her breasts. She could not see her cousin's murderer, but she knew he was out there and she would be next on his list unless she made her move.

De Mona darted across the street, holding the hemp-bound package close. The sharp scent of fresh cloves singed her nose, but it was a necessary evil. When she hit the street she was blinded by lights as a speeding car plowed towards her. The driver slammed on his brakes but couldn't stop in time. The impact sent De Mona flying through the air and skidding down the street before she finally slammed into the fender of a parked car.

"Dear God!" the driver shouted, jumping from the late-model Ford. When he took in the prone form of the girl he prayed that she was still alive, but at the speed he'd been going when he hit her it didn't look good. In the distance police sirens sounded, and they were getting closer by the minute. The man had barely checked her for a pulse when the girl's eyes popped open. In one swift motion she was back on her feet and scanning the block for danger. She still didn't see her cousin's murderer, but she knew he was out there waiting for her. Picking up the burlap sack, she began backing away cautiously.

"Jesus, are you okay? I didn't even see you." The driver approached her. "Listen." He looked off and saw the flashing police lights in the distance. "Help should be here any minute. If you're okay I'm just gonna—" That was as far as he got before a bullet struck him in the right cheek and sprayed De Mona with his blood. Eerily the darkness rolled forward and swallowed the driver's body.

A tendril of darkness latched onto De Mona's ankle, spilling her to the ground. The more she fought, the tighter the darkness wound itself around her legs. The darkness encircled her waist and continued upward, but when it reached the parcel she clutched to her chest it recoiled as if in pain. Using all her strength, De Mona was able to kick free of her shadowy band and scramble clumsily to her feet. The darkness made a second attempt, but De Mona was already across the street. When she reached the corner she took a minute to look over her shoulder, which proved to be a bad move. The darkness itself opened up, spilling three men out. The one bringing up the rear was the shooter. His face and uniform were splotched with blood, but he didn't seem to notice as he tried to draw a bead on her with his service revolver. She was too quick for him to catch her in a flat-out footrace, but the two leading the charge were closing the distance at an alarming rate.

They looked like dime-store versions of Siegfried & Roy, but the patches of rotted flesh on their faces revealed the truth of what they were: Stalkers.

De Mona willed every ounce of her strength to her legs and got out ahead of her pursuers. She had them by about a half block and was gaining distance, but eventually she would tire and they wouldn't and then it would be on unless she came up with a plan. As if in answer to her prayers, she spotted an alley a few yards down. Increasing her speed, she grabbed a streetlight, doing a 180, and propelled herself into the alley. When she crossed the threshold of cool darkness she realized it had been a mistake.

The streetlight on the curb still shone, but its beam stopped in a perfect line at the mouth of the alley. It was as if something had come through and swallowed the light. It was a setup and she ran right into it.

"Don't look so grim, child," the darkness directly in front of her spoke. From it stepped a man dressed in faded blue jeans and a black T-shirt. Along his arms De Mona could see tattoos that she knew to be symbols of dark magic. Though his face was pleasant, the unnatural shine to his eyes said trouble. "Give it to me, and I'll keep you as my whore instead of letting Titus have his way with you."

"Stay the hell away from me," De Mona growled, backing up slowly the way she had come. She thought about bolting, but that thought died when the three men who had been on her heels blocked the mouth of the alley. She was caught between the frying pan and the fire.

"You know what I've come for." His eyes flicked and the darkness seemed to fill the whites. De Mona felt the hairs on her skin begin to stand up and knew she had her hands full with that one.

Where demons were hell's minions, the Stalkers were

the foot soldiers. They were lesser demons and poltergeists that could inhabit the bodies of the dead, provided that they had been murdered or died tragically. Though the Stalkers often maintained their supernatural strength, their full power couldn't cross the void. They amounted to little more than half-witted slaves, serving Belthon for the promise of chaos.

The more powerful demons were another case. Because their powers were stronger they were able to not only bring more of their full powers across but also to take living hosts. There had been more than one story of a demon making promises to the weak or sickly, neglecting to mention that the host's soul would have to take the demon's place in hell until the body was returned or destroyed. The man in the black T-shirt appeared to be such a case.

"There is no escape," he said to her, smiling to reveal jagged fangs and blackened gums. "Alive or dead, you will give it up."

De Mona tried to control her fear but found it difficult. Already her fingers were involuntarily curling into hardened spears. Her control was slipping and she couldn't afford that. Her mission was too important to compromise, but they were leaving her little choice. Slowly she drew her hunting knife from the pocket of her fatigue pants. Looking from the man in the black T-shirt to the Stalkers, she whispered, "Let's do this."

Following her challenge De Mona heard two very disturbing sounds. The first was a battle cry as a Stalker charged her and the second was a gunshot from a police officer. The Stalker was quick, but so was she. Dropping the sack to the ground, she caught the Stalker by the throat with one hand and let him taste her blade with the other. She had already stabbed him three times before he realized he was getting the short end. She delivered a backhand that snapped the Stalker's neck back, exposing the soft flesh, which she slashed open with her blade. Without missing a beat she drove the knife into his head and kicked the body away from her.

The second Stalker was on her out of nowhere. She caught it in midair, by the wrists, but that didn't stop the thing from trying to clamp its razor-like teeth on her cheek. De Mona wasn't worried about the bite turning her, but her body would still have to recover from the infection. The Stalker garbled something in a tongue she didn't care to decipher just before yanking one of its arms free and trying to tear her head off. De Mona countered with a straight palm to the chest and released the breath she had been holding. She felt its ribs cave in first, then the soft thump as its heart exploded. Though its heart no longer beat, it was the foundation of the demon's hold on the body, so hitting it served just as well in dispatching a demon as decapitation.

Duck, she heard in her head just as she spun out of the way of a wayward bullet. "I'm gonna off you, bitch, and write my own ticket!" the crazed cop screamed, firing.

De Mona went in low, with her left arm stretched outward. She connected with the officer's midsection, doubling him over. She came up behind him and grabbed the man by the back of the neck, shaking him like a rag doll. Unlike the Stalkers, the mortal wasn't very sturdy.

"You picked the wrong demon to worship," she breathed in his face. The officer trembled as he thought he smelled faint traces of sulfur. Yanking his head viciously to one side, she snapped his neck and let him crumble to the ground.

With the alley mouth now being clear, her mind screamed for her to flee, but the bloodlust had her and it needed a new target. She pivoted, snarling like an animal, and turned her rage to the man in the black T-shirt,

but to her surprise he was charging her with a very large
knife.

"You should've just given it over, bitch." He grinned as
he drove the blade into her stomach. The smile melted
from his face as the weapon snapped in half on impact.

The man's terrified stare went from the broken point
on the ground to the face of the girl he had been hunting.
His veil of darkness still blanketed the alley, but there
was a glint of moonlight in her eyes that shouldn't have
been. It was then that he saw what he had been too arro-
gant to see earlier.

"You ain't the only game in town," she said in a voice
that sounded like she had too many teeth in her mouth.
"Now." She moved slowly towards him, with her body
seeming to bulk up as she went. "Let's talk about that
whore's position you offered me earlier."

Five minutes later De Mona came out of the alley at the
end she hadn't been able to see due to the man's spell. Her
hands were stained with something too black to be considered blood, which soaked into the sack. The item inside momentarily pulsed and then went still again. She
shook off the haze that was trying to settle over her brain
and cursed her parcel. In the short time she had been in
possession of the thing, it had cost her everything and
everyone she'd known. Redfeather had been the name on
her dying father's lips, and she intended to find him at all
costs.

The pain in Sam's gut was so intense that he found it hard
to walk straight. His blond Mohawk was dingy and wilted,
and there was no luster left in his normally crisp blue eyes.
The seemingly endless river of snot running from his
nose had begun to cake around his nostrils and just above
his top lip, but appearances were the least of his concerns

at that moment. If he didn't get a fix soon, he doubted that he'd make it through the night.

Sam had stopped at the mouth of an alley to catch his breath when he heard what sounded like a faint moaning. He tried to peek into the alley, but the darkness was too thick. He was about to keep walking when he heard the voice.

"Help," it called weakly.

"Who's there?" Sam called back.

"Please, help me."

Sam leaned farther into the alley to see if he could get a better look and something grabbed hold of his neck. He grabbed at it, but his hands passed right through the tendril of darkness. The grip was so intense that he could neither scream nor move. All he could do was whimper as the darkness invaded every hole in his body.

CHAPTER TWO

"And that, in short, was the rise and fall of the Spanish colonization of the Americas," Professor Garland was saying while the bored students of his history class listened. He was a bear of a man, with a salt-and-pepper mane of messy hair. "Now." He turned his Coke-bottle glasses on the students. "Who can tell me the names of three of the last four Spanish colonies to be occupied by the United States after the Spanish-American War ended?" The room was silent. "Come now; we've only been talking about this over the last week since over sixty percent of you flunked my exam. I'm sure someone can name me three?" He looked around the room, and save for the young man sitting closest to the window no one would meet his gaze. "All right then, I'll choose." His eyes swept over his students and landed on a pretty blonde who was playing with her BlackBerry. "Ms. Reynolds!" His deep voice startled her so bad that she dropped the device. "We're waiting."

Katie looked around dumbly because she had no idea what exactly Professor Garland was waiting for. She was more interested in her Facebook page than what he was saying. "I'm sorry?" she said sheepishly.

"You certainly are, Ms. Reynolds; it's only a pity that you have to be so on my time," he said in disgust. It was common for Professor Garland to go into one of his famous rants on a student he felt was slacking off. These rants were legendary throughout all the universities he'd ever taught at, even rumored to have reduced men to tears, and from the look on his face he was about to let Katie have it.

"Cuba, Puerto Rico, Guam, and the Philippines, not necessarily in that order," a meek voice called from the corner. All eyes turned to see who would be stupid enough to put themselves in Professor Garland's crosshairs when he was working himself up to a rant. Gabriel adjusted his glasses on the bridge of his nose and looked around trying to figure out why everyone was starting at him. He was a very attractive young man, with sandblasted brown skin and shoulder-length black hair that he never seemed to comb, but as attractive as he was, Gabriel was about as much fun as Professor Garland's course. Gabriel was the quiet kid who sat in the corner, staring out the window and never saying more than a word or two in class unless it was to Katie Reynolds, and even then his tone was always hushed. He'd sounded confident when he spoke up on behalf of Katie but with Professor Garland's eye boring into him he wanted to shrink into invisibility.

"Correct, Mr. Redfeather, but I don't recall presenting that question to you," Professor Garland said.

"Technically you were. See, you first posed the question to anyone who could answer it. I just chose not to answer at that moment." Gabriel smiled dumbly as the class erupted with laughter. The only reason he even replied was to keep from vomiting in front of the entire class.

"Okay, Mr. Wiseass." Professor Garland picked up a thick textbook and flipped through it until he found the section he was looking for. "Since you're so versed in the subject, let me ask you this: when Columbus failed to gain the support of the king of Portugal whom did he—"

"The monarchs of Castile and Aragon, they financed his little adventure because they wanted a quicker route to reach the traders in Asia," Gabriel said triumphantly as the class backed him with a chorus of cheers. Katie blew him a kiss, which he caught in his palm. This only pissed Professor Garland off more.

"I'll see the two of you after class." Professor Garland slammed the textbook on the table.

Professor Garland spent the better part of twenty minutes chewing out Gabriel and Katie for their little display of defiance in his class. Garland was a man who didn't take well to *usurpers*, as he called them. He was so upset that Gabriel thought one of the massive veins in his forehead was going to explode. When he'd finally dismissed them, Gabriel looked like he was going to fall apart and Katie could barely suppress the giggle that was rattling around in her gut.

"You were awesome in there," Katie said to Gabriel while they were walking through the hall.

"He seemed pretty pissed off; I thought he was going to have a heart attack in there," Gabriel said, fumbling with his glasses. The arm was loose, so they kept sliding down his nose.

"I wish. If old man Garland falls over dead, then maybe we won't have to take the final exam," Katie said half-jokingly. "Dude, I thought I was going to shit myself when he asked me about the Mexican-American War."

"Spanish-American," he corrected her.

"Whatever." She waved her hand dismissively. "I wouldn't know one from the other, which is why I know I'm going to fail that exam and end up back here for summer classes."

"Katie, have you ever considered studying?" he asked seriously.

"Ew, studying is for geeks." She covered her mouth

when she realized she'd offended him. "No offense, Gabe, it's just that I can't manage to sit still long enough to get through half of that garbage."

"It's not garbage, Katie; it's the required material for the class." He adjusted the large stack of books he was carrying. No sooner had he gotten them into a comfortable position than a hulking young man bumped him and knocked all the books on the floor.

"Watch where you're going, nerd," the young man said over his shoulder, never breaking his stride.

"Oh, why don't you grow up?" Katie called after the young man. "Are you okay?" She bent down to help Gabriel pick up the books.

"Yeah, I'm cool," he lied. He was more angry that he'd let Katie see what happened than at the actual offense. While she was helping him pick up the books a strand of her hair brushed his face. He inhaled deeply of her scent. He loved the way Katie smelled. She had a naturally sweet scent, like a flower, mixed with whatever she used in her hair. It was a smell that he would always carry in his memory. Again Gabriel found his mind wondering, *What if . . . ?*

"Gabriel, you've gotta learn to stand up for yourself," she told him, placing the last textbook atop the pile. "With all these books you carry around I'd bet you're as strong as an ox." She pinched his biceps playfully and found that his arm felt like coiled steel.

"I do stand, when I believe in the cause," he told her.

"What can be a better cause than keeping people from picking on you?"

"The greatest battles are fought with our heads and our hearts," Gabriel said as if he was imparting some great wisdom to her.

"Well, your heart can't keep from getting your head cracked." She knocked on his forehead softly. He was still giving her that blank-puppy look of his, so she let it alone. "Getting back to what I was saying, I know that nothing short of a miracle is going to get me over the hump in Professor Garland's history class."

"Then you'd better get yourself over to the church and start praying," Gabriel said, continuing down the hall.

"Hold on, Gabe." She caught up to him. "I was kind of hoping—"

"No, Katie," he cut her off.

"You didn't even let me finish."

"Doesn't matter; the answer is still no."

"Gabe, I just need a little help." She stroked his cheek.

The heat from her body and the heady scent of her perfume brought a tingling sensation below his waist. Katie was a beautiful girl. She stood a hair over five-three and had sandy blond hair. Gabriel had often fantasized about what it would be like to be with her, even just once, but he knew they would never be more than friends.

"Nothing doing, Katie." He shook the fog from his mind. "The last time you got me to help you with something I ended up doing the paper for you while you talked on the phone."

"That is so untrue. I helped out."

"Katie, handing me a textbook doesn't count as help," he informed her.

"Gabriel, I *need* this. If I don't pass this class I'll have to stay here for the summer and take it again. My parents are treating me to Rio and I don't want to miss out. Please?"

Gabriel looked into her pleading blue eyes and felt his heart flutter. Katie was a spoiled rich girl from the Howard Beach section of Queens. As the daughter of two renowned surgeons, she was afforded the best that life had to offer. Most of the other students frowned on her and the other girls in her privileged circle, but in his two years at the university Gabriel had learned a different side of her. Katie was really just a girl trying to crawl out from under her parents' shadows and find her own place in the world. It was the child-like innocence, beneath the shallow exterior, that had drawn Gabriel to her and forged the bond between them.

"Okay," he conceded. "I'll help you out this one last time, Katie."

"Oh, thank you!" she squealed, kissing him on the cheek. "You're the best, Gabe."

"Yeah, yeah." He blushed. "I've got some research to do at the library, so meet me there around ten."

"Tonight? Gabe, it's Friday. Can't we meet earlier?"

"No, we can't. I told you, I've got research to do."

"You and your research." She pouted. "I don't see why anyone would give a shit about languages that no one uses anymore anyhow."

"Well, I give a shit. Those are my terms, Katie. You can show or not; it's up to you."

"All right, you big wet blanket. But you're still the best friend a girl could ever have!"

"Whatever," he said, trying to hide the smirk on his face. Gabriel looked around to see if anyone was watching, and when he was satisfied that they were alone he decided to finally make a move on Katie. "Listen, I was wondering if you—" Katie's ringing BlackBerry cut his question short. She answered the phone and was immediately engrossed in what the person on the other end of the line had to say. Katie finger-waved good-bye and walked off down the hall, chatting away on her phone.

". . . wanted to catch a movie this weekend," he said to the space where she had been standing.

CHAPTER THREE

During the day Hunter College's massive library was usually bustling with students, but at night it was a ghost town. It was rare for students to be in the building after dark and nearly unheard of for a Friday night. This didn't apply to Gabriel Redfeather. The library was one of his favorite places, especially at night. He had worked out an arrangement with the custodian to tutor his daughter in exchange for the use of the library after hours. During the wee hours, Gabriel could do his research in peace.

Gabriel was a certified genius. He had numerous scholarship offers to universities all over the country and abroad, but he chose to attend Hunter. His major was history, but his love was linguistic studies. It was something Gabriel had become interested in as a child, and it had followed him into young adulthood. Hunter wasn't the best school in New York, but it was a respectable university with a slightly smaller campus than some of the others in the city, which suited him. Besides that, attending Hunter allowed him to stay close to home to help his aging grandfather.

Settling into one of the rickety wooden chairs, Gabriel thumbed through a book on South American cultures. Currently he was researching a long-forgotten tribe that was said to inhabit the hills of Argentina. Gabriel pored through photos of wall markings and was scribbling onto a notepad, trying to decipher the language, when the lights flickered and died.

"Shit," he cursed. The room was completely dark, save for a sliver of light coming from the adjoining hallway. When he stood to look for a light switch, he heard footsteps. "Who's there?" There was no answer.

Gabriel felt his way along the tables and chairs until he found a bookshelf. Placing his back to it, he scanned the darkness for the intruder. The only light was the slither seeping under the door from the hall. Gabriel caught something break the beam and disappear behind the quantum physics shelves. His heart began to quicken. He rubbed his palms against his jeans, in an attempt to remove the film of sweat that coated them. He looked around for a weapon but doubted that the *Webster's Unabridged Dictionary* would do him much good, despite its massive size.

Craning his neck, he made one last attempt. "All right, this isn't funny. For the last time, who's in here?" In response to his question, a shadow darted at him. Time suddenly moved at a crawl. The blur of darkness slowed and he was able to make out the shape of a man. Gabriel grabbed a handful of clothing and twisted his body in the direction the blur was moving. The momentum of the lunge propelled the shape over Gabriel's head and sent it crashing into the table where he had been studying. Not bothering to identify his attacker, Gabriel made a mad dash for the exit. When he got within feet of it, the room was flooded with light.

It took his eyes a while to refocus, but when they did, he made out the shape of a man standing in the doorway. Gabriel spun around to make for the second exit and froze. Lying on his back near the overturned table was Gabriel's good friend Carter.

"What the hell, Gabe!" Carter said, still lying on his

back. Carter was a six-two junior, who played shooting guard on the basketball team. He had a kind heart but was deadly in a fight. A year and a half prior, Carter was about to flunk off the team when Gabriel helped him to pull his grades up. They had been friends ever since.

"This fool put you on your ass, C.," the young man said standing near the light switch. Vince also played on the basketball team, but he and Gabriel weren't friends. Vince was amongst the number of students who often ridiculed Gabriel for his bookish nature.

"Carter, what the hell is wrong with you?" Gabriel asked, helping him to his feet.

"Damn, kid. I was just coming in here to play a prank on you, and I get tossed into a bookshelf. I'm the fastest guy in the division, and you dodged me. How the hell did you do that?" He rubbed the knot that was rising under his tapered Afro.

This was a question Gabriel honestly couldn't answer. Ever since he was a child he had always had keen reflexes. He was always quicker and more agile than most kids his age. It wasn't something he could explain; he just was. This was part of what had made him such an asset in his late parents' carnival show.

"Carter, how'd you let this nerd do that to you?" Vince asked, strolling over.

"Watch your mouth, Vince," Carter warned. "I'm the only one who can give Gabe shit."

"It's cool, man," Gabriel said, casting a glare at Vince. "What're you two jokers up to?" He turned his attention back to Carter.

"I came by to ask if you wanted to hang out tonight. A bunch of us are going down to this spot in the Village called Six-Six-Six or something like that."

"Yeah, Carter's mom is away for the weekend, so orgy at his place," Vince added.

"Man, why don't you shut the hell up?" Carter snapped. "Yeah, Mom Dukes is gone, so we got somewhere to slide if we get lucky, you wit' it?"

"I can't," Gabriel said, picking up the books Carter had knocked over. "I've gotta study and Katie needs my help with a project she's got coming up."

Carter and Vince shared a look. "Gabe, Katie left with Molly and June about fifteen minutes ago. Guess she took a rain check on your little date." Vince placed a hand on Gabriel's shoulder and had it knocked away.

"Knock it off, Vince," Carter snapped at him. "Gabe, it's Friday, man. Those dead guys will still be here on Monday. Just come out for a little while."

Once again, Katie had set him up to be the patsy. It amazed him how she would be able to barhop and be in the library studying simultaneously. Those pleading eyes and angelic face did him in every time. He looked over at the pile of scattered books and decided he would think of himself this night.

"All right already, just let me clean up around here and lock up." He glanced at his watch, which read: 9:52. "I'll meet you guys there at quarter to eleven."

"That's my dawg." Carter slapped him on the back. "For a minute you were beginning to scare me. You keep poking around with these dead guys and you're gonna find yourself in a Kelly Armstrong novel," he joked.

"Hardly." Gabriel blushed. He'd often imagined himself as a dashing sorcerer or brave werewolf. "Those are fictional novels; what I study is *real*."

"Whatever, man. Just make sure you're at the spot," Carter said, heading towards the door.

Vince let his stare linger on Gabriel before he turned to follow Carter. "Who knows?" he called over his shoulder. "You might even get laid tonight." His mocking laughter still rang in Gabriel's ears long after they had left.

* * *

In a back alley not far from where Gabriel found himself cleaning up Carter's mess, an old man sat huddled near a Dumpster. His dingy white beard brushed the lap of his worn jeans as he sat cross-legged, rocking back and forth. A cat that had made the mistake of passing too close to the man hissed and darted off under a fence. The man smiled and stood, heading for the mouth of the alley.

The leather on the soles of his dingy running shoes slapped against the concrete beneath but made no sound. Even as he walked through the shallow puddles the rain had made on uneven ground, there wasn't even a splash. At the mouth of the alley he leaned against the wall and waited for the inevitable.

He smelled her before he had actually seen her. It had been quite some time since he'd smelled her particular fragrance, but he would know it anywhere. Hugging the shadows to him, he waited for her to pass.

She was an attractive young woman with olive-colored skin and sharp facial features. Even through the baggy jeans he could see that she was curvaceous, though it would be a few years yet before she finally reached womanhood. Her dark braided hair and Latin features reminded him of an Aztec princess he'd once known, but her posture was of that of a warrior, as it was with all her lot. The old man waited until she was almost right on top of him before he stepped into the light.

The old man removed the wool cap that was doing a poor job of containing his long white hair and bowed from the waist. "What a pretty bag; might I help you carry it?"

The girl spun, braids whipping about her face and knife at the ready. After what had happened the night before she wasn't taking any chances. "Mister, if you knew like I did you'd get lost. This is a problem you don't want!" she snarled. He could smell the rage mounting in her, so he took a step back, knowing what would come if he pushed.

"My stars and garters, I've offended you, haven't I? Forgive an old man for overstepping his bounds, ma'am. I just thought that with such a heavy parcel you might've needed a bit of help."

"It's not that heavy; I'll manage," she said, and continued on her way.

"The weight of an item isn't always a physical thing," he called after her. The girl ignored him and kept going. The old man watched her form disappear in the direction of the campus and rubbed his hands together. "The Iron Maiden meets the Hunter. This should be interesting," he mused before fading back into the shadows.

Fifteen minutes later, Gabriel had just about cleaned up the mess that Carter's prank had caused. Fortunately for Gabriel, nothing was broken. As he was replacing the volumes he'd been reading through back on the shelves, he heard footsteps in the hall. He sighed. "Carter, why don't you stop being a dick? That joke is old already."

"I've been called worse," a female voice called behind him.

Gabriel spun and saw that it wasn't Carter approaching. The girl standing in the doorway looked to be about his age, possibly younger. She wore a black, form-fitting T-shirt and baggy blue jeans over black boots. Pushing a loose braid behind her ear, she sized Gabriel up.

"Oh, ah . . . sorry, I thought you were someone else." He tried to hide his embarrassment but did a horrible job of it.

"Apparently so. Listen, I didn't mean to barge in on you, but the door was open."

Gotta remember to lock the damn door, he thought to

himself. "Yeah, I planned to lock it on my way out. The library's closed."

"Yeah, I know." She started towards him. "I wasn't actually looking for a book but a person. You know a guy named Redfeather? I think he works here."

Gabriel raised an eyebrow. "And why might you be looking for him?"

A look somewhere between aggravation and impatience crossed her face. "Look, if you ain't him then it doesn't concern you. I need to find him; it's a matter of life and death."

"Well, look no further." He half-bowed.

"You're Redfeather?" she asked suspiciously.

"Yes, Gabriel Redfeather." He extended his hand.

She looked at it for a minute as if it were a trick before taking it. "De Mona Sanchez." She pumped his hand. "Sorry, I just didn't expect you to be so young, the way my father spoke of you."

"Your father?"

"Yeah, Edward Sanchez." She waited for a reaction but got none.

Gabriel shrugged his shoulders. "Doesn't ring a bell."

De Mona eyed him suspiciously, trying to see if he was lying. She had never met the man called Redfeather, but her father had always spoken of him as some great scholar and Gabriel didn't appear to be more than a college kid. Moving closer to him, she asked, "What do you know about Lifeless Tongues?"

This did get a reaction. Lifeless Tongues was an Internet group composed of men and women who shared a curiosity in ancient languages. Gabriel had joined the group six months prior but soon lost interest. There were only a few members who took the art as seriously as he did, so he limited his visits to the site to the occasional pop in to see what was new.

"Oh, is that what this is about? Listen, if you're looking to join the group then you should really be talking to Harvey Klein; he's the moderator. If you want, I could give you his e-mail address," Gabriel offered.

"So then you're not the same Redfeather who deciphered the infamous lost Babylonian text?"

"Yes, that was me, but it's really not as complicated as it sounds. The guy who posted the text was a fraud. His text was nothing more than a dialect of Portuguese, with a splash of eleventh-century Romanian. The reason it read so funky was because he purposely misspelled the words, making it seem like something more than what it really was. It was a simple trick actually," Gabriel said as if anyone could've figured it out.

De Mona's eyes narrowed to slits. "Either you're pulling my chain or I've made a hell of a mistake, which I've been doing a lot lately. Look, I was told that a man named Redfeather would be able to translate something for me. Something my father lost his life protecting." She tossed the sack onto the table. Gabriel looked at it as if it were a poisonous snake. "Don't worry; it isn't anthrax."

Cautiously Gabriel undid the hemp and peered into the bag. The smell of cloves wafted up into his sinuses, causing his nose to twitch. It was strange that someone would stuff a sack with cloves, but it was the item inside the sack that was more baffling. It was the rusted head of a pitchfork that was broken at the shaft and missing its middle point.

Holding the fork in his hand, he looked up at De Mona. "Is this a joke?"

She glared at him as if she had been insulted. She placed her knuckles on the table, tipping it a fraction of an inch. Gabriel was so fixed on her walnut brown eyes that he didn't even notice. "Mr. Redfeather—"

"Gabriel," he cut her off.

"What?"

"My name is Gabriel. Mr. Redfeather is my grandfather."

"Whatever." She waved her hands. "My father was killed and it had something to do with that thing." She nodded at the fork. "Now all I know is that you or your grandfather is my best bet at finding out what it is. Will you help me or not?"

There was a harshness to her voice that made him afraid, but it was the pleading undertone that struck a chord with him. He too had lost his parents tragically, so he understood her pain and aggravation. "I'll try." He put on his glasses and commenced to examine the fork. "I don't see anything." He turned it end over end.

"Hold it to the moonlight." She nodded towards the library's window.

Gabriel gave her a suspicious look, then walked over to the window. He held the fork up, so the light of the moon kissed the shaft. At first he still didn't see anything, but to his surprise the fork began to vibrate slightly. The light of the moon was absorbed into the metal, revealing faint letters. "Well, I'll be damned! There's something written on the side, but I can't tell what the language is. It could be Aramaic, but I don't recognize the dialect offhand." He rotated the fork. "Give me a day or so to consult my textbooks and—" He gasped as the markings began to change.

" 'The two are one, as it must always be. I am the Nimrod, release me and know my name,' " he read out loud.

CHAPTER FOUR

Ontario, Canada

The home office of the Titus Corporation was located in downtown Ontario. It was a massive structure that stood sixty-six stories above the ground and was the only building for several blocks around that wasn't owned by the city. The office and living quarters of its CEO, Maxwell Titus, were located on the top floor and could only be accessed by a special card-key. The majority of the time, it was from his sanctuary on the top floor that Titus conducted his business, but that night he was engaging in pleasure.

The man, who for the last hundred years had been known as Maxwell Titus, or Maxwell Titus Jr., depending on whom you asked, lounged in his double-wide Jacuzzi, with the back of his head resting against the cool marble. He was a well-built man, with muscular arms and a barrel-like chest. The bare skin was flawless, save for the pinkish scar just above his heart. He had a handsome face, with a neatly trimmed black beard, sprinkled with gray. Though physically he looked to be in his late thirties to early forties, he had lived far longer than that. Maxwell Titus had seen more than his mind cared to remember. From the rise and fall of kingdoms to the automobile replacing the carriage, he had seen it. But no matter how much the world around him changed, Maxwell Titus remained trapped in the middle of his life.

Before he heard the soft knock, Titus felt the presence outside the door. "Come in, Flag," he called, without bothering to cover himself or his ladies. The first one was pale, with hair the color of sunrise, rinsed with molten gold. Her partner, in contrast, had a cinnamon complexion, with chocolate brown eyes and hair so black that it reflected no light. The attendants were beautiful, so beautiful in fact that to stare at them for too long was to risk your own free will. They were vampires. Titus had found them masquerading as whores in New Orleans' red-light district, preying on tourists and those ignorant of the supernatural. They had been living as little more than scavengers until they had met Titus. The favorite son of the dark lord had given them shelter, purpose, and power . . . so much power.

The man who stepped cautiously into the room was a hair over six feet and about as thin as a pipe cleaner. Hair so blond that it was almost white hung loosely down his back and spilled over his shoulders. Behind his wire-framed glasses, his clear blue eyes went from the naked trio down to his tie, which he busied himself straightening.

"My lord," Flag said in a crisp British accent, keeping his eyes on the tiles.

"Surely you're not embarrassed by a little flesh?" Titus taunted him, fondling one of Raven's breasts.

"Of course not. I just didn't expect to find you indisposed."

"Even the favorite son of Belthon still has mortal urges." He kissed Helena, then Raven. "Ladies, leave us."

"Yes, Lord Titus," they said in unison. The women slid naked from the tub and moved for the door. Their hungry eyes were locked on Flag as they passed him, but they knew better than to touch the mage uninvited.

"I trust you have news from Moses," Titus said, rising from the pool. He grabbed his black robe from a chair and slipped it on.

"Another failed attempt," Flag said, just above a whisper.

Faster than Flag's eyes could follow, Titus had crossed the room and was standing directly in front of him. "You've interrupted me to bring news of failure?"

Flag swallowed and went on. "The Stalkers were destroyed and Moses lost his host's body. Thankfully, he was able to procure another, but it will still be some time before the vessel is battle ready. It seems that the body is suffering from a severe case of withdrawal."

Titus hissed. Flag flinched at the smell of sulfur coming off his master's breath. "How could the so-called master of shadows and a small pack of Stalkers be undone by two teenagers?"

"The boy was slain, he was human, but the girl wasn't. What we didn't know until she showed herself was that she wears the mark of the Valkrin. From what I've gathered from my intelligence she's the progeny of Mercy."

Titus shook his head as he thought back on the defiant demon captain. "No matter which side she's fighting on, Mercy continues to give me grief."

"On a lighter note, we've recovered Judas' ring. One of the goblin troops discovered it in the Dakota mountains. It's being secured in the vault as we speak," Flag offered.

Judas' ring was the wedding band crafted for one of the First Guard and the eldest daughter of Judas and wielded by a warrior maiden during the siege. It was a diamond set in a gold band that gave its wearer the power to distinguish the truth from a lie. When someone lied, it would turn red, when they told the truth, it turned green.

It wasn't the most powerful of the artifacts, but coupled with the others it was a power unto itself.

Without warning Titus had shot out and gripped Flag about the throat. Titus lifted him from the ground as if he were a small child and began crushing his windpipe. "Fool," Titus snarled. "What care I for trinkets that can do no more than parlor tricks? I seek the most powerful of weapons, the eternal prison of the cursed Bishop, the Nimrod."

"As do all the servants of Belthon, Lord Titus. This is just a minor setback. We know that the girl hasn't left the city and the Stalkers are out in force searching for her. Shall I send the hag to speed along Moses' progression so he can resume his search?"

Titus thought on it for a minute. "No, let the so-called master of shadows dwell in the hell of his new body for a time. Now, on to the next order of business, by the next full moon I expect—" Titus' words were cut off when a sharp pain exploded in his chest. On shaky legs he staggered over to the chair and braced his hands against it.

"What is it?" Flag asked nervously.

Titus turned his now-glowing red eyes on Flag. "The Bishop stirs."

New York City

"What the hell is a Nimrod?" De Mona asked, staring at the fork.

"I don't know." Gabriel continued to inspect it. "If I'm reading it correctly, that's what the fork is called. Did your father tell you anything about the fork, maybe how he came across it?"

"My dad owned an antique shop, so it wasn't unusual for him to bring home some of the more rare items to store in our basement vault," she began. "About a month ago he came back from Africa with some stuff he'd brought from another antique dealer and that's when things got weird." She paused to reflect on the last few days she'd spent with her father. "My father was the kind of guy who wouldn't even raise his voice during an argument, so I was shocked to find a gun in his bedroom closet. Not your run-of-the-mill 'protect your home and family' kinda thing. I'm talking M16. Then he tells me that we're selling our house in Queens."

"Maybe he just thought the neighborhood wasn't safe anymore and wanted to move away?" Gabriel offered, trying to believe it himself.

De Mona looked at him. "Gabriel, my father had the house built when he found out my mother was pregnant with me. Even when she ran out on us and took our life savings," there was scorn in De Mona's voice, "he still wouldn't sell the house. Something in Africa rattled him."

Gabriel nodded, still studying the fork. "And this," he held it up, "did he bring this back from Africa too?"

De Mona shrugged. "I had assumed so, since I had never laid eyes on it before three days ago. When I asked him what it was, all he would say was that it belonged to some friends he had at the church and that we'd be returning it as soon as we relocated."

"Don't suppose you knew who these friends were or what church he meant?"

"No," she half-lied.

"So what made you bring it to me?" Gabriel asked. He motioned to put the fork back in the bag but found himself reluctant. Beneath the tarnish he found it quite beautiful.

"The name," she told him. "Every so often my father would bring up the name Redfeather. Mostly when it came to the unknown; it was another one of my father's hobbies.

Often he'd say that the only human he knew who knew more about the arcane than him was this Redfeather. He wanted to consult with your grandfather about the fork before returning it to the church. Since I had never met this Redfeather, I Googled him and came up with you, though I think it was off by a generation or two."

"Grandfather." Gabriel nodded. "My granddad knows a great many things about a great many things. He might be able to tell us a little more." Gabriel glanced at his watch. "He's probably still up."

"You think your grandfather can help out?" she asked with hope in her voice.

"Only one way to find out." He stuffed the fork back into the sack.

When they exited the library, the first thing De Mona noticed was the silence. She looked up and down the darkened block and there wasn't a soul in sight, which was odd for a Friday night in New York City, on a college campus no less. A tickling wave rolled up her arms and across her neck, tightening the skin as it moved.

"Something wrong?" Gabriel asked, noticing the change in her facial expression.

"I was just thinking how quiet it was," she said, concentrating on not letting her control slip. "You got a car?"

"On a student budget, are you kidding? What's the matter, De Mona?"

De Mona sniffed the air and frowned. "Which way to the closest subway station?"

"Just over on Lexington." He motioned with his head. "De Mona, what's wrong with you? What's going on?"

Without warning De Mona grabbed Gabriel by the arm and yanked him towards her. He was surprised by the suddenness and the force as he flew by De Mona and into a parked car. He'd almost thought she was attacking him until he heard the loud crashing behind him. When he was able to see straight he saw a man dressed in an off-the-rack brown suit that had its back cut out, like the corpses they dressed in funeral homes. The creature turned its dead eyes to Gabriel and hissed, showing broken and jagged yellow teeth. Gabriel started to bolt, but he was cut off by another man.

The man was handsome. Not movie-star handsome, more like an easy-on-the-eyes pro athlete. He had a thin, angular face with Asian eyes and skin the color of soft moonlight. His stringy hair, that was so black that it could've passed for blue in the right light, hung freely around his broad shoulders. A black motorcycle jacket hugged his frame like armor, bearing patches from different wars. In ancient times he was the warlord of the death god Thanos, but now he served Belthon.

"Knight!" he roared. "I am called Riel, Shepherd of the Dead and King Maker. By the will of my lord Belthon, I have come to claim your weapon and your head!" he shouted, and waved the blade in a low arc, leaving an eerie trail of greenish smoke. Under the streetlight Gabriel could see the scorch mark that ran up the blade's crease and fanned out to cover the point. It was called Poison, the burning death, and a strike from it would cause just that.

"I've already sent one of you boys home packing this week, hell spawn; don't make yourself number two," De Mona warned.

"You shouldn't throw stones, little girl," Riel laughed. He turned and addressed the walking corpses: "The hunt has been called and the prize is flesh!" Riel pointed Poison at De Mona.

"Flesh!" the Stalker in the brown suit snarled before slamming its shoulder into Gabriel, sending him crashing over the hood of the car. He hit the ground, shattering his glasses and feeling like he'd cracked a rib, but it was nothing compared to what the advancing Stalker was going to do when it reached him. The Stalker had just about closed the distance when something grabbed the back of its tattered suit jacket. It turned to see a pair of moonlit eyes staring at him from the face of the girl. With Gabriel being out of sight she could take the gloves off, and that meant trouble for the Stalker.

When Gabriel hit the ground the fork slid down the street and lodged itself under a car's wheel. The dazed boy managed to stagger to his feet and move his gut out of the way as Riel tried to splay him. The demon came around in an arc, trying to split Gabriel in two with his cursed blade, but the former acrobat was able to bounce out of the way. When the blade hit the concrete it left a scorch mark.

Gabriel shuffled his feet once and hit Riel in the jaw with an awkward right cross. Riel smiled the blow off and retuned the favor with a blow to the chest. Gabriel hit the ground and bounced twice before landing in the middle of the street. Before he could even shake the cobwebs, Riel was lifting Gabriel by the front of his shirt.

"What cowardice." Riel shook the frightened young man as if he were an unruly child. "One of God's chosen shakes in the face of evil." He pulled Gabriel close enough so that he could smell the sickly stench of the grave on Riel's breath. "Where is your God now?"

In response Gabriel grunted and slammed both of his legs into Riel's chest and rolled backward into a crouch. Riel swung the blade, but Gabriel was quicker and managed to scramble under a car.

"Come out, Knight. I promised to make your death painless," Riel taunted.

Gabriel lay under the car shaking like a leaf. He had

come across some unexplainable things in his studies of the forgotten and unknown, but nothing compared to what he was witnessing in the flesh. He shut his eyes as he saw Riel's fingers grip the edge of the car's fender and begin to lift. Slowly the automobile began to come off the ground, and Gabriel knew he would soon be exposed. "Somebody please help me," he whimpered, covering his head with his hands.

"Release me."

Gabriel almost jumped out of his skin when he heard the voice. It sounded like the speaker was whispering in his ear, but there was no one else under the car.

"Release me and know my name," the voice went on.

Gabriel looked near the front wheel and saw the fork peeking out of its wrapping. As if of its own accord, his hand shot out and grabbed it. This time it was hot to his skin, almost to the point of burning. A wave of energy went from the fork up through his arm and settled around his heart like a warming calm. Holding the fork by its broken shaft, he rolled out from under the other side of the car. If the thing intended to kill him, then Gabriel would die on his feet.

"So, you've decided to fight?" Riel smiled. "Good." Bounding over the car, he charged Gabriel.

Gabriel stood with his head half-bowed, waiting for the death blow that the demon would surely deliver. Overhead there was a rumble of thunder somewhere in the distance, but the meteorologist had predicted clear skies that night. Lightning whipped from the ground, running up through the fork and dispersing into the sky. The dull fork began to glow softly, radiating power through Gabriel's body. The power soon pulsed so brightly that Riel had to back away, but the light didn't harm Gabriel. He looked curiously yet knowingly at the fork as it began to change. The shaft extended until it was twice the length of a man's arm, with runes appearing along its side. The two points straightened, passing lightning messages between each other, occasionally consulting the shaft. The broken fork was now a glowing rod of tremendous power.

CHAPTER FIVE

De Mona danced around like a pro boxer, landing quick punches on the thing's exposed chin. Her fist landed with the force of small jackhammers, breaking its jaw and eye socket, but the thing kept coming. The brown-suited Stalker charged her awkwardly, slashing its claws at her midsection. She managed to avoid one clawed hand, but the other tore the front of her shirt.

"You gotta do better than that," she said just before delivering a roundhouse kick to the thing's head, cracking its skull. The Stalker backpedaled but was back on her before she had a chance to catch her breath. The creature raked a hand across her face, causing De Mona to reflexively reach up to protect her eyes, leaving her stomach exposed. With inhuman strength it drove its talons into her gut, tearing through the shirt, but when it made contact with her stone-like skin the bones in the borrowed fingers snapped. The air around De Mona wavered and her body seemed to bulk up beneath the tight black shirt. The full light of the moon shone in her eyes as she let her gaze roll over the thing in the brown suit. Her control had slipped.

De Mona let out a sound that couldn't be produced by anything human. The Stalker swung its good arm around

and raked its nails across De Mona's face, but they couldn't
even break the skin. Drawing on all its might, it slammed
a fist into De Mona's gut, breaking every bone in the
already-damaged hand. Just before she plunged her index
and middle fingers into its eyes, spearing its brain, the
monster got a glimpse of the face beneath the mask and it
shuddered.

Tossing the already-decomposing corpse to the side,
De Mona looked for Gabriel, intending to rescue him
from the thing that called himself Riel. What she saw
froze her. The fork had changed into its true form in the
hands of young Redfeather. Though he claimed to be
ignorant concerning the artifact, the thing answered to
his every whim as he matched Riel strike for strike.
The way Gabriel moved, you'd have thought he and the
relic were old friends. She still intended saving his ass,
but when the battle was done he would tell her what
she needed to know about the fork whether he wanted to
or not.

Before she could move to help, another Stalker seemed
to appear out of thin air and slammed into the distracted
girl. This one must've been a pro wrestler in life, because
it was built like a tank with tree stumps for limbs. At the
same time the creature made its second lunge, De Mona
threw herself out of the way. Pain shot from her scalp and
spread throughout her face as the Stalker grabbed a handful of her hair and yanked. Instead of trying to pull away,
she spun towards the creature like a tiny cyclone, ripping
away chunks of flesh each time her clawed hands struck
the creature. The flesh just over the corpse's ribs and
heart sizzled as the poison from her nails killed the flesh.
The creature howled and loosened its grip enough for her
to slip out of its reach.

De Mona snapped her hands at the wrists, flicking the

Stalker's bodily fluids and the excess poison to the ground. She raked her nails across one another, causing a faint spark, and glared at the Stalker. "Come get it."

"You'll need more than a light show to save you, Knight," Riel said, circling Gabriel while trying to shield his eyes from the trident's glare. "But it's good to see that you do have at least a little fight in you." He tossed his blade from one hand to the other. "Let's have at it then."

Riel moved with inhuman speed as he charged Gabriel, Poison swinging in a high arc, only to meet the head of the trident instead of Gabriel's throat. When the two ancient weapons collided they sent a ripple of power out like a stone hitting a still pond. Riel tried to force Poison into Gabriel's neck, but the man's strength rivaled that of the demon. Gabriel's brown eyes seemed to melt in on themselves, leaving behind two silver pools. Within these pools identical storm clouds rolled over a barren hill, lightning flashing in their wake.

"This cannot be," Riel hissed, with fear edging into his voice.

Gabriel smiled triumphantly at Riel. "Ah, but it is, lapdog of the dark lord. The storm master has returned." With the force of his will Gabriel pushed outward, flinging Riel backward. "And my rain shall cleanse the earth!"

"If it's all the same to you, I'll stay dirty for a while," Riel said smugly, staggering to his feet. When inhabiting a host's body he also adapted some of the demon's resilience but could still be broken. The host's ribs had been cracked, but the body was still functional. "Lord Titus will have your heart for this, dog!"

Gabriel cocked his head as if he'd heard something in the distance. His face suddenly twisted and the thunder became louder. "You serve the betrayer? The whore of Belthon was supposed to be as a god, but instead he commands an army of half demons and walking corpses," Gabriel chuckled in the voice that wasn't quite his; lightning webbed his lips when he spoke. "I think his death shall be sweetest. But first, back to hell with you." Gabriel pointed the trident for emphasis.

Riel took a defensive stance. "Surely I'll be sitting with my master soon enough, but not this night," Raising his Poison in the air, he shouted, "Attend me!"

The air whistled behind Gabriel and he moved barely a second before another Stalker shot out from behind him. Gabriel grabbed the thing by its decomposing neck and held the head of the trident near its face. The Stalker cringed as the skin on its cheek began to smoke.

"Behold what the mighty armies of hell have been reduced to." Gabriel tossed the Stalker roughly to the ground. "Borrowed flesh!" Gabriel howled as he raised the trident high above his head and plunged it into the Stalker's heart. White light began to pour from its eyes, mouth, and ruined ears. For a brief moment Gabriel could see what the host had looked like before becoming a victim of Belthon's evil. The portly man even seemed to be smiling as his spirit rose from his body in a wisp of smoke. His soul was finally free, and all that was left of his body was the clothes he had been buried in and a pile of charred flesh. Gabriel turned his attention back to Riel, but the demon was gone.

De Mona seemed to be holding her own against the wrestler, but the hulking corpse was wearing her down. She threw a wild punch at the thing, which grabbed her and slung her onto a car, breaking the windshield. De Mona tried to recover, but the hulk had her by the neck and was lifting her off the car. She hit it with a series of lefts and rights, but it didn't seem to want to let go.

Gabriel raised the trident over his head and began twirling it like a baton. With every pass the wind picked up until he found himself standing in the center of a small storm. Lightning rolled up his legs and passed through his arms, like veins transporting blood. With all his might he hurled the trident at the creature. The creature shrieked as the trident buried itself in the hulk's back and released its soul.

Gabriel stood over De Mona with a strange look in his eye. The storm was gone, but he was changed somehow, almost as if he had aged since they'd met in the library. Reaching down with his free hand, he helped De Mona to her feet. Her skin felt a little rough, but otherwise she had returned to normal.

"You okay?" he asked.

"My throat is sore as hell, but I think I'll live." She massaged it for emphasis. "Neat trick." She motioned towards the trident.

"I didn't do it. One minute I'm about to get my head chopped off, and the next I'm all fuzzy. I knew I was fighting, but it was like I was moving off instinct rather than courage. This won that battle." He tapped the shaft twice on the ground as if he was trying to test its authenticity. The shaft vibrated and began to shrink. Within seconds it was the head of a fork again but had retained its luster. "Unreal." Gabriel shook his head.

"I got the feeling you ain't telling me everything, Red-feather," De Mona accused.

"I could say the same. I don't see a weapon on you, yet the thing that jumped you is dead." He nodded towards the rotted corpse.

She shrugged. "I got lucky."

Gabriel clearly didn't believe her, but he didn't press it. "You and me are definitely gonna do some talking, but not here and not now. With all the noise we made, the police are surely gonna come, and I really don't think they'll believe us about how these bodies got here."

De Mona looked around at the damage they'd caused. "Okay, you got that one. Where to?"

"Harlem, to see my grandfather," Gabriel told her, stuffing the fork down the back of his pants.

CHAPTER SIX

The first patrol car had barely been at the scene for five minutes when it was joined by a midnight blue Dodge Viper. The officers hadn't had a chance to call the crime in yet, so they knew it couldn't have been one of theirs. The senior officer on the scene went to tell the driver to move along, but the door swung open before he had a chance.

The man who emerged from the vehicle was tall, with an athletic build. A subtle wind played with the hem of his leather jacket, exposing the two Colts holstered under each arm. If you looked closely you could see the runes carved into the barrel and grip of the one on his left. His face was a smooth chocolate color, with an angular chin and a wide nose that he had inherited from his Guyanese mother. Though there was no sun, he wore heavily tinted shades over his eyes. Neatly twisted locks were pulled into a tight ponytail, which hung down his back. A lit cigarette dangled from his full lips, sending flecks of ash floating on the breeze. He was quite handsome, yet most people tended to forget his face right after seeing it, which was how he preferred things. Secrecy was his edge. Flicking his cigarette away, he approached the crime scene.

"Sir, I'm gonna have to ask you to get back in your

vehicle and move along. This is a police matter." A chubby cop with a beet-red face blocked his path.

"It's cool, man. I'm with the department." Rogue flashed his identification.

The chubby officer squinted to read the name beneath the blurred picture. " 'Jonathan Rogue,' " he read aloud. "I've heard of you. You aren't a cop; you're some kind of bounty hunter or something."

Rogue grinned. "*Or something*, that's cute."

Rogue's name was notorious amongst law enforcement in New York. He had once been a third-generation cop, who had a promising future with the Dade County narcotics division down in Florida until his temper got him suspended. A little girl had overdosed on heroin in one of Carol City's housing projects. Rogue's own sister had overdosed years earlier, so he took the girl's death personally and took the law into his own hands. He hadn't intended killing the dealer, but things got out of hand and Rogue found himself sitting in front of the Internal Affairs review board. Because of his family's deep connections in the department, the death was ruled a justifiable homicide, so Rogue was able to avoid jail time, but because of his history of being especially brutal on dealers he was kicked off the force.

The fact that Rogue had been a good cop earned him the respect of criminals and law enforcement, but it was his gift for spell casting that made him the scourge of the supernatural world. In addition to being a third-generation cop, Rogue was also a seventh-generation mage. The mages were spell casters, but not like witches or sorcerers. The difference was something like that between a pancake and a crepe, the same but different. Though hardly as gifted in the blood as sorcerers, mages made up in knowledge what they lacked in natural ability, dissecting and reconstructing age-old magics to suit their own dark purposes.

The mages represented another spectrum of the magical wheel where light and dark were irrelevant and only power was absolute.

Like the witches, the mages also had covens of sorts called houses. Rogue's family represented the house of Thanos, the death cult. Thanos was one of two remaining mage houses in the modern world. The followers of the fallen god were said to be masters of death magic and traffickers of the dark. Some even whispered that their powers derived from the spirits they held prisoners in their black towers.

However, Rogue and his family didn't adhere to the general practices of their lineage. Since Rogue was a little boy his father had always taught his family that their gifts should only be used to help humanity and uphold the law. A sound philosophy until you learn that the line between law and lawlessness has become so blurred that doing the right thing feels wrong. Still, law and order was in Rogue's veins and the situation demanded his attention.

"I prefer the term 'consultant,'" Rogue continued, "and I consult you jokers more than I handle my own cases. Hell, it's a wonder that I even stay in business."

"I don't care what and who you are; you can't cross the line. This is a crime scene," the chubby officer shot back. He folded his arms and stared at Rogue defiantly.

Rogue sighed. He'd been hoping that he could use just his fast tongue to get what he needed from the crime scene, but the cop was being a prick about it and Rogue didn't have time to play twenty questions. He was hoping he didn't have to rattle the cage, but Rogue wasn't big on twenty questions. "Let me talk to you for a second." Rogue moved closer to the officer. Peering over the top of his shades, he said, "I just want a quick look to see if this is related to a jumper I'm looking for. I won't disturb the scene."

The chubby officer knew that it was against procedure to let a civilian onto a crime scene, but there was something about the soothing tone of Rogue's voice that made him feel wrong for denying the man. "I guess a quick look won't hurt anything; just don't tell the sergeant," the officer said, not quite believing the words coming out of his mouth as he spoke.

"Good man." Rogue patted him on the back and crossed the yellow tape. His guest snickered quietly, but Rogue blocked him out. As he got closer, he could see body parts and broken glass strewn all over the parking lot. At the edge of the crime scene there was a second officer leaning against a car, spitting up the leftover Chinese food he'd had for dinner.

"What've we got here?" Rogue asked, startling the second officer.

"Hey, you're not supposed to be back here," the officer said, wiping his mouth with the back of his hand.

"It's cool; I'm with the department," Rogue told him, infusing his words with power.

The man's face was unsure, but his words came out steady. "It's like nothing I've ever seen." He nodded towards the scene. "It's as if somebody dropped a bunch of rotting corpses all over the street. I count at least three of them."

"Rotting corpses?" Rogue raised an eyebrow behind his dark glasses.

"If that's what you wanna call 'em," the chubby officer said as he joined them.

Rogue turned his back on the officers and stepped close to one of the corpses. Behind his sunglasses Rogue let the boundaries of the physical world fall away and examined the scene with his *other* eyes. The fluids on the ground were fresh, but the corpse had died long before that night. The corpses were without a doubt Stalkers, which was what concerned him. These were the foot soldiers of hell and had no business being so far away from the keeps and estates that hid their masters away from the world. It had been the sixth sighting in almost as many nights, definitely a bad sign. If these beasties were running loose in his city, then something big was going down.

Rogue removed a small penknife from his pocket and knelt beside one of the corpses. The stench reminded him of a murdered dealer he'd come across in his days on the force. The man had had his throat cut and was stuffed into a meat locker. He'd been in there for at least a week before his body was uncovered. Rogue collected a sample on the tip of his knife and scraped it off into one of the small glass vials he kept in his pocket for such things. It would take a day or two to complete the spell that would lead him back to whatever had destroyed the monsters, but from the way the Stalkers had been dismembered he wasn't sure if he wanted to.

"What do you make of it, sir?" the chubby officer asked, a little unnerved by how still the bounty hunter had gone.

Rogue stood and turned his shaded eyes to the chubby officer. "I think it was a classic case of vandalism. Some kids probably got drunk and trashed a few cars." He shrugged. "Not much to do except contact the owners and hope their insurance is paid up."

The chubby officer looked at Rogue as if he had taken leave of his senses. "Rogue, I don't know if this is getting through to you or not, but we've got three stiffs here. I think this goes way beyond drunken kids. I gotta call it in."

"Couldn't agree with you more." Rogue removed his sunglasses and stood directly in front of the officer. The chubby officer froze when he looked into Rogue's eyes . . . the eyes of something that was clearly not of this world. They were black, but not like the color. They were the black of the universe before the supposed big bang that created the world. A black so deep that even if you shone a flashlight in them, they still could not reflect the light. Dancing within the blackness were dozens of star-like flakes. Staring into Rogue's eyes was like looking up at a Nebraska sky on a crisp September night. The eyes were a gift and a curse from a demon his youngest brother had been foolish enough to summon and lose control of. With the combined efforts of Rogue and his father and uncle, they were able to coerce the demon back to the pit it had crawled out of, but not without a price. When you are dealing with demons there's always a price.

Through the soulless eyes Rogue was able to see the world as no mortal ever would. He could see people for what they truly were and sometimes what he saw was horrifying, which was why he wore the sunglasses, to help block out the ugliness of the world. And just as Rogue could see as the demon would, the same held true for the donor. The demon could see the world with the simplicity of a mortal without leaving the solitude of its pit. The eyes bound them not only in sight but also in power. Because of their connection Rogue found that he was able to tap into the darkness to add to his own magic, magic that he used to banish the creatures of the dark and sometimes those of the light. No one escaped the bounty hunter when he was set on a trail.

Locking gazes with the chubby officer, Rogue called his power. The starry night in his eyes brightened and the flakes began to swirl in the darkness. "When you call it in, you will report it just as I said. Some kids got drunk and made a mess of some cars, do you understand?" The chubby officer was so enthralled that you could've slapped him in the face and he probably wouldn't have noticed. This was just a sample of the centuries-old magic Rogue commanded.

"Sure thing," the chubby officer said, through a goofy grin. His partner stood beside him nodding. By the time their heads cleared they wouldn't even remember having spoken with the bounty hunter.

Rogue made one last circuit of the parking lot, sprinkling a brown powder over the corpses he passed while mumbling in Swahili under his breath. When he was back behind the wheel of his Viper he began processing what he'd learned, and it didn't sit well with him. One or two Stalkers he could've shrugged off as a coincidence, but six sightings meant that something nasty was about to go down in the rotten Apple, and he'd more than likely find himself in the middle of it. Throwing the car in gear, Rogue peeled out onto the road. In his rearview mirror he could see the effects of the aging spell he'd cast as the wind began to take what was left of the decomposing corpses.

CHAPTER SEVEN

After a very cautious trek to 86th Street and Lexington, Gabriel and De Mona boarded the 4 train. It was only one stop to 125th, but the ride seemed to take forever. People spared the soiled couple a brief look, but no one commented on their appearance. In New York City you were liable to see far stranger things on the subway than two people in dirty clothes.

After exiting the train station they headed west, crossing 127th Street. Both of them were wrapped in their own thoughts but still very alert. De Mona watched Gabriel curiously as he led the way through the streets of Harlem. She had known there was something unusual about the fork but never imagined how much so. If the grandson was able to bring it to life by touching it, then the grandfather would surely know how best to use it against her father's murderers.

When they got to 127th and Fifth Avenue, Gabriel motioned for her to stop. Within the shadowy doorway of a building he detected movement. His immediately removed the trident from his pants and tried to activate it. To his surprise, it did nothing. Though it was still warm to the touch, he could not will it to life as he had done in the parking lot. Just as they were about to break and run, a homeless man with a shabby white beard stepped from the doorway. He gave them a curious glance and continued foraging through trash cans.

De Mona let out a breath. "What happened? I thought you were gonna make with the light show again?"

"I don't know." Gabriel turned the fork over in his hand. "Maybe I busted it in the fight. I'll check it when we get to my house."

"Well, how much further is it? I'll feel a lot safer once we're off the streets."

"It's just up the way." Gabriel motioned up the street.

They continued deeper into the block until they came to a brownstone. It stood about four stories, with a small iron fence blocking the entrance. The brownstone wasn't as well kept as some of the others on the block and wasn't in the best condition.

Bypassing the main entrance, Gabriel led De Mona down the three steps that led to the basement of the building. The door was made of a very thick wood and De Mona could make out faint markings in its finish. When she mouthed them a stale taste settled at the back of her throat. She knew just what they were but wondered how well they were cast.

Gabriel looked in the window. "He's here, the light is still on." He slipped his key into the door lock and turned. "Come on." He cleared the threshold, pulling her by the hand.

De Mona took a deep breath and stepped forward. There was nothing at first, but when she tried to step fully into the house, fire shot up her arms. It was so intense that De Mona couldn't even scream; she just whimpered and fell backward into the trash cans.

"Jesus, are you okay?" Gabriel rushed to her side and helped her up.

"I'm good." De Mona rubbed her arms. There were small welts crossing them, but her body was already beginning the process of healing them over. "Just give me a second."

"What was that all about?"

"A ward," a deep voice answered. "Set to keep out the enemies of my lord. Now, who and what are you?" The speaker cocked the slide of the twelve-gauge he was holding. He was a large man, with hawk-like features. His silver hair hung loose down his back. Though he had a pleasant face, there was a hard edge to him. He was a man who had seen some horrible things in his lifetime.

"Granddad, wait!" Gabriel stepped between them.

"Move aside, Gabriel," his grandfather said sternly. The shotgun was firmly pressed against his shoulder, not even wavering when his own flesh stepped into its deadly line of fire. "That ward was set to only go off when something truly vile tried to cross it. Who is this girl, and what evil have you foolishly tried to bring into our home?"

"Mr. Redfeather, I can explain." De Mona took a step towards him.

He aimed it at her face. "As God is my witness, if you take another step I'll blow you clean back to hell, demon."

Gabriel looked at his grandfather as if he had completely lost it. "Granddad, De Mona's no demon. Please, put the gun down before someone gets hurt."

De Mona discreetly took stock of her situation. She didn't want to fight, but she would if the issue was forced. She reasoned that even if the old man did manage to get a shot off, she could take him before he managed to inflict any serious damage, but Gabriel might present a problem. She'd seen what he could do, even unintentionally, under the thrall of the trident, and the idea of being rent limb from limb didn't sit well with her. Even if she was able to defeat Gabriel, the discharge from the trident would attract the Stalkers, and in her exhausted condition it'd be a lopsided fight. No, reason had to prevail where violence wouldn't.

"Mr. Redfeather, we don't have time for this. I assure you that I didn't come here to fight. All I want is answers and I was led to believe that this is where I'd find them. Now, we can stand out here and bicker until the Stalkers regroup and swoop down to kill us all, or we can go inside and talk like normal people." She made to take a step in the old man's direction and the gun went off.

The stench of gunpowder in the cramped space was so pungent that it made Gabriel's eyes water. When the smoke cleared and the ringing in his ears subsided he looked at the aftermath of his grandfather's paranoia in wide-eyed shock.

The shotgun blast had burned several large holes in De Mona's already-tattered shirt, but the skin beneath was still smooth and unblemished, save for the powder residue that stained it. Her face was still beautiful after the change, if not more so with the soft glow of the moon dancing in her now-black eyes. A small spine of bone started at the bridge of her nose and went up to her forehead, while two slightly thicker ones went from her eyebrows to her hairline. Her full lip drew back, revealing elongated canines as she glared at the man holding the smoking shotgun.

"Sweet Jesus." Gabriel stumbled backward. He was shocked by the revelation, but Redfeather wasn't.

"I cast thee back!" Redfeather tried to get off another shot, but De Mona moved with inhuman speed. She snatched the gun from him with so much force that he feared she broke his fingers. She belched a low growl as she curled the butt and barrel of the gun until they formed a U. The animal inside her screamed for the blood of the last of the Redfeather clan, but luckily the rational side was still the ruling force.

Redfeather slid a hunting knife from his belt and held it, poised to strike at the thing. "Leave us be," he half-commanded, half-pleaded.

With great concentration De Mona tried to make her face look as normal as possible. The spines and fangs had receded, but the moon still flashed in her eyes. "I told you that I didn't come here to hurt you, but if you attack me again, you'll learn that this trick works on bones too." She held up the mangled shotgun. She waited until some of the tension had eased before continuing. "My name is De Mona Sanchez; you knew my parents, Edward and Mercy."

Redfeather's eyes showed recognition. "Mercy's child?" he said. He knew full well the story of Edward and Mercy. Redfeather had happened upon Mercy years ago while working as a researcher for Sanctuary. She had been a refugee of a war that still raged in the farthest corners of the world, seeking amnesty in America. Like most of the demons who immigrated, she had to be processed at Sanctuary.

Edward had volunteered himself as her sponsor, someone who would familiarize her with the laws of Sanctuary and humanity to help with the transition. Next to the goblins, the Valkrin were the most feared warriors of the Dark Order and, until then, the most loyal to their cause. To hear an account of their culture as told by one of their own was a rarity, and he jumped at the chance to record it for the Order of Sanctuary's database.

Edward was taken aback when he first met Mercy. She awaited him in the garden, dressed in a simple white linen gown, with her thick black hair tied into a French braid. When she smiled up at him it was as if the sun shone a little brighter. He knew that the Valkrin were amongst the few demons who had a human form, but he hadn't expected her to be so breathtakingly beautiful. Had she been of this realm he would've placed her heritage with one of the Aztec tribes. Physically, Mercy didn't appear to be more than thirty or so, but at the time she was well over two hundred years old. Mercy was battle hardened, as was expected, but she was also very well-read and intelligent. During their first session she confided in him that she had spent a great deal of time amongst humans, studying them for the Dark Order as well as her own curiosity, and found herself attracted to their almost child-like weakness. Amongst her kind the weak were shunned and often cannibalized by the stronger warriors, but amongst the humans there was no shame in weakness. When she was away she found herself longing to be back amongst her humans she studied, so on her last outing she had decided that she would remain amongst the strange creatures and sought protection from the Order of Sanctuary.

Sometimes they would just sit for hours, talking like two schoolkids about everything from the differences between the nine hells to the superiority of DVDs over VHS tapes. Eventually their relationship grew beyond his just being her sponsor to their actually becoming good friends. In him she found someone whose intelligence rivaled her own, and in her he found a willing student, eager for not only knowledge but also love and the understanding of it.

It came as no surprise when Edward sponsored her visa, but it caused quite a stir when the two became lovers. Redfeather had been there to witness the waves Edward's decision caused amongst those who still hadn't quite adjusted to the idea of demons living amongst us. And a few months later when he decided to marry Mercy it made him an outcast. After a while it became too much for the couple, so Edward left Sanctuary, choosing to live a quiet life with his bride. He and Redfeather kept in touch for a while, but the letters and e-mails became less and less frequent as Edward's antiquing business expanded.

"My Lord in heaven." Redfeather's eyes got wide as if he was just realizing what she had been trying to tell him. He lowered the knife but didn't re-sheath it. He studied De Mona carefully while she studied him in return.

"Would you like me to pose so you can take a picture?" she asked sarcastically.

"I don't mean to stare, but you're the first progeny of a demon/human that I've ever seen in person. Where are your parents? Are Edward and Mercy well?" he asked. From the concerned look on his face you'd have never known that he'd shot De Mona a few moments prior.

A flicker of movement across the street caught De Mona's eye, causing her to stiffen. Thankfully it was only a hungry alley cat in search of food, but the next time it could be one of Belthon's killers in search of their heads. "Mr. Redfeather, to make a long story short, I have no idea where my mother is and my father was murdered a few nights ago, apparently for that thing your grandson has in his pants." Gabriel blushed when she said this. "I'll be happy to fill in the blanks, but there's a demon lord trying to kill us and I'd much rather not make the job easier by standing out here in the open like three lost crackheads. Now can you douse the wards so we can go inside and talk like normal people?"

After disarming the wards Redfeather led them to what he called his study. More accurately, it was a basement storage area filled beyond capacity with clutter. Three bookcases, each easily a head taller than a man, dominated the back wall. It was bursting with literature covering just about everything known to man and some things that weren't. For as interesting as Redfeather's library was, it was the wall closet just behind a desk that you could barely see for the papers and scrolls covering it. On the shelves of the cases were books in every shape, size, and color. Some were new paperbacks, while others were older, leather-bound works. Dominating the left wall, the one closest to De Mona, was a tribute to books and different oddities. There were bookshelves dominating every wall in the small basement apartment, on any- and everything imaginable. They lined shelves, were stacked on tables, and in some places were strewn all over the floor. De Mona didn't think she had read even a quarter as many books in her entire life.

With a sweep of his arm, Redfeather cleared away some books and loose papers that had been hiding a worn green love seat and motioned for them to sit. De Mona, feeling quite weary, plopped down on one of the lumpy pillows. She looked up at Gabriel, who was just staring down at her, rooted to the spot over by one of the bookshelves. She hated to spring it on him like that, but his grandfather had taken away the choice when he got trigger-happy.

"I'm sorry to hear about your father." Redfeather perched himself on the edge of a cluttered desk. "What happened?"

De Mona tore her eyes away from Gabriel and looked up at Redfeather. "To tell you the truth, I'm still trying to figure it out." De Mona went on to tell Redfeather the abbreviated version of what she'd shared with Gabriel. She told Redfeather of the night that she and her cousin had come back from the movies and found her father. "He was in a bad way," she recalled. "They'd bled him to the point of death, and to add insult to it he was bound to a chair by his intestines." She paused, nearly choking on the words. "It's a miracle that he lived long enough to say good-bye. I wanted to call for help, but he wouldn't let me. He said that getting this fork back to the church took precedence over everything, even his life."

"Wait a second," Gabriel interjected. "You said that you needed to find out what it was?"

"I *do* need to find out what it is. My father died because of that fork, and I intend to find out why."

"Fork?" Redfeather asked, looking from De Mona to Gabriel.

"Oh, with all that was going on I almost forgot." Gabriel pulled the fork from his pants and held it up to eye level. The fork pulsed once in his hand, sending faint waves of heat up his arm.

Redfeather made the sign of the cross and stepped back as if the fork would strike him. "The Nimrod." His voice quivered.

"You know what this thing is, Granddad?"

Redfeather tried to hide the panic that was creeping into his voice. "The greatest gift and curse ever bestowed upon the world by the gods. Quickly." He tossed Gabriel an old jacket that had been draped over the back of a chair. "Wrap it!"

"What's wrong?" Gabriel asked nervously.

"Just do as I say!" Redfeather snapped.

Gabriel took the coat and began wrapping it. The vibrating got stronger, and the warmth was trying to shift to a burn. Only after he had completely wrapped it in the coat did the thing go still.

"If they know that's the Nimrod, they'll swoop down on us," Redfeather said, pacing back and forth nervously. Every so often he would spare a glance at the wrapped fork as if it would leap up through the jacket and smite them all. Having an item of biblical fame in his midst clearly made him uneasy.

"If by 'they' you mean the demons, it's too late. They jumped us outside the library at Gabriel's school."

His pacing stopped. "You've seen them? The dark agents?"

"Not only did we see them, but Gabriel kicked their asses." De Mona smirked.

"Is this true?" he asked his grandson.

Gabriel looked at his shoes. "Not exactly. De Mona helped."

"That thing," De Mona pointed to the lump under the suit jacket, "came to life in his hands and went all mystic. He claims to have no knowledge of it, though he handled it quite well." She looked at Gabriel and then back to Redfeather.

Redfeather looked at his grandson, his eyes pleading for it to be a lie, but the truth shone in Gabriel's face.

"I'm not really sure what happened, but I was scared and needed to get out of there, and the fork knew it." Gabriel shrugged. "This relic," he nodded at the bag, "the things that jumped us in the parking lot . . . It's like an old wives' tale used to scare children. Scientifically this is all impossible."

"Two things I've learned in life are that not all things can be explained by science and that there's a truth in even the tallest tales, Gabriel," Redfeather told him. "You coming into possession of the Nimrod is amazing, but it answering to your touch is something that I've dreaded my whole life."

Redfeather looked from the angered De Mona to the confused Gabriel. If the fork came to life in the hands of Redfeather's grandson, that meant it had chosen him. "Why?" was still an unanswered question. Seeing the Nimrod brought back a rush of memories Redfeather had buried deep within his mind. Most of the others thought that the stories the elders had told them about the Seven-Day Siege were just stories, but Redfeather knew better. He knew firsthand not only that the dark horde was real but also what they were capable of. It had been one of the main reasons for his leaving the order.

For as much as he would've liked to believe that the second war was a myth, the thing lying wrapped on the floor of his study was more reality than he was ready for. As it had centuries ago, the Nimrod had answered to the touch of a Redfeather. The pendulum was set swinging and the battle for souls would begin. Though he'd hoped he'd never have to, it was time to tell Gabriel their family secret.

CHAPTER EIGHT

Gabriel and De Mona watched Redfeather for at least five minutes, but he didn't say a word. He paced the carpeted office, occasionally casting a glance at the lump of cloth. A thousand lies couldn't avert what he knew was coming. Whether he liked it or not, the vengeful thing had chosen his grandson, and he needed to be prepared.

"This thing is a curse dating back to the siege," Redfeather finally said.

"The siege." Gabriel absently ran his hand through his slightly mussed hair. "Isn't that the story you used to tell me when I was a kid? It was something about a battle between saints and demons, right?"

"Knights," De Mona corrected. "They were called the Knights of Christ. My dad told me the story a time or two."

"I always thought that it was something you used to tell me just for kicks," Gabriel said to Redfeather. "The idea of demons actually existing just seemed a little out there . . . no offense," he said to De Mona, who just grunted.

"No, the siege really happened, and Ms. Sanchez," he nodded towards De Mona, "should be proof enough for you that they walk amongst us." Redfeather moved towards one of the massive bookshelves, running his finger along the spines. He selected a thick, leather-bound book and tested its weight in his hand. "The story of the Seven-Day Siege was passed down from parent to child since after the last demon was slain. When our enemies were lain low, the Knights were disbanded and entrusted with the anointed weapons. It was our job to guard the weapons and the story in case the Knights would one day be called back to arms. We were to be prepared in case the forces of hell moved on humanity again. Though the Order of the Knights was disbanded, our ancestors made sure that we would never forget the men and women who died in the battle, or would we be ill prepared if the forces of hell tried to move against humanity again."

Gabriel's face suddenly went placid. "Granddad, why do you keep saying 'we'?"

He looked up into the questioning face of his grandson. "Because it was our blood that won that day, and our blood which was to be hunted for all time by the dark agents. They will not rest until the last of the Hunters are no more."

"Grandfather, I'm a vegetarian, remember? I'm no more of a hunter than you are." He smirked at his grandfather.

Redfeather looked at his wrinkled hands and flexed them as if he were holding something. "But I was not always the man you see before you. It wasn't so long ago that I stood proudly with the order, and my son with me. Your father was amongst the bravest of our brethren until he fell victim to the dark."

"My father?" The subject of his father and that faithful night brought back painful memories. When Gabriel was a child, he had been a part of his parents' carnival act, the Flying Redfeathers. They would wow the crowd every night with their death-defying acts; they had even traveled with a French circus troupe for a time. Those had been the best years of Gabriel's life, until a freak fire in a trailer had put an end to it all. The only thing that had spared Gabriel's life was the fact that he had been in town with some of the other performers getting supplies when the fire broke out. The blaze had claimed parents, uncle, and older brother, leaving Gabriel alone in the world until he was taken in by his grandfather.

"But they all died in an accidental fire," Gabriel said emotionally.

"It was a fire that claimed them, but it was no accident; it was the work of hell's minions," Redfeather admitted. "I'm sorry that I lied to you, Gabriel, but I did so to hide the terrible truth from you."

"And what is that truth?" Gabriel asked sharply. He couldn't believe that the one person he had trusted most in the world had lied to him.

The tone of his voice stung the old man, but Redfeather understood Gabriel's pain. Redfeather placed his hand on a large Bible that was on the bottom shelf and looked up at his grandson. "Gabriel, before I go on I must know that you are ready to accept what I have to tell you."

"I wanna know," Gabriel said in a low voice.

Redfeather nodded. "Very well then," he said before pulling the Bible halfway off the shelf. A grinding sound came from the bookshelf to Gabriel's left, just before it unhitched from the wall and slid to the side. Behind it was a glass display case, which crept forward on its wheeled stand. Inside the case was a breastplate that looked to be made of animal bones. Resting on a slender pole just behind it was a headdress of beautiful brown and white feathers. Gabriel found that it was extremely difficult to tear his eyes away from the hidden treasure, to pay attention to his grandfather's explanation.

"This is the armor that protected our ancestors and our lineage during the Seven-Day Siege." Redfeather traced the angle of the display case. It had been over ten years since he had last had reason to lay eyes on the armor. "He was the most skilled tracker in the Black Hills, when they still belonged to us, and friend to both animals and beast people. It was even said that he had one day taken one for his bride, but let me not get ahead of myself. He was to lead the hunt against the evil, but as it turned out, he ended up being the one to win the battle."

"Wait a second, I'm no expert, but wasn't someone called the Bishop supposed to be their general?" De Mona asked, trying to remember the whole tale in her head.

"Yes, Bishop Michael Francisco was indeed chosen to wield the Nimrod, but the last strike was not his," Redfeather informed her. "When the Bishop was slain by the dark forces, it was the Hunter who picked up the trident, and to everyone's surprise it answered to him. The Hunter turned the tide that day and closed the rift, sending the demons back to hell. Though some of them escaped, the nastiest were purged from this world."

"So you think that this is that trident?" Gabriel knelt beside the fork. He hadn't really meant to, but he rubbed his hand across the fabric of the jacket, tracing the outline of the fork with his fingers. It was like angels dancing along his arm and singing the sweetest melody in his ears.

"If the things you've told me tonight are true, yes," Redfeather said. "There were thirteen anointed weapons in all, one for each of the chosen, but the trident was the most powerful. Over the years the items were lost, resurfacing here and there every so often. The forces of the light have been able to recover some, but so have the dark forces. There are a few floating around somewhere, but I have no idea how many."

"Well, if these things were so damn dangerous, how come they were able to get lost in the shuffle? I mean, didn't the Knights or the pope think to safeguard them in some way?"

"They did." Redfeather knelt to unlock the case. "The Knights who survived agreed to keep their artifacts in case they were ever called to duty again. Some of the order stayed on to serve the church or Sanctuary, while others faded, living their lives as if the siege had never happened. It was peaceful for a while, but the peace was short-lived. It took several years, but one by one the Knights and their descendants were hunted by the dark forces and slaughtered. Families, friends, livestock . . . the demons spared none. Very few of the original lines survived, the Redfeathers being one of them."

Gabriel walked over to the case and examined the items inside closely. His eyes drank in the beauty of the feathers in the headdress and how well preserved they were. Attached to the headdress was a faceplate, also carved from bone. The eagle's powerful beak curved down into a near razor-sharp slope, hooking slightly at the tip. He stared into the dark pits that would've been the bird's eyes, feeling a tickling whisper in the back of his head, while they spoke without speaking.

"I am the master of the storm."

Gabriel looked around to see if anyone else had heard the whisper, but neither De Mona nor his grandfather gave any indication that they had.

"It was said," Redfeather snapped Gabriel out of his daze, "that the king of the eagles gave of his own feathers to make that band." He nodded at the headdress. "It endowed Redfeather with great sight. The bones," he nodded to the breastplate, "were donated by the wolves. They felt that the souls of their kills would reinforce the armor to protect him from harm."

"Whispering Hound," Gabriel breathed.

Redfeather stared at his grandson. "That was one of

the names given to him. He had the nose and instincts of a tracker, but the sweet tongue of a politician. The Bishop often kept council with the Hunter, and it was the Hunter's sweet words that convinced the animals to throw in their lot with the Knights against the demons."

Gabriel reached up and removed the headdress from its stand. He inhaled deep of the eagle's wings, letting the knowledge embroidered into the feathers seep through him. When he spoke, it was his voice, but words from another time. "Our ancestor was a great hunter, and always brought more meat back to the village than any two men. What most didn't know, not even his brothers, was that he spoke the language of the animals. While others shunned the wolves and fierce things that hunted the plains, Redfeather befriended them. He had hunted with the mountain lions of the great slopes, and taken vengeance with the wolves when their packs were being poached." Gabriel raised the headdress to place it over his head but hesitated.

"Gabriel?" Redfeather touched his shoulder. His grandfather's hand brought Gabriel back to the here and now.

"I'm fine," Gabriel said, fighting off the nausea that was trying to get him to embarrass himself. "Please, continue." He placed the headdress on the seat next to him.

Redfeather nodded. He was hesitant to pick up the worn gauntlet. Though in all the years he'd been in possession of it, it had never reacted to his touch, it still made him uneasy. "This was Redfeather's anointed weapon, the Dagger of Fate." He held up a rusty dagger that Gabriel hadn't noticed before. Its blade was bent and worn, but the bone handle was still smooth. When Gabriel reached for the dagger, Redfeather almost snatched it back. It was so faint that he almost didn't notice it, but he was all too familiar with the allure of the anointed weapons.

Redfeather placed the dagger on the table and pulled

another volume from the shelf. "The details are sketchy on this one, as it wasn't one of the original thirteen weapons."

"I thought all these fabled weapons came from the guys in the pretty robes," De Mona interrupted.

"For the most part they did, but the dagger had belonged to the Hunter since he was a boy. It was passed down from his father." Redfeather went back to studying the book. "It wasn't the most imposing of the weapons, but it was a power unto itself and when wielded by the Hunter it always rang true."

"Doesn't look like much to me," De Mona said in a very unimpressed tone.

Redfeather turned to her. "I'd think that you, if anyone, could attest to the fact that surface appearances don't count for much."

Gabriel picked the dagger up off the table and tested its weight. It was subtle, but he could feel the power answering to his blood. Like the Nimrod, it pulsed under his touch, but the power felt different . . . cleaner. "For as long as I hold you, my people shall never go hungry." The words came from somewhere inside Gabriel's head.

De Mona eyed him suspiciously. "Funny, a few hours ago you acted as if you'd never seen that Nimrod thing, but suddenly you're very knowledgeable about all this. Is there something you want to share with me?"

He looked up from the dagger that he had been studying intensely. "I don't . . . I mean, I didn't. It's just like seeing all this stuff is filling my head with information." He massaged his temples. Feeling nauseous, he went back to sit beside the headdress. Something magical passed between the dagger and the headdress and he again found himself touching the feathers.

"It has to be the Bishop," Redfeather spoke up.

"What's a guy who's been dead for three hundred years have to do with what's happening now?" De Mona wanted to know.

"The Nimrod forms an almost unbreakable bond with its wielder. It had formed such a bond with the Bishop before he was consumed by it."

"What do you mean, 'consumed'?" Gabriel stared at the trident cautiously. Even though it was wrapped in the jacket, he could still see it perfectly in his mind. It was glowing and calling to him. The call was so intense that he had reached out and touched the jacket before he realized he had even moved.

"Exactly what it sounds like, the Nimrod was not only the Bishop's weapon, but it ultimately became his prison. Trapped within the trident is the soul of the Bishop," Redfeather explained, but Gabriel was only half-listening. "Gabriel?" Redfeather's voice fell on deaf ears.

The Nimrod had begun to pulse hard enough for Gabriel to feel the vibration through the couch. De Mona must have felt it too, because she looked at the wrapped jacket like it was a poisonous snake. "*The power is in the blood, the blood restores all,*" the voice whispered in the back of Gabriel's head. He looked to see if De Mona had heard it, but she was still staring at the wrapping. "*The power is in the blood,*" the voice said more sharply. Gabriel went to cover his ears and realized that he was now holding the dagger. "*The blood restores all,*" the voice repeated. Gabriel was confused at first, but when he looked at the faint glow that was emitting from the dagger he understood what needed to be done.

"What are you doing?" Redfeather moved to stop Gabriel, but it was already too late.

Gabriel watched his hands move of their own accord and placed the blade of the dagger in his right palm. A thin line of blood welled in his palm and dripped along the edge of the dagger. He watched in wonder as the blade absorbed his blood and the rust began to fall away. When the transformation was complete, it was as beautiful as it had been when the Hunter had wielded it.

"How in God's name did you do that?" Redfeather bent to inspect the dagger, but not close enough to actually touch it. In all the years he'd kept the thing it had never answered to his touch.

"I wish I knew." Gabriel started at the dagger. "These things, or whatever is empowering them, are speaking to me. Haven't either of you felt it?" He looked from De Mona to Redfeather, who were staring at him as if he were losing it. "Don't look at me like that," he snapped. Gabriel suddenly had a theory and picked up the jacket concealing the trident. "If the dagger responded to my blood, I wonder if the Nimrod will." He unwrapped the fork.

"Gabriel, you mustn't; we can't risk it binding itself to you further," Redfeather tried to caution his grandson.

"*The blood is the restorer*," the voice enticed Gabriel. Nervously he touched his bloody hand to the trident, and the room was flooded with light.

De Mona was the first to recover from the blast. A powerful wind whipped through the room, soaking both her and everything in it in rain, but there were no windows in the basement. It was as if a storm had materialized out of thin air. She looked for the humans and found Redfeather on all fours in the corner. Like De Mona, the blast had knocked him senseless. She peered through the increasing rainfall, trying to see what had become of Gabriel, and her eyes went wide. Not only was he unaffected by the freak storm; he was also the source.

He was standing in the middle of a vortex of wind, with papers and books swirling around him at an incredible rate of speed. In his hands he held the Nimrod, which had returned to its full jeweled brilliance. Lightning jumped from the trident and traveled through his body before dispersing at his feet. She tried to move to help him, but every time she tried to get up from behind the sofa the wind threatened to carry her away.

"It's the Nimrod!" Redfeather shouted over the wind.

"I know what it is, but how in the hell do we shut it off?"

"We must break the connection," Redfeather said, pulling himself along the bookshelf. He had almost made it to Gabriel when the young man turned his eyes on his grandfather, eyes that were not his own.

"The Hunters." Gabriel let out a demonic-sounding cackle. "Your lot were always the most selfless and most foolish of us." Gabriel slowly raised the trident and aimed it at his grandfather. The power flared between the broken points and died as De Mona broke a chair over Gabriel's back.

The reptilian eyes that had been watching the Redfeather brownstone from the shadows squinted against the blinding flash that had just consumed the lower level. The Stalker's natural instincts bid it to flee, but the greater fear of its master rooted it to the spot. The flash only lasted a few seconds, but the mystic print it left was a very distinctive one. The Stalker would be well rewarded when it took the information back to its master.

When the Stalker turned around to leave, a massive hand grabbed it about the neck. With enough force to shatter nearly all the bones in the creature's back, it was slammed to the ground. The Stalker clawed frantically at the meaty forearm of its attacker but found that the skin was rock hard. Gray eyes stared out from a face that was almost entirely covered in thick red hair, and the creature knew that its time within the host's body had come to an end.

"Spawn of hell," the bearded man said in a Bostonian accent, laced with a bit of his mother's Irish heritage. "In the name of my Lord and my family, I cast thee back to the pit which birthed you!" With a swing of the bearded man's massive arm, he slammed his jeweled hammer through the Stalker's skull and webbed the concrete below.

The bearded man spat on the rotting corpse of the Stalker's host body. "May your black-hearted master punish you for your failure." He pulled the hammer from the ruined mass of the body's skull and examined the black gook that now coated the head of his hammer. Before his very eyes the hammer began to absorb the substance. No matter how many times he had seen the feat, it always amazed him.

"Another one down," he said into a two-way radio's headset.

"*Good riddance*," the metallic voice squawked back. "*Any sign of more shitheads?*" This was a term the bearded man and his partners used when referring to Stalkers. Their favorite method of incapacitating Stalkers was by crushing their skulls. Whatever it was that passed for their brains always looked like shit when it oozed out.

The bearded man looked around before answering. "Not that I can see. Satan's little ass kissers have probably scuttled back to whatever holes they crawled out of."

"*I'm still gonna have Jackson look around to make sure. Morgan, you might still want to make a quick sweep of the block*," *t*he voice said.

"Not to worry, Jonas. If there are any more lurking about, Jackson and I will make short work of them, you can bet. Any idea what the hard-on is about that they have for the cute couple?"

"*Not just yet. All we've got to go on is the fact that the shitheads jumped them in the parking lot. They don't usually just attack out in the open like that. Someone sent them to pay that visit. My gift doesn't come with video feed and you guys arrived at the scene too late to actually see what happened. All we can do at this point is speculate, or ask them what happened.*"

"In a pig's eye, my friend," Morgan replied. "What would you do if a six-five Irishman and a reject from the movie *Colors* come calling about a run-in you had with a pack of zombies?"

"*They're demons who have taken possession of corpses,*" Jonas corrected him. "*You may be right about the direct approach. What I really want to know is how in the nine hells did they manage to escape? There were at least two shitheads and a demon that I haven't been able to identify yet.*"

"Maybe they told him they were going to call the police," Morgan said sarcastically.

"*I seriously doubt that. We'll keep an eye on them for now until we find out what their angle is.*"

"We aren't the only enemies the demons have out there. What if they're working for another nasty faction of this little dance?"

The line went silent for a few beats before Jonas' distorted voice came back. "*We kill them.*"

From the shadows another set of eyes was watching the turn of events. Only when he was sure the bearded man was gone did he come out to assess the situation. Casting an expressionless glance at what remained of the Stalker, the old man wrinkled his nose.

"Poor soul," he said to no one in particular. "I would beg the Lord to have mercy on you, but I'm afraid my prayers would go unanswered. There is no salvation for the servants of Belthon." The old man looked in the direction of the Redfeathers' brownstone and smirked. "Be wary, young Hunter, for the Bishop sleeps no more and his thirst for vengeance is all consuming. Keep to your faith, for only it will save you from what lies ahead." The air around the man rippled once before he vanished.

CHAPTER NINE

"You fool girl, you could've killed him." Redfeather picked his way through what was left of his study. Furniture was smashed and books that contained centuries of knowledge were now ash resting on what was left of the massive bookshelves. The Nimrod had shown its might.

"If I recall correctly I stopped him from killing you!" De Mona shot back.

Redfeather ignored her, and continued on to his grandson. Gabriel was lying in a heap, with his clothes smoldering. The Nimrod had vanished, but the air was still thick with magical residue. When Redfeather went to check for a pulse, he jerked his hand back. Gabriel's skin was almost too hot to touch.

"Gabriel!" Redfeather called out, but the boy didn't stir. Frantically Redfeather rushed into the study's small bathroom and wet a towel. When he first touched it to the young man's forehead, steam began to rise from it. After a few moments he cooled off enough for Redfeather to carry him to the couch.

"What the hell was that?!" De Mona came to stand next to the sofa, where Redfeather was attending to Gabriel.

"That was a sample of the Nimrod's power," Redfeather said, still trying to rouse his grandson.

"*Sample*?" De Mona asked in disbelief. "Jesus Christ, that storm almost ripped this whole place apart!"

"Dear girl, that was but a drop of water in an ocean," Redfeather said seriously. "In the right hands the Nimrod could level a city block, but in the hands of the Dark Order it could enslave humanity."

"Is he okay?" she asked, noticing the faint smoke that was still rising from Gabriel's clothes.

"I hope so," Redfeather said, placing his ear to Gabriel's chest. "He's breathing, but I can't wake him."

"Is he in some kind of coma?" De Mona asked, cautiously making her way to the couch.

"No, I fear this is the work of the Nimrod and whatever dark designs it has for my grandson." Redfeather raised his hands to the heavens and muttered something over Gabriel's prone form.

"What was that, another spell?" De Mona asked.

"No, a prayer," Redfeather said seriously.

"Yeah, we'll probably need plenty of those," De Mona said, examining Gabriel. When her eyes passed over his arm, which was dangling over the edge of the couch, her breath caught in her chest. "Holy shit!"

Redfeather looked to where De Mona was staring and his mouth also dropped open. The relic hadn't vanished at all; it had etched itself into Gabriel's arm. Where the skin had once been smooth and clear, there was now a tattoo of a trident in the center of a storm.

"Was it supposed to do that?" De Mona asked.

"I . . . I . . . This is most unusual," Redfeather said, moving to get a closer look. The picture was raised and still glowing slightly, as if it would come to life at any second.

"What's it doing?" De Mona asked, backing up.

"We won't be finding out." Redfeather wrapped Gabriel's arm in what was left of a curtain. "We don't need a repeat performance of what just happened."

"This is unreal." De Mona began pacing the floor, trying her best not to stumble over the debris.

"I'm afraid it's all too real. I should've seen it coming; I should've seen it." Redfeather slumped to the ground and placed his head in his hands.

"There's no way you could've predicted that this thing would've come to your grandson, let alone come to life," De Mona said.

"But I did." When he looked up at her his eyes were glassy. "We are the last members of our tribe, and direct descendants of the great Hunter, but not all of us carry whatever spark it was that made our line so special. In all the years that I was in possession of the dagger it never answered to my touch, but it did for my son, Gabriel's father. As it had been passed to me by my father, I gave it to him. In all the years I'd had it the thing had never so much as reacted to me, and I expected as much for my son. When the dagger reacted to my child I allowed him into this," he motioned around the ruined room, "and it proved to be his undoing, as the Nimrod threatens my grandchild."

De Mona studied him for a time. When she'd originally sought the Redfeathers out it was only to use them to gain the answers she needed to the mystery of the trident, but as she was coming to know them she saw the same goodness in the clan that her father always spoke of.

"We're not gonna let that happen to him." De Mona placed a reassuring hand on Redfeather's shoulder. This time he didn't recoil from the demon's touch. "Maybe these Sanctuary guys can help?"

"That's it!" Redfeather sprang to his feet so quickly

that he startled De Mona. "Help me get him upstairs; we have to go." Redfeather grabbed Gabriel by the legs while De Mona took him under the arms. In all truthfulness the Valkrin could've carried him on her own, but she allowed Redfeather to help.

"And where exactly are we going? We can't leave him here alone," she asked as they made their way to the upper levels of the brownstone.

"We won't; I have a friend who I can call to sit with him while we're gone. If anyone can make sense of what's going on with my grandson, Brother Angelo can."

"Well, what do we have here?" Morgan leaned over the rooftop. When his pale hand touched the concrete rail it darkened, taking on the hue of the rail. "It looks like someone else has joined the party."

"That's not the same guy we saw her with earlier." Jackson absently twirled a silver stiletto between his gloved fingers, stepping closer to Morgan. When Jackson moved, it was like watching a shadow. Peering over the ledge, his unnaturally sharp eyes spied their quarry leaving the brownstone.

"A brilliant observation," Morgan said sarcastically.

Jackson flashed his diamond and gold teeth at his partner. "Don't be a wiseass, Red. Who's the old guy?"

"Why don't you ask the wizard?"

"*I heard that,*" Jonas' voice came in over Morgan's earpiece. "*Can you get close enough to get a visual for me to work with?*"

"I could probably get close enough," Jackson offered. He had the uncanny ability to move unseen when he wanted to. It wasn't the same as becoming invisible, but you wouldn't notice him unless you were looking directly at him, another unexplained side effect of what they now only referred to as "that night."

Back then Jackson was a hard-ass teen born in the Bronx and raised by the streets of New York. In those days Jackson ran with a gang of vicious young punks who were the scourge of their housing projects. One night Jackson and his gang had chased what they thought were two rival gang members to a deserted section of Hunt's Point. When Jackson's gang finally managed to corner them inside a meatpacking facility they learned the ugly truth. The two men had been posers, and Jackson's gang had walked smack into a nest of vampires. The creatures moved so fast that by the time he was able to scream his crew had already been wasted.

By the time Morgan came upon Jackson, there wasn't much left of him. Jackson fought with all that he had and was rewarded by the vampires literally tearing him limb from limb before bleeding him out. As Jackson lay there, taking what he knew were his last breaths, fate threw him a bone in the form of a blinding flash of light. Most of what happened was a blur, as he was in and out of consciousness, but he remembered flashes of a red beard and the sounds of screams.

The vampires were vicious but hardly a match for Morgan's jeweled hammer. When the Irishman was done there wasn't enough of them left for the morning sun to cook. His wrath was swift but, unfortunately for Jackson, not swift enough. His body was a mass of bruises, bloody gashes, and mutilated limbs. Morgan had assumed the man was dead until he started dousing him with kerosene, drawing a low moan from the broken body. Jackson's breathing was faint but steady and the fire that burned in his eyes could've melted the polar caps. He was a man who wasn't quite ready to die, and knowing this touched Morgan and he didn't kill Jackson.

When Jonas found out what Morgan intended to do, he all but ordered him to finish Jackson off before the infection could take hold, but Morgan couldn't do it. Much like the young man, Morgan too had once been a victim. The forces of hell had slaughtered his wife and children, leaving him to die in a gutter. As Jonas had done with Morgan, he would give the broken man a fighting chance. Gathering up the body and ignoring Jonas' rants about the man carrying the infection, Morgan disappeared.

The first week was the hardest. The vampire infection ravaged the young man's body. It was like watching a heroin addict go through withdrawal but ten times worse. Day and night Morgan watched over the young man, ready to dispatch him if he showed signs of the change. To Morgan's amazement, he didn't. Though his wounds were healing faster than anyone had expected, he didn't seem to carry the infection. Morgan nursed the young man back to health, helping him adjust to being handicapped. Jackson's mind seemed whole enough, but his body was still broken.

Jonas was irate and had even personally tried to finish Jackson off, but thankfully Morgan was able to stop him. He had seen too many young men and women fall victim to the dark to not give the stranger a fair chance. Not only did Jackson's body fight off infection, but he also seemed to be healing alarmingly quickly. After three weeks Jackson was walking again and the worst of his wounds had healed. Jonas thought that it was a delayed reaction from the turn, but all Jackson's tests had come back negative. He may not have been infected by the vampires, but something had triggered a biological reaction in him. A month later, Morgan presented the former victim with two gifts that would change his life.

After six long months of physical therapy and a crash course in the supernatural, Jackson was well enough to venture back out into the world, but he had nowhere to go. His gang had been his only family, and much like Morgan and Jonas the forces of hell had made him an orphan, so it was no surprise when Jackson asked to stay. He couldn't go back to living an everyday hood life with what he'd seen and been through. Morgan and Jonas had snatched the blinders off, and Jackson now saw the world through a new set of eyes, and what he saw wasn't pretty. From then on, the duet had become a trio. They would find themselves in some tight situations over the next few years, some better than others, but one thing was apparent about their newest member: Jackson might not have contracted the vampire infection, but he did acquire a taste for blood . . . the spilling of it.

"Negative, we still don't know if they're really human or posers. Morgan, I need you to head back here so we can see if we can make heads or tails out of the data we've already gathered. Jackson, I want you to follow them, but by no means are you to approach, is that understood?"

"Come on, dawg, can't I have a little fun?" Jackson whined.

"Yeah, it'll be fun until you find out you just drew down on two Weres and they make a candlelit dinner out of you," Jonas warned. *"Fall back, Jackson. We can't take any chances until we know what their deals are."*

"You got it," Jackson said, cutting off his radio. He mumbled something under his breath and punched the brick wall beside the exit door, chipping it.

Morgan waited until he was sure Jonas wasn't still on the line before speaking to his friend. "So, are you gonna do like the man has asked or do what Jackson wants to do?"

Jackson looked at Morgan as if he had asked a stupid question. "Man, how long have you known me?"

"Jesus, lad, why can't you just do things the correct way for once?"

Jackson shrugged. "Because I might wake up one day, discover how boring my life actually is, and kill myself." Jackson winked at his partner and leapt over the side of the building.

Morgan just shook his head and calmly walked to the stairs.

CHAPTER TEN

Titus balanced himself against his desk, waiting for the pain to pass. It was similar to what he had felt earlier yet more intense. Somewhere in New York, the Nimrod stirred.

When he had made his pact with Belthon, Titus was promised that all his suffering would come to an end. The fire exploding within his chest was a definite indication that someone wasn't keeping up his end of the bargain. When the pain finally passed, two things happened. Titus was able to stand up straight, and Flag released the breath he had been holding.

"My lord," Flag called in almost a whisper.

"A moment." Titus rolled his broad shoulder to ease the tension. When he looked at Flag, his eyes were glassy, as if in either extreme ecstasy or pain. "Speak," he ordered.

"We have word in from New York," Flag said, tensing up.

"The Nimrod?"

"Yes, Lord Titus. Riel encountered the trident, but there was a problem retrieving it. He—"

"Hold your tongue." Titus waved him silent. "You know I'd rather receive bad news firsthand."

Flag bowed, thankful that he wouldn't be punished for delivering the news. "Of course, my lord. I'll ready the mirror." Flag moved to stand in front of the silver-framed mirror, which stood just a hair over five feet and was mounted against the wall in Titus' office. Whispering an incantation, Flag waved his hand across the mirror, which filled with smoke. When the smoke cleared, a distorted image of Riel stood in the reflection.

"And what news does my most efficient captain bring this night?" Titus asked, as if he already knew the answer.

Riel didn't answer right away. There was no doubt in his mind that his master would not like the news he was about to receive, and Riel had become quite fond of his host's body. Though New York was hundreds of miles away, distance mattered little when dealing with magic. Though the looking-glass spell couldn't be used for travel, it still made Riel accessible to a point.

"Lord Titus, favorite son of Belthon, I humbly greet—," Riel began but was cut off by a dismissive gesture.

"Riel, please skip the formalities and get to the point." While Titus' voice was neutral, there was a dangerous glint in his eyes.

"As you wish." Riel swallowed. "This evening I did battle with a Knight who wielded the Trident of Heaven."

"Seeing that you're alive, I would assume that you have recovered it for the dark father?" Titus asked.

Riel cast his eyes to the ground. "No, the Stalkers were destroyed and I barely managed to escape with my host's body intact."

Without warning Titus' hand shot out at the mirror. When it made contact with the surface there was no breaking glass but the low thud of something being dropped into place. Gnarled hands clutched Riel about the throat while blackened nails bit deep into his borrowed flesh.

He could feel the skin blister as Titus threatened to incinerate him.

"The Old Ones call you King Maker, but I call you a failure!" Titus' eyes blazed, as well as his hands. "For centuries we have searched for the remaining weapons of the cursed Knights, and you manage to lose the most powerful of them to an offshoot of a bygone era. Riel, you as well as all who follow the Dark Order know the price of failure."

Riel was one of the most feared and powerful demons in the history of the world, but his efforts to break Titus' hold were useless. The looking glass's main function was communication, but the most skilled at using the object, or the spell where its abilities derived from, could send or receive items through the glass, as Titus was showing Riel. Being that the glass's transmissions were channeled across the demon plain, it allowed Titus to call on his demon form without the normal restrictions of the mortal realm. Titus was powerful in the mortal realm, but on the plains he had the power of Belthon himself at his call.

Riel gasped. He was quietly still trying to call his powers against Titus, but he had not the strength. Figuring he'd never overpower Titus, Riel tried diplomacy. "He called the Storm!" he croaked.

Titus loosened his grip. "Impossible. Petty lies will not undo your fate."

"It is the truth," Riel insisted. "Storm clouds danced in his eyes, master, as he slew an entire troop of Stalkers. I swear to it, Lord Titus; the Bishop himself spoke to me through the boy!"

Releasing Riel completely, Titus withdrew his hands from the mirror. They had taken back their normal forms, but the skin around the knuckles was a bit scorched. He studied Riel, measuring his words. "Tell me about this, offshoot," Titus demanded.

Riel went on to recount the tale of the bookish young man he had clashed with earlier that night and the light that had threatened to send him to the same black place the Stalkers had gone. Of course he added his own twist and omitted the part about his calling Shadow's Cloak to escape.

Titus doubted most of what Riel said had happened. Demons were excellent liars by nature. What Titus did know to be true was that the Nimrod has been awakened and with it the soul of the cursed Bishop. The reoccurring throbbing in Titus' chest confirmed that. In the recesses of his mind he could've sworn he heard the Bishop laughing at him. But even with the Nimrod active and the Bishop's soul stirring, the power was incomplete. Only with a willing and capable host could the Bishop cross the plains. There was still a chance that they could capture it, unless Riel spoke the truth and the fabled Nimrod had chosen. As unlikely as it might've sounded, Titus couldn't deny feeling the power of the relic coursing through him.

Over the last few centuries the Nimrod had mostly remained dormant. It had passed through several hands, with most people mistaking it for just what it looked like, a broken fork. There was one instance when it had flared to life briefly, but before going back to sleep it ended up consuming the poor soul who had happened across it. If the trident had chosen a master, it could mean the beginning of another war. If they were on the threshold of another seven-day siege, then Titus knew he would need his most valued demon warriors at his side.

"Riel, you have served the order faithfully for centuries, and proven yourself to be more of an asset than a liability. It is for this reason alone that I do not cast you back into the fire to answer to Belthon," Titus told him.

"Thank you, my lord," Riel said, almost groveling.

"I don't need your thanks, worm. I need results. I don't care if you have to raise an entire cemetery to slay the boy and capture the trident, I want it!"

"Your will be done," Riel said as his image faded from the looking glass.

"Incompetent," Flag mumbled. Titus looked at him as if just realizing Flag was in the room. "Not you, Lord Titus. I was speaking of Riel," Flag quickly explained.

"Flag, Riel has been shedding blood, human and demon, for longer than you or I have been alive. Though he failed to capture the Nimrod, he has just taught us two very important lessons." Seeing the confused look on Flag's face, Titus explained, "The first is the fact that the Nimrod is very much alive. The second is never underestimate an opponent. Riel thought because it was humans he was seeking that they would be weak, but magic can turn even the most timid sheep into a fierce lion. This mortal must be found and the Nimrod captured before the Bishop gains a foothold in this world." There was no mistaking the nervousness in Titus' voice.

"Should we inform Belthon?" Flag asked, praying Titus would say no. Flag's master was a beast of a man, but the demon lord made him seem like a pussycat. Though the mage had been working closely with the Dark Order since he was a child, the more powerful entities always made him uneasy, even if they weren't full demons.

"Not yet. I can't see that a lone mortal is more powerful than the forces of hell, trident or not. We must formulate a plan, but first we will need answers. We'll see what Leah says of this."

"Sir, do you really think consulting her is necessary?" Flag stopped. His face suddenly wore a worried expression.

"Flag, surely you haven't become that prejudiced that

you can't stand the company of a sprite?" There was a mocking tone to Titus' voice.

"Leah is more than just a sprite," Flag grumbled.

"Indeed, she is the answer to our questions. Attend me, mage; there are plans to be laid," Titus ordered, leaving his office.

CHAPTER ELEVEN

The elevator took them two floors below the one that housed Titus' office. Like most of the upper levels, this one could only be accessed by a card-key and boasted a state-of-the-art security system, but unlike the business-functional floors of the building, this reeked of magic . . . old magic. The unmarked floor was the most heavily guarded level of the building, including Titus' own lair. The floors, walls, and ceilings had all been heavily warded with magic that was almost as old as civilization. Only Titus could call even a slither of magic while on this level; all others were neutralized. The greatest of care was taken when fortifying the unmarked level, but it wasn't to keep others from getting in; it was to keep someone from getting out.

Two females dressed in military fatigues stood guard outside a sculpted bronze door. They were armed with high-caliber assault weapons, but if the wards didn't hold their guest, then the guns would be useless. Inside the room there were two more guards, who were also females. Titus had seen the games his guest could play with the minds and hearts of men, even without magic, and he wasn't taking any chances. The only man who was even allowed to enter the room unsupervised was Titus.

The inside of the room seemed totally out of place in

the office building. The entire eastern and western walls were screens that showed realistic views of downtown Ontario, which changed according to the time of day or season. No sun- or moonlight was allowed in the room. There were bookshelves filled with just about every kind of book, except those dealing with magic, not even fairy tales. Resting amongst the throw pillows of a large canopy bed, in the center of the room, was Titus' guest and the object of Flag's fear, Leah.

She was sitting on the bed, with her back to them and her knees gathered to her chest. From that angle all you could see was her spill of soft pink hair. Her shoulders were straight and proud even in light of her situation. She tilted her head, showing the beginnings of her keen nose and angular jaw, indicating that she had acknowledged their presence but would not give her visitors her full attention. Even in bondage, Leah still carried herself like royalty. "Titus." She purposely left the title off his name as a sign of disrespect, but Titus wasn't easily goaded.

"Good evening, Leah," Titus said in an almost affectionate voice. "I trust you are well?"

"As well as can be . . . considering." She raised her hand to point at the wards etched into the posts of her bed, letting the soft silk of her nightgown slide into a bunch about her elbow. Her pale skin seemed radiant even in the dim light. "Have you come to grant me my freedom or to taunt me further?" she mused.

Titus' lips curled into a smile. "Come now, Leah. Has your stay here been that miserable? Have I not been a gracious and loving host?"

"Loving?" The air rippled slightly, blowing her hair like a gentle breeze. "Where is the love in caging me like an animal? Or clipping my wings?" She turned and faced them for the first time. Her doll-like face was hard, and fire danced in her molten gold eyes. "This is not love, Titus, betrayer of his brother. . . . You've condemned me to hell!" At the force of her voice the wards flickered to life, illuminating the room in a dull glow. Flag stepped back, but Titus held his ground.

The tone of Leah's voice was that of an adult, but her appearance was anything but. She was frail, with just the beginnings of breasts pushing out against the silk. Her full beauty hadn't yet come to her, but she was still stunning. It wasn't in an attractive way as yet, but more like seeing the sun rise for the first time. At the height of her glory Leah had been hailed in some cultures as a goddess, but thanks to Belthon's magic she was a woman trapped in a child's body.

"Leah, *hell* is such a relative term." Titus approached the bed but didn't get within arm's reach. Though her magic had been suppressed within the child's body, she could still inflict physical harm. "Besides, most women would kill for the chance to be forever young."

"I *was* forever young." She folded her slender legs beneath her. Though she seemed calmer, there was still murder in her eyes. "A woman who would be twenty for all time . . . a goddess, but you've robbed me of that."

"I robbed you of nothing, dear girl, only delayed the maturation process of your powers," Titus said as if it were all quite simple.

"By murdering me?" she said in an almost-pleading tone. "If I were myself, I would show you true hell, betrayer," she hissed.

"I'm sure you would, Leah. And this is the reason you will never grown into womanhood," Titus taunted her.

Like most sprites, Leah had a fascination with mortals. One of her favorite pastimes was masquerading amongst them. Leah would swap souls with a mortal girl and take a lover for a night or two. She never worried about the mortal making off with her body because without the sprite's spirit to insulate it from the lingering magical residue, the human would either literally go mad over time or combust. In that event Leah would keep the borrowed body and be re-made when it reached the proper age. It was during one of her little games that she ended up in the hands of Belthon.

The mortal lover she had chosen was a follower of the dark forces. They enjoyed wine and carnal sex all through the night and into the morning. While Leah slept in her borrowed body the forces of Belthon captured her. Belthon also knew the legends of the sprites, which was why he worked a dark spell on her. Every host's body she had inhabited would be murdered before it could reach its twentieth year and replaced with another preteen girl. Leah would be old enough for her powers to be of use to the Dark Order but never old enough to become the goddess again.

"Enough reminiscing, I have need of answers that only you can give," Titus told her.

Leah smiled warmly. "Lord Titus, you are a fool to think I will willingly help you. Murder this body again if you must, but I will not serve you or your master." Leah sat back with her arms folded like that was the end of it.

"Oh, but I think you will." Titus' hand lashed out and he had the female guard by the throat. She struggled but was no match for him with his supernatural strength. Titus waved a hand across her exposed flesh, leaving a red welt as it passed. There was nothing at first, but within seconds blood started to pour over his hand from the wound.

"An offering." Titus smirked, holding out his bloody hand. Blood dripped from his fingertips, splashing against the lavender bedsheets, almost hitting Leah's bare foot.

"No." Leah scampered farther back onto the bed, as if the blood would scald her. "I will not serve you!"

Titus dragged the guard over to the bed where Leah was cowering. "You don't have a choice," Titus said, before digging his fingers into the wound, causing the blood to spray in an arc, splattering the lace veil that covered the bed. "I make an offering, sprite. Blood and bone, that is the dowry." Titus flicked excess from his fingers at Leah.

When the blood touched her skin she shrieked like she'd been scalded. The blood that had landed on Leah's skin sizzled, before seeping into her pores. The corpse of the guard shook violently, as the rest of her blood spilled forth and as if by magic was sucked into the sprite's skin. Soon there was no trace of the blood or the body of the guard, only Leah's glowing form levitating slightly off the mattress.

"The tribute is accepted." Her voice was rich with the power of the blood sacrifice. "Ask what you will at your own peril, and receive the goddess's truth."

"I seek the Nimrod, Goddess," Titus said.

"As do all the forces of light and dark. The Nimrod has been unearthed and the Bishop sleeps no more. Three hundred years ago the Nimrod answered to the call of the Hunter as it does this night." Her gold eyes seemed to glow brighter. "Even now the magic seduces him with whispers of its dark secrets. Beware the Dark Storm, Halfling."

By now Flag was near the door, trying to fight off the panic attack he felt coming on. He had never been comfortable with feeding Leah's power to call the visions, because he knew just how dangerous she could be, but Titus was confident that he could control the girl, as Flag had been until now. He could feel raw energy dripping off the girl and pushing against the wards. It seemed as the awakening of the trident was affecting even the oldest magics. Flag intended to suggest that they consider killing Leah's host earlier than scheduled when Titus was done with his questioning.

"I fear nothing but the dark lord himself." Titus tried to sound confident. He could feel Leah's power running up and down his skin like ghostly fingers. "I will command the Nimrod."

The laugh that came from Leah rattled the bookshelves. "None may command that which no longer has a master. It was God who created it and it is revenge that fuels it. Magic like that cannot be contained or mastered, only conspired with, or have you forgotten what has become of your brother? Abandon your quest for the Nimrod, Halfling, for I see unholy blood spilled by its unforgiving strike. Heed well my warning, Titus, betrayer of his brother."

She hovered closer to Titus so that he could see the scene unfolding in her eyes. It was the moment that the Nimrod had been plunged into his chest, but it wasn't quite right. It wasn't the stretch of open field in Naples but a modern street. Though the wielder in the vision was slightly younger than Titus remembered the Hunter to be, their faces were almost identical.

"Trickery," Titus hissed, throwing the force of his will forward, trying to send her into the wall. The power whipped around Leah like a strong gust of wind, rocking her form, but she continued to hover in place, legs crossed beneath her and back erect. Calling as much of his magic into his hand as he dared in the warded room, Titus rose for a strike. "Enough games, sprite. The price has been paid and you still haven't told me what I need to know."

"The goddess knows only truth, Titus, which is what you need to know, but what you ask for is the blueprint for disaster. So be it then." Her form floated softly to the bed. "The Bishop has chosen his vessel and only death shall break their bond, and empowered by the Nimrod the

Hunter will not die easily. No living thing can part them as long as the two hearts beat as one."

"Then the only way to wrest the trident from him is to find a way to kill him?" Titus was speaking more to himself, but Leah chose to answer him.

"Yes, but it is not as simple as it sounds. The Nimrod was made to be wielded by a god; thus through it the vessel shall become more god-like the more connected the two become. Even acting blindly, he still slaughters your foot soldiers like cattle, and each time he uses the weapon it becomes stronger. I fear that he is already past the point where anything of this world can part them."

"But they can be parted?" Titus pressed.

"Even the ocean was able to be parted."

Titus turned the riddle over in his head. "I will take your words into consideration, Goddess. Now, where can I find the Hunter?"

"If you are insistent on going to your doom, then I will gladly light the way for you. The Hunter's progeny roams the city of glass towers, with unsolved mysteries rather than pelts as his game. The Bishop motivates his actions now, so it will only be a matter of time before he finds you." With those last words, Leah's skin began to dim and she was back to herself. She cast sleepy blue eyes up at Titus as if just coming out of a dream, before curling up under the blanket and nodding off like nothing had ever happened.

"I find the trips to see Leah becoming less and less pleasant," Flag was saying as they made their way back to Titus' office.

"I'd never known the mages to have differences with the fairy folk," Titus said with a smirk.

"It's not the sprites as a species, just Leah. Even in the host's body her power feels stronger than it should be, especially when she's made to call the visions. If I were you, I'd seriously consider murdering her host sooner this time," Flag suggested.

"Then it's a good thing you aren't me," Titus said. "Finding the proper host for one as powerful as Leah is no easy task, mage. This isn't the Middle Ages, when young girls could go missing regularly and it wouldn't arouse suspicion. No, Leah will keep that body for a time longer. We have a more pressing problem ahead of us: capturing the Nimrod."

"It will be no easy task. As Leah said, the boy and the Nimrod may be past the point of being parted," Flag reminded him.

"She said that they may not be parted by anything of this world, so I will seek help outside this world. I will have the *Night Hawk* fueled and ready for you by the time you're done packing. Prepare to be gone for as long as I have need of you."

"Where am I going?" Flag asked.

"To New York. Riel is a loyal servant, but there are things that require a more subtle touch that I need you to handle. I fear the resurgence of the relic in a city as powerful as New York will draw more than a bit of attention, from both light and dark armies. We must be ready when our enemies show their bleeding crosses. Go to the Iron Mountains and tell Prince Orden that we have need of his lot."

CHAPTER TWELVE

The taxi turned into a quiet residential block off the Prospect Park Loop in Brooklyn. Before it had even come to a complete stop, Redfeather tossed a wad of bills at the driver and hopped out. De Mona followed Redfeather onto the curb. Her body fell in step with the older man, but her mind was on the youngest Redfeather.

The Nimrod had literally used him as a conductor for its power, nearly frying Gabriel and drowning them in the process. His body still seemed to be intact, aside from the bruises he was sure to have from being crowned with a chair, but as near as she could tell his mind was gone. A part of her wondered if it had been sucked into the Nimrod, as the last host's spirit had been, but that wouldn't explain why it had bound itself to Gabriel. Both the Nimrod and the youngest of the Redfeather clan were mysteries that De Mona was now even more determined to solve.

De Mona had been hesitant about leaving Gabriel at the brownstone in the condition he was in and still wearing the Nimrod's mark, but Redfeather assured her that Gabriel would be safe with Meg. Though the old woman offered little more than a halfhearted smile in the way of a greeting, De Mona could smell the magic coming off her. When De Mona asked Redfeather about her he simply said that she was an *old* friend.

They found themselves on the steps of an old building that was clearly older than the park it stood across from. De Mona started up at the sharp details of the gargoyles that guarded the six posts of the structure's roof. For a minute she thought she saw one of them move, but she brushed it off as nerves. The building wasn't quite a church, but it gave off the feeling of something holy and powerful, which it was. It was Sanctuary, the place her father had been attempting to reach when he was killed.

Sanctuary was composed of several buildings located at various points around the globe. All were respectively impressive, but the Prospect Park location, though not the largest, was the most vital when it came to information. Erected long before New York was called New Amsterdam, the building was a waypoint for demons who wanted a different way of life, or protection from those they'd betrayed. Sanctuary was to migrating supernaturals what Ellis Island had been to America's own immigrants. In exchange for the services provided by Sanctuary, the demons were required to share their histories and cultures to help further the research of the order.

The order was initially started by a group of wealthy scholars and mystics, whose original names had been forgotten long before the siege ever erupted. Its original purpose had been simply to study paranormal activity, but the scholars soon learned that sometimes just watching wasn't enough and action was called for. In these cases they sent in the Inquisitors. These men were more soldiers than scholars and were unwavering in their loyalty to the order and man. Trained from birth in combat, the Inquisitors would die or kill in the name of the order.

There were several sources that they could've tapped into to get the answers they needed, but both Redfeather and her late father believed that Sanctuary was the best shot they had. Redfeather had a relationship with the man who ran the order, Brother Angelo, and seemed to think that they could trust him, but something still had him on edge. With the kind of power coming off the place, she hoped Redfeather's trust was well placed.

When De Mona's foot made contact with the first step she felt an immediate tingling run up her body. It wasn't a malicious sensation, more like a curious prodding. The muscles under her skin rolled, trying to force the change to come, but she held fast. Something inside the place was communicating with her demon side, and she didn't like it.

The steps were made from a fine marble, and though they were heavily treaded and cracking, you could still see the sculpted quality. These led up to a massive door, which stood at least twelve feet in height. Along the edges De Mona could make out faint runes, slightly different from the ones on the Redfeather home but powerful nonetheless. De Mona reached out and traced the runes with her finger. These didn't hurt like the ones the old man had cast, but she knew they could. She was about to study the markings on the other side of the door when it suddenly came open.

Standing in the doorway was a man as black as midnight, with two gold hoops hanging from each ear. The muscles beneath his black leather vest looked like coiled steel when he moved. There were tribal tattoos running from his jaws to the corners of his eyes, eyes like glaciers that took in Redfeather but lingered on De Mona. There was a twinge of recognition in his face before his lips rolled back into a fierce sneer.

Jackson coasted his late-model Ninja motorcycle to a stop at the tip of the block the taxi had disappeared down. Trailing it down the FDR had proven to be a trickier task than he had expected. With the sparse traffic on the freeway between Manhattan and Brooklyn it was hard to follow them unnoticed. He tried to stay far enough behind where they wouldn't notice him but close enough not to lose them. He almost flipped the bike making the sharp cut over to exit at the Brooklyn Bridge.

Trailing them once they got into the borough was a little easier because of the increase in traffic. Even at that hour, Brooklyn was rank with cars leaving various after-hours spots or going to late-night suppers. He was glad when the passengers of the taxi had finally decided to stop a few yards away from an old church. Using his heightened sight, he identified the address of the place and radioed Jonas.

"J., I've tracked them to Brooklyn." Jackson fed the address into the microphone.

Jonas was quiet for a minute before coming back over the air. *"Jackson, check the place for magical residue."*

"Jonas, this place looks more like a flophouse than Castle Grayskull."

"Humor me, Jack."

Jackson muttered something under his breath and dug in his pocket for the item he would need for the task. He produced a small crystal that hung from the end of a leather cord and held it up to eye level. At first there was nothing, but suddenly the crystal began to sway on the cord. It was subtle at first, as if the wind were moving the thing, but eventually the crystal began to sway faster. Quite unexpectedly the crystal swung out and dangled in midair, pointing in the direction of the building. The pull had gotten so strong that Jackson had to cover the crystal with his hand before it snapped the cord.

"Whoa," Jackson said, trying to put the crystal back in his pocket. "Jonas, I'm not sure what's going on in there, but it must involve some serious magic. The crystal is going nuts."

"Just as I thought," Jonas said, over the faint clicking sounds of his laptop's keys. *"Jackson, this place is off-limits in a major way. If you have to lose the tail we'll pick it up again somewhere else, but I don't want you going near that place."*

"What the hell is your deal, man? I thought you wanted the four-one-one on these cats?" Jackson asked.

"I do, but not enough to risk you going near Sanctuary when we still haven't diagnosed your condition. It's too risky."

"Man, it's been years and I still ain't sprouted fangs, fur, or a damn sixth toe, so why don't you chill?" Jackson snapped.

"Jackson, I don't mean it like that. . . . Look." He took a breath. *"There's always some real bad shit lurking around those places, bad shit that specializes in ripping supernaturals to pieces, and I'd hate for somebody to get the wrong idea about you snooping around that place. Just maintain a safe distance and we'll see what their next move is."*

"You know, I hate to be a wet blanket, but this cloak-and-dagger crap is starting to get old. I say let me hog-tie the both of them and we force the information out of them." He flexed his fists beneath the leather gloves, imagining he could feel the lethal blades easing up his forearms.

"You know we don't operate like that, Jackson. We start tying up potentially innocent people and we become no better than the shitheads and their bosses. I'm still not sure quite what their roles are in all this, but if the Dark Order wants them dead, we might be able to use them."

"My boy Jonas, a regular army recruiter," Jackson teased.

"Call it what you want, but we're gonna need all the help we can get against the forces of hell. Keep your eyes peeled and I'll see what I can come up with on this end."

"You got it, boss," Jackson said sarcastically, and ended the connection. He loved and respected Jonas, but sometimes they didn't see eye to eye on how to handle certain situations. Jackson had been a soldier all his life and was used to handling things directly, while Jonas believed in a diplomatic approach. His way had worked more often than it hadn't, but that still didn't change the fact that war loomed in Jackson's heart. Jonas could have his diplomacy as long as Jackson got to kick some ass in the end.

CHAPTER THIRTEEN

Gabriel felt like he had just gone five rounds with Antonio Tarver. He could feel the fog beginning to lift from his head, but he still felt like his body was asleep. With some effort he stretched both arms at his sides and began wiggling his fingers. When he thought he had gotten enough feeling back in his arms he rolled over onto his stomach and pushed himself off the ground.

He expected to feel the worn carpet of his grandfather's study, but instead it was moist grass. Checking his surroundings, he was thoroughly startled to find out that he was in what appeared to be a dense forest. Before he had a chance to process how or why he was there, a low growl came from somewhere to his left. Gabriel found himself being approached by a pack of very large wolves, with pelts of varying colors.

Gabriel tried to backpedal away from the advancing wolves but found that he was suddenly unable to keep his balance. Slipping on the moist grass, he landed on all fours. He tried to brace his hands and lift himself again but found that they had been replaced by paws. His arms were now thin and covered in thick black fur. The wolves were still advancing, with curious glances, but he sensed no malice from them. Instead there was sort of a kinship.

Unexpectedly the wolves took off running through the

thick brush. The wolf bringing up the rear motioned for Gabriel to follow, and for some reason he did. He loped along in his wolf form, trying to keep pace with the pack. The rush of wind felt good against his muzzle as he cut thorough the foliage. Branches slashed at his fur, but he kept running, oblivious to the nicks and scratches. He knew that instead of galloping through the forest he should be trying to figure out what the hell had happened to him, but it seemed secondary at that moment. All he cared about was the rush of excitement he was overcome with chasing *his* pack through the forest.

He cleared the last thicket and could make out the shapes of the pack just ahead of him. Tongue hanging loosely over his fanged lower jaw, he broke out into a dead sprint. Loose rocks bit into his paws as he ran across the open plain, but he ignored the slight pinching. The pack disappeared through a dense patch of fog, with Gabriel close on their heels. He picked up on the scents of his pack and added speed to his run. No sooner had Gabriel broken through the fog than the ground below disappeared. With deformed limbs flailing, Gabriel plunged over the side of the cliff.

The wind rushed up at Gabriel so violently that it tore off thick clumps of fur in its passing over him. His muscles cramped and became wracked with pain as his limbs contorted and straightened. Gabriel found himself as naked as the day he was born, about to collide with the concrete. He closed his eyes and braced, but to his surprise he landed as softly as a blade of grass. He started to say a prayer of thanks for being spared, but when he opened his eyes the words caught in his throat.

The natural surroundings had transformed into something out of a horror movie. The sky overhead had gone from a beautiful blue to a pale orange. Winged things that he had only seen in books flew overhead scanning the ground for prey. The freak sandstorm that had appeared from nowhere made it hard for him to see, but he could hear very clearly the screams of someone or something being tortured. Something slick slithered across his foot, but he was so afraid that he didn't even look to see what it was. Gabriel just took off running.

As he ran, the layout changed again. Through the blowing sand he could make out what looked like the tall buildings that decorated the Manhattan skyline, but they were rotted and burning. Skeletal creatures similar to the things that had attacked him in the parking lot hissed and lunged at him. A few even managed to touch him, but he was able to easily throw them off. He didn't try to study the creatures, for fear of being consumed by the warm ground if he stood in one spot too long. Gabriel just kept running.

Directly in front of him a man appeared. The man wasn't skeletal or rotting like the things that were now pouring from every doorway and window of the hellish city. He stood fully clad in armor bearing the sign of the cross on the breastplate. His midnight hair was neatly combed back and tied into a ponytail. He raised an armored hand at Gabriel and a blinding light washed over him.

The intense light sent a searing pain through his limbs and stung at the backs of his eyes. He went to shield them with his hands but recoiled when he saw the skin on his right knuckle moving. Gabriel watched in awe as the tattoo of the Nimrod danced in the center of the terrible storm, seeming to grow stronger with every crack of thunder. His hand suddenly felt like the skin was being peeled off as the Nimrod peeled itself free and took substance between him and the Knight.

"My will be done," the Knight said in a ghostly voice as the Nimrod came to rest in his hand. Gabriel tried to turn away, but the voice seemed to pull him closer. "My will be done," the man said again. For some reason, Gabriel couldn't take his eyes off the Knight. He was as beautiful as an angel, but the merciless eyes of something wicked stared back at Gabriel. "My will be done!" the man said again. This time the voice was so loud that Gabriel's ears began to bleed.

"What do you want from me?" Gabriel cried, unable to take it anymore.

"Justice," the Knight sneered just before he swung the Nimrod. Gabriel closed his eyes and awaited the killing blow, but to his surprise it never came. When he opened his eyes the Knight was gone, but the Nimrod remained.

The relic pulsed softly as it moved towards Gabriel. He hadn't meant to, but it was so beautiful that he needed to touch it. When his greedy flesh made contact with the ancient thing his mind was assaulted with images of a great battle. He knew what he was seeing had been the Seven-Day Siege. The gruesome scene played over and over in his head until he could bear it no longer and began to scream. When he finally came to his senses he was back in his bedroom, still holding the trident. In the distance he could hear the Knight's ghostly decree: "*My will be done.*"

Gabriel reached up and touched his bookshelf to make sure it was real, and was beyond thrilled when he felt the old wood under his fingertips. He took a deep breath and tried to tell himself that everything was okay, but when he noticed the body lying outside his bedroom door he knew that it wasn't.

Megan Cromwell, known as Meg to her friends, was a woman in the twilight of her life. At the age of sixty-five she had seen enough to last her two lifetimes. Meg was a witch but not currently active in the affairs of the coven of witches and warlocks. After the mystic wars of the early eighties she chose to live a quiet life in a New Jersey suburb. She was content to stay at home and tend her herb garden, making home remedies for the locals and supernaturals, but found herself in the middle of the city that never slept to help an old friend.

When Redfeather called and asked her to come to his home she feared the worst. As they often spent hours chatting on the phone, he understood her reluctance to venture away from her home, but he insisted that it was of the utmost importance and would say no more. Only when she arrived did he tell her what had happened. The Nimrod had induced a trance-like sleep and Redfeather had no idea how to break the spell. Meg was an old and powerful witch, but even her magics couldn't stir the boy. All she could do now was keep watch over the boy until his grandfather returned from Sanctuary.

For the last two hours Gabriel had been still, not so much as snoring or changing positions. But a few moments ago she could've sworn she heard voices. Meg quietly made her way upstairs to where he was sleeping and placed her ear against the door. "My will be done," she heard him utter over and over. Fearing he might be delirious, Meg opened the door to check him. What she saw left her momentarily speechless.

Gabriel was not only awake but also standing in the middle of the room. He was naked from the waist up and sweating like he had run a marathon. His black hair blew on a breeze that should not have been one as he chanted over and over. In his hand he held a thing that Meg had thought to never lay eyes on in her lifetime, the Nimrod.

Meg wasted no time waving her hands in a complex design, raising every magical defense she could think of. She knew in her heart that there wasn't much her magic could do against a god, but she was going to give it her best go. Speaking in a long-forgotten language, Meg called on the power of the goddess. "In the name of all that is pure, I cast thee back to the pit, demon." Meg gave it everything she had, but the magic dissipated before it could get within three feet of Gabriel.

With a mocking smile he laid a hand on Meg's barrier and shattered it. "All who would challenge the word of my lord shall burn in the fire!"

The trident burned so brightly that Meg had to shield her eyes against it. She backpedaled and collided with the door frame. "Gabriel?" she called to him. For a minute she saw the flash of brown beneath the storm clouds, but it disappeared no sooner than it had come.

"For too long the unclean things have sullied the green pastures of my lord." He grabbed Meg about the jaws and lifted her as easily as if she were a child. "Fear not, witch, for you shall be cleansed." Gabriel placed the Nimrod gently against Meg's chest and she felt her lungs fill with water. She tried to cough it out, but it kept coming until her struggling had ceased. "How fragile the magicians have become." He cast her into the hallway, breaking the banister. Gabriel sat on his bed as if nothing had happened and lay back. "Go forth, my vessel, and show me this world," the voice faded. Gabriel shook his mind clear and recoiled at the horror of what he'd done.

"Meg!" Gabriel tossed the Nimrod on the bed and ran to her side. "What have I done?" He knelt beside Meg's prone form with tears in his eyes. A trickle of blood ran down the side of her head, which he wiped away tenderly. "Meg, can you hear me?" He prayed for her to wake up, but she didn't.

"What have you done?" He turned on the trident, which was starting to dim. Gabriel grabbed the cooling rod from the bed and held it at arm's length. "You did this." He expected to hear the ghostly voice again, but the thing was silent.

Suddenly it occurred to him that his grandfather hadn't come up to see what the commotion was. "Granddad!" Gabriel bounded down what was left of the stairs and made his way to the lower levels of the brownstone. When he entered his grandfather's study Gabriel's heart sank. Everything was destroyed. Relics and everything else his grandfather had held dear were gone, thanks to Gabriel. He searched the rubble and found no sign of De Mona or his grandfather, so maybe they'd escaped the Nimrod's wrath, but where were they?

There were a lot of questions to be answered, but first Gabriel had to get away from the brownstone. Depending on how much noise the Nimrod had made, the police could very well be on their way there, and he'd be hard-pressed to explain a dead body and a lost relic from the church. He needed to find somewhere he could go to try to make heads or tails of what was going on, and when he looked at the clock he knew just where. It was just after midnight, so chances were that he could catch up with Carter at the Triple Six. If there was anyone Gabriel could turn to, it would be Carter.

Trying not to look at Meg's dead body, Gabriel threw on a fresh pair of jeans and a T-shirt. He threw a green army jacket over his arm and moved to find something he could wrap the trident in, but when Gabriel looked on the bed the thing was gone. Before he could even pose the question, he felt the wriggling on his arm and found that the tattoo was real. The storm was settling and the Nimrod was still, but for how long he couldn't be sure.

Though it hurt him to do so, Gabriel said his good-byes to Meg. "I'm sorry you had to get caught up in all this, Meg, but I'm gonna make it right." With tear-filled eyes he looked at the tattoo on his arm. "One way or another, this debt will be settled."

CHAPTER FOURTEEN

"What line are you?" the tattooed man asked, looking from De Mona to Redfeather and back.

"Excuse me?" De Mona looked up at him quizzically.

"Demon line," Redfeather told her, knowing that De Mona was ignorant of the customs of the Great Houses. "He can sense the taint on you and wants to know what demon line you're from."

"Oh," De Mona said, trying to hide her confusion. "Ah . . . Valkrin, my mother was a Valkrin. Her name was Mercy," she added, trying not to squirm under the guardian's accusing glare.

His eyes suddenly became more hostile, as if he weren't already giving her a look of disgust. "What business do you have here, child of Mercy?"

"We're here to see Brother Angelo," Redfeather spoke up.

The guardian sneered at him. "I was speaking to the Valkrin, *human*." He said the last word as if it left a foul taste on his tongue. He turned back to De Mona. "Your people have made their position clear, little one, so there is nothing here for you."

"Man, I ain't got no peoples, so you got the wrong chick," De Mona informed him. "Now we got business here, so why don't you let us handle it."

"You'd do well to watch your mouth when speaking to me, abomination," he sneered. De Mona couldn't be sure, but she could've sworn the temperature on the stoop dropped a few degrees as he got more agitated.

Fearing the worst, Redfeather cut in, "Good sir, I assure you that if you just mention the name Redfeather, Brother Angelo will see us."

"Brother Angelo is unavailable at the moment, human, and as I've said, the Valkrin have given up their place here. You," he glared down at De Mona, "are not welcome!"

"All who seek peace and knowledge are welcome in Sanctuary." A voice came from behind the doorman. The speaker was a petite Asian woman. The young girl's skin was a beautiful blend of a freshly ripened banana with a hint of gold in the undertones. She was dressed in jeans and a polo shirt. Her doe-like brown eyes were very alert but saw nothing as she navigated her way across the room with an ivory walking stick. The girl had been blind since birth but moved more gracefully than someone with twenty-twenty vision.

"Lydia, you shouldn't be here," the guardian said, softening his tone when he spoke to the girl. "I know how to do my job."

"Oh, I don't doubt that, Akbar, but sometimes you can be a bit biased regarding these things. The Valkrin have abandoned us, but we still have an obligation to provide Sanctuary for those who seek it; that is the purpose of this Great House." She tapped her staff on the ground for emphasis. "Now, why don't you stand aside and let these people in out of the cold?"

Akbar looked at Lydia but didn't say anything. He allowed Redfeather to pass without more than a slightly distrustful glance, but the look Akbar gave De Mona was one of pure hatred. As she passed him she could feel an icy chill emitting from his body. It was so intense that her arm started to go numb when she brushed against him to clear the doorway. *Definitely not human*, she thought to herself, and would make it a point to find out just what he was.

Redfeather went to offer his hand but, realizing that Lydia couldn't see, withdrew it. "Thank you, young lady. My name is—"

"Yes, I know who you are, Mr. Redfeather. I may not be able to see, but my ears work just fine," Lydia informed him.

"I . . . ah—"

"Don't apologize, Mr. Redfeather; it was only a joke." She smiled in his direction. "Akbar," she turned to the giant, "could you see if Brother Angelo is available, please?" He mumbled something under his breath and went off to do as he was told. She turned back to Redfeather and De Mona. "We can wait in the chapel for Brother Angelo. If you'll follow me." She started forward.

De Mona followed Redfeather and Lydia through a door on the opposite side of the one that Akbar had disappeared through. The room was large yet cozy, equipped with a fireplace and comfortable chairs. There were several people sitting, reading, or talking amongst themselves. Some said "hello," while others completely ignored the visitors. To De Mona's surprise, they weren't all human. She doubted that Redfeather had picked up on it, but there were several very strong demon presences gathered in the building.

They had gone down at least two levels when the stairwell emptied out into a circular foyer. Thin pillars ran from the ground up to the fifteen-foot ceiling. Symbols were etched into the pillars and the floor space directly below them. She recognized them from old texts her father used to show her. Each symbol represented a demon line, but she could find the mark of the Valkrin nowhere. She wasn't sure what her mother's people had done, but from the way she was being gawked at she imagined she would find out before they left the place.

As they made their way to the other side of the chamber De Mona couldn't help but notice several doors lining the walls. One of them was open and there were hushed voices coming from within. Curiously De Mona peeked inside. There was a man dressed in a leisure suit, speaking to someone De Mona couldn't quite make out. The figure was standing partially in the shadows of the room, with a large hood obscuring her view of its face. Who- or whatever it was must've felt her intrusive glare and turned around. De Mona let out a small yelp as she saw the horns and ringed nose. The creature snorted something and rudely slammed the door.

"This way please," Lydia said over her shoulder. De Mona's eyes lingered on the door for a few more seconds before she followed her group.

Lydia continued to navigate the building, occasionally stopping to speak with someone. Though she didn't appear to be any older than De Mona, everyone treated Lydia with great respect. As she walked she tapped her stick along the ground in an odd rhythm. Every time it made contact with the ground De Mona could feel power vibrating from it, which aroused her curiosity.

"That's a pretty staff," De Mona commented.

Lydia stopped and raised the stick to eye level as if she could see it. "Brother Angelo gave it to me, it originally belonged to my great-great-grandfather." She traced her fingers along the runes, letting its familiar power run up through her fingers. "They say that he was one of the emperor's greatest magicians."

"So you're some kinda witch?" De Mona asked, still admiring the staff.

"Me? No, my talents lie elsewhere." Lydia smiled slyly, twirling the stick once before going back to her tapping. "It's not much further," she said, leading them through another door. Within this chamber was the chapel. It had been a great many years since Redfeather had seen the room, but it was every bit as amazing as it had been in those days. The chapel was easily the size of a small train station, with arched ceilings and hardwood floors. It actually resembled a real church with its wooden benches and altars, but the walls were adorned with symbols of every religion from both the mortal and supernatural worlds. Both man and mystic were represented in the chapel.

De Mona could feel the familiar energy of her people in the room and it made her almost giddy. She had gone to brace herself against one of the benches when her hand brushed against something soft. She looked at the bench but saw nothing. As she scanned the shadows her focus began to blur. It wasn't as if something was wrong with her eyes, more like something was wrong with the space she was staring at. The shadows moved and a pair of eyes, so black that they appeared to shine, stared back at her. De Mona blinked and the eyes were gone.

Lydia led them farther down the carpeted aisle to a padded bench that sat in the shadow of the tallest of the altars. She motioned for them to be seated while she balanced her weight on her staff. "So, Mr. Redfeather—"

"Just 'Redfeather' is fine," he interrupted.

"Sorry. . . . Redfeather, what brings you and . . ."

"De Mona."

"Right. . . . What brings you and De Mona to Sanctuary? Have you come to petition for your people, or just yourself?" Lydia directed the last question at De Mona.

"Petition? No, I don't even understand what's going on. What did Mr. Clean mean by the Valkrin aren't welcome?"

"I was going to ask the same thing." Redfeather spoke up. "What has transpired that has made the warriors outcasts?"

"You mean you didn't know?" Lydia's face saddened. "I will tell you what I know about. It was the lesser demons who first started defecting. The demons that were too weak to be soldiers and had no stomach for war. As time went on some of the stronger ones began filing in. The Ghelgaths, the elementals, all the weary, came when they tired of the fighting. The number of demons coming to our side was surprising, but we got our biggest shock when Mercy showed up at our door to petition for refuge. The Valkrin were the strength of the dark hordes, so when she and the others came we thought we may have been on the cusp of ending a war that's raged since the beginning of time. We learned a lot about the Valkrin during their time with us, especially Mercy. She and Edward helped out a great deal with acclimating some of the arrivals to the modern world and laws. Then one day the Valkrin begin disappearing."

"What brought this on?" Redfeather asked.

"At first we thought that it was the work of the dark lords, punishing the warriors for betraying the order, but then the reports started coming in and we discovered the horrible truth about what had happened to the Valkrin." She turned to where she heard De Mona's rapidly beating heart.

"And what did you find out?" De Mona asked, not sure if she was ready for the answer.

Lydia took a breath before continuing. "The dark lords weren't punishing them; they were calling them home. Our sources informed us that the dark forces were gathering, for what we still aren't sure. The Valkrin left us to answer the call to arms. Those who didn't answer the call and anyone close to them within the Order of

Sanctuary were destroyed. Mercy was amongst the first to leave us."

"My mother?" De Mona asked in disbelief.

"Yes, that's why when you showed up I thought that maybe she had sent you to broker a new peace."

De Mona scoffed, "My mother bounced on us, so if she was down with this little uprising or whatever, I wasn't in on it."

Lydia's brow creased. "She didn't take you?"

"No, why?" De Mona asked.

"Because all the Valkrin are bound to combat; it's one of their culture's oldest traditions. If Mercy didn't take you with her, then you must be a secret to the elders. To not stand beside your sisters in battle is punishable by death. I'm sorry; I thought you knew all this."

De Mona shook her head. It seemed that every time she thought she had her mother figured out, something new was revealed to De Mona. Hearing all the new information about her mother and her people took De Mona back to the day she had discovered the truth about what she was. For her first eleven years on earth, she had been a happy little girl living a seemingly normal life, with two loving parents. Her mother, though always forceful and strong-willed, was every bit the television housewife, tending to things around the house while De Mona's father worked to support them. One day she had been playing in the park near their house when a stray pit bull had wandered over. Not knowing any better, she tried to pet the dog, and it bit her. Seeing the blood all over her new white dress, De Mona went into shock.

The next few moments were fuzzy, but she could remember the smell of burning wood and the sound of whimpering. When she snapped out of it the dog lay crumpled at her feet, its neck at an uncomfortable-looking angle. When she went to touch the spot on her arm where she had been bitten, she discovered that not only had the wound healed, but she had also changed. Her dainty hands were now gnarled talons and her skin as smooth as leather. When she touched the talons to her face, she felt the bumps under the skin on her forehead. De Mona tore off screaming for her mother, hoping that she could fix whatever was wrong, but was horrified when she reached her. Mercy's face was no longer that of the loving mother De Mona had always known but the demon she had just discovered. After calming her, Mercy took De Mona home and together her parents told her the truth of what she really was.

When Mercy disappeared, De Mona's father let her believe that her mother had just run off, but her sins went far deeper. In De Mona's heart Mercy had abandoned not only her but also the very world that had taken Mercy in. De Mona had always been angry at her mother for leaving them, but to throw in her lot with the dark forces? It was no wonder Akbar hated De Mona, because at that moment she wasn't sure how she felt about herself.

"As if I wasn't a big enough loser already." De Mona sagged in on herself.

"But as we teach here, one cannot be judged by the actions of their kin, only on individual deeds," Brother Angelo said, strolling into the room with Akbar on his heels. Brother Angelo was a handsome man, who walked erect and proud. His hair was still as thick and as curly as Redfeather had remembered it, but it was now flecked with gray. Angelo was dressed in a tight-fitting black shirt, showing off his well-developed body. Along his thick arms he sported tattoos similar to the ones on Akbar's face. Though Brother Angelo seemed normal enough, De Mona could sense there was a great power about him.

Brother Angelo Annapolis was what was called a High Brother, or Core. He was the living embodiment of the power that dwelled within the Great Halls of Sanctuary, and leader of their order. Each house had a High Brother, but even amongst the others Brother Angelo was one of the most respected. Since birth he had been groomed to one day serve the order, as was their way. When Angelo was elected to his position he was bound by the oath and empowered by the magic trapped within the walls of the house. Because of the power within Sanctuary and the bond it created with the High Brothers, they could call on the power of the halls, as it could call on them in times of need. Though not quite immortal, they were very hard to kill.

Angelo nodded to Redfeather and gave De Mona a cordial smile. "Welcome, child of Mercy. What can we do for you here?"

"I . . . ah . . ."

"She was attacked by Stalkers," Redfeather answered for the girl.

"Wow, you actually saw a real Stalker?" Lydia asked excitedly. "The closest I ever came was when we took this guy in who had been bitten. When he started going through the change from the infection Akbar had to—"

"Enough, Lydia." Angelo raised his hand. "I don't think now is the time to rehash old stories. Why don't you go and see if Fin needs your help in the hall of prayer."

"Brother Angelo, how hard could it be to wipe off the benches?"

"Good-bye, Lydia." The girl sucked her teeth but left as she was told. When she was gone, Angelo turned back to Redfeather. "You know how teenagers can be." Angelo shrugged. "Lydia has been under my care for almost ten years now and a ward of the Sanctuary since she was born."

"Gabriel is slightly older than her." Redfeather thought back on Gabriel, who still hadn't woken. "He is the reason we've come here tonight."

Angelo studied Redfeather for a minute. "The last time I saw him we were laying his father to rest." Angelo crossed himself. "As I recall, you turned your back on the order and your duties shortly after."

"Yes, Angelo. I understand that you may still hold some bitterness in your heart for my decision, but you have to understand my circumstances. I had lost my entire family to Belthon's lot and I did not have the heart to send my grandson into the fire, as I had my sons."

"None of us would, but to pretend that they are not amongst us is delusional, old friend. You know the legacy of your people."

"Indeed I do. And it is the legacy of my people that has stirred the most disturbing of things, the Nimrod."

Angelo's smirk was suddenly washed away. "The Bishop's prison? Impossible."

"I wish that were so, Angelo, but it isn't. The Nimrod has resurfaced and answered to the touch of my grandson," Redfeather said seriously.

Angelo gave Redfeather a look that said he wasn't quite convinced. "Redfeather, even if the Nimrod had resurfaced, only one of the Bishop's line could wake his spirit, let alone control the thing. Anyone else would probably do little more than incinerate himself."

Redfeather raised his eyebrow and asked, "Need I remind you who stopped the Dark Storm the first time?"

"Yes, the same man who accidentally slew several of his own with the cursed thing," Angelo spat.

"That was the work of Nimrod, not my ancestor!" Redfeather said heatedly. Arguing was getting him nowhere, so he tried to rationalize. "Angelo, the Nimrod has done something to my grandson, and the more we bicker the worse his condition could become. Whatever your feelings about me might be, you know I've always been a man of my word. If you do not believe me, then believe your own eyes." Redfeather pulled the handkerchief from his pocket and laid it on the table. He folded it open and showed Angelo the dagger. "The Bishop sleeps no more."

Angelo had a hard time taking his eyes off the dagger. It had been ages since he'd seen it, and longer still since he'd seen it shine so brightly. "It came alive for Gabriel?"

Redfeather nodded. "As did the Nimrod."

Angelo watched Redfeather for a while, trying to gauge the sincerity of his words. The dagger being restored was proof enough that something was afoot, but if what Redfeather was saying held any truth then it could mark the beginning of the next battle for humanity. Taking Redfeather's claim lightly could potentially leave them open to an assault by the dark forces.

"Tell me, how did your grandson come into possession of the Nimrod?" Angelo asked, still weighing his decision.

De Mona raised her hand. "Afraid I'm responsible for that." She went on to tell Angelo the tale of how the trident came into her possession and of her father's murder.

Angelo shook his head sadly. "I'm sorry to hear about your father, De Mona. Edward was a good man and didn't deserve that. Tell me, where is the Nimrod now?"

"With Gabriel," Redfeather answered.

Angelo turned his eyes to him. "Redfeather, the Nimrod is one of the most powerful religious artifacts ever known and you left it with your grandson?"

"It was through no choice of mine. I'm afraid the Nimrod has bound itself to my grandson in more than just spirit." Redfeather went on to explain about the tattoo and Gabriel's coma.

"God in heaven, how could this be?" Angelo gasped.

"We came here for answers, but it seems like you guys are asking all the questions," De Mona said. She hadn't meant to be short with Angelo, but her mind was reeling from the last few days' events.

"Hold your tongue, demon," Akbar warned. Just as it had in the doorway, the temperature dropped in the chapel.

De Mona stood directly in front of him. She could feel the change coming as her fingers hardened, and welcomed it this time. "If you're trying to scare me, you ain't doing a very good job."

"Then maybe I should increase my efforts?" Akbar challenged. He held his palm up and a shard of ice appeared in the center of it.

"Enough," Angelo said. Though he never raised his voice, it seemed to echo throughout the chapel. "Akbar, this girl has been through a lot and deserves a little compassion."

"Angelo, surely you're not being taken in by their lies?" Akbar was still tense, but the ice had melted away to water dripping from his hand. "You've seen how the Valkrin abandoned us; surely you won't take the word of Mercy's child?"

"No, but I'll take the word of an old friend." He glanced at Redfeather. "We'll have a team assembled within the hour to recover your grandson. I will lead them personally."

"Impossible," Akbar cut in. "You're too valuable to the order to lead the investigation, Brother Angelo. You are the Core of the power which dwells in this place; we can't risk losing you. I'll lead the team."

"Akbar, I appreciate your concern, but I don't think me being gone for a couple of hours will result in the dissipation of this house. I will go with Redfeather to bring his grandson in."

"Thank you, Angelo, but I would rather just be rid of the trident. Gabriel has been through enough," Redfeather told him.

"I understand, Redfeather, but I'm afraid they'll both

have to be brought here. If it is as you say and the trident has bonded with Gabriel, he's as much a part of the puzzle as it is."

"I cannot agree to my grandson being brought here to be studied," Redfeather said heatedly.

"I'm afraid you don't have a choice." Angelo locked eyes with his old friend. "The weapon is too powerful to be left in the hands of the uninitiated. The trident has awakened for your grandson and we need to know why. In the wrong hands, the trident of heaven could upset the balance of light and dark, and that cannot be allowed."

"Angelo, you are making a mistake," Redfeather insisted.

"Don't try and tell me how to do my job, Redfeather. I have served the order faithfully, while others have chosen to turn a blind eye to the vile things that prey on humanity. Akbar will escort you back upstairs to wait until the team is ready to go. I am sorry that your grandson is caught in the middle of this, Redfeather, truly." Without giving Redfeather a chance to protest further, Angelo turned and left.

De Mona looked from Angelo to Redfeather, who wore a worried expression on his face. "Some freaking friends."

CHAPTER FIFTEEN

On a commercial flight it took an average of between six and eight hours to get from Ontario to New York, but the *Night Hawk* did it in fewer than three. It was a sleek eight-passenger jet that could travel at mach 2 for over two thousand miles before compromising its hull integrity. As far as luxury jets went, it didn't get any more top-of-the-line than the gift to the Dark Order from the Russian government, but it still made Flag nervous.

Flag hated flying, especially in an airplane. The flying machines were the ultimate display of modern technology and therefore the best at interfering with magic. Between the minerals used in their construction and the radio waves, they made casting a spell three times as hard as it would be standing in an open field. If something went wrong, Flag wouldn't be able to totally depend on his magics, and working with a handicap didn't sit well with him, especially in light of the mission Titus had sent him on.

Flag knew he was going to have his hands full overseeing their troops in the city while they searched for the Nimrod, but the e-mail he'd just gotten on his BlackBerry threatened to complicate things even more. His spies had reported that Mercy's daughter had last been seen going into a church in Brooklyn. Flag knew that it had to be the stronghold of the Inquisitors and they could cause a serious problem.

Since the days before the witch hunts, the Inquisition and the Order of Sanctuary had been the most hated enemies of the Dark Order. Unlike the church, the Inquisitors were willing to tap into the great beyond to accomplish their ultimate goal of casting evil from the world. They were a relentless and merciless lot, who once they'd been set on you wouldn't stop until you were destroyed. Flag's being a man wanted by the Order of Mages and a servant of the Dark Order would be more than enough reason for the Inquisitors to put him in their sights, so he wanted to get in and out of the city as quickly as possible.

When Flag stepped off the plane he was greeted by Riel and two Stalkers that, thankfully, looked to be freshly dead. Flag understood the necessity for Riel's abominations but had never been comfortable with the animated corpses. The mages believed that spirits were best utilized by stripping them of their power, rather then giving them an opportunity to stab you when your back was turned. Flag stopped at the bottom of the folding stairs and regarded the demon.

"Well, this will truly be a glorious night if Titus has sent his favorite lackey into the heart of the battle," Riel said smugly.

"If the choice had been mine, I wouldn't be here, demon." Flag stared him down. "Sadly, fate has thrust us together, so I suggest we get on with our assignments so we can be done."

"Agreed." Riel led Flag to the waiting limo.

"I trust that your people are still looking for the Nimrod." Flag settled into the backseat of the limo. Behind the wheel was a man who had no eyes but seemed to see clearer than any of them.

"The Nimrod burns brighter than a hundred stars; even as it tries to hide, my people see it. We've got the best tracker in the kennels of the Gehenna on the trail and he places it somewhere in uptown Manhattan. We will find this boy and his whore and I shall drink from both their severed heads." Riel wiped his mouth with the back of his hand.

"What you do with their blood is your business, demon. I'm only concerned with concluding Titus' business so I can be away from this place." Flag looked out the window nervously. Though he couldn't see them, he could feel the different supernatural presences moving around him. In New York almost nothing was as it seemed, and the sooner he could be away the better he would feel.

"The shadow master has been cured of his sickness and has been dispatched to the warlocks' stronghold to administer his special brand of interrogation to some of the young ones. If they know something, Moses will find out. We will not fail the dark lord again," Riel assured Flag.

"You should hope so, Riel. Titus has entrusted you with a heavy task, and failure could leave a blemish on your impeccable record. You've long been the faithful right arm of Titus, so I gather it wouldn't go over well for you if it seemed like that arm's strength was wavering." Flag smirked.

"The day that I can't defeat a novice I combat is the day that you boy-loving magicians will rule the underworld." Riel laughed.

"Your performance earlier says otherwise, but that's a conversation for you to have with Titus."

"So it is, but you have a far more interesting conversation ahead of you. I hear that the goblins prefer the flesh of magicians only second to fairies," Riel taunted him. "But fear not; I've provided you with two able bodies to see you through." He pointed to the Stalkers. They were menacing but would be little more than food if the goblins turned on them.

"For your sake I hope they're up to the task. If I were you, I'd get moving. Raising the dead must be time-consuming," Flag said.

"Only to the unenlightened. Don't worry, mage; Titus will have his army and I will have my glory." Riel disappeared into a wisp of acidic black smoke.

"I hate demons," Flag said to the empty space.

The driver of the recently missing Greyhound bus that had been traveling from Atlantic City back to New York braced himself against the cemetery fence and continued throwing up until he felt like his body would turn itself inside out. When he'd been approached by the young biker his good mind said to refuse, but the money the biker was offering was too good to pass up. He made it seem like a simple kidnapping that would net the driver fifty large, but he was now seeing that the stakes were for something far greater than money.

Riel had instructed the driver to drive the bus to the closest cemetery, where he proceeded to unload the passengers, aided by the few Stalkers that hadn't fallen to the Nimrod. Most of the passengers knew they were done, but some held on to hopes that they might be ransomed or rescued. But those thoughts fled when the first blood was shed. Riel executed all of them. The loser, the newly-weds, even a woman who had been huddled in the back with her teenaged son. The demon spared no one. Their blood would be a tribute to the god Thanos for sharing his power, and their flesh would fuel his troops.

"Listen, can I go now? I can pick my money up in the morning?" the driver asked, not being able to take it anymore.

"Hold your place, mortal." Riel pointed Poison at him. "None may break the circle until Titus has his army."

The driver felt the first chills of the wind as it whipped at his thin uniform jacket. He tried to huddle against the cold, but it seemed to seep into his bones. Watching the demon work, the driver wondered if it had been such a good idea to strike a deal with him.

Riel's face had lost its rugged appeal and become something more twisted as he invoked his magic. He could feel the dimensions of man and demons colliding, threatening to singe every nerve in his host's body. Riel had performed mass summoning before, but never had he attempted such a grand rising on the mortal or the demon side of the rift. On the mortal side he could raise a few Stalkers to do his bidding, but he couldn't draw on enough of his demonic powers to raise the number of foot soldiers Titus wanted. The only thing that was keeping Riel's host's body intact was the power of his cursed blade, and even that could only take so much strain. Still, losing his host failed in comparison to what Titus would do if Riel didn't capture the Nimrod.

Riel began the ritual from within a circle of bones that he had erected on the far side of the cemetery, closest to the position of the moon. Raising his hands heavenward, he chanted the words in a language that was as familiar to him as the blade he had wielded for over a thousand years. The ground trembled as he flushed his power into it, tilling the dry earth as it gathered. The dirty drank greedily of the blood Riel had sacrificed, connecting the war demon with the land. He manipulated the streams of blood as if they were his own fingers, touching the souls that rested beneath in the graves and through them calling to his minions on the demon plains. The spirits of those buried in the cemetery wisely shied away from the dark magic, but the vile things that worshiped chaos swarmed to it, anticipating the chance to become flesh again.

The driver jumped back as he felt something tickling his boot. He looked down expecting to see a rat or some other small animal but instead saw the bloody hand of the young girl whom he had helped with her bag when she was getting on the bus. Her eyes had been cool blue then, but now they were gray and lifeless as she looked up at the driver. The driver tried to run but ended up tripping over his feet and landing on a soft path of dirt that was in the shadow of a marble angel. "What is this, man?" The driver scrambled for the concrete path.

Riel looked over at the man, still standing within the circle of bone. "It's your reward, mortal. For your betrayal of your own, you shall feed my newborns." Riel laughed menacingly. The demons shot up through the corpses in the ground and passed through Riel before choosing their hosts' bodies.

The realization had finally set in and the driver knew that the demon had lied to him and there would be no riches, only horrible death. He struggled as much as he could, but one of the Stalkers had an unyielding grip on his pant leg. One by one the bodies of his dead passengers came to life, hungry and crawling in his direction. The driver would've screamed had it not been for the Stalker who had just chewed through his vocal cords.

CHAPTER SIXTEEN

The Triple Six nightclub was located in the Village, right off the West Side Highway. Though it wasn't the most well-advertised spot, there was never a shortage of people trying to get in. The Triple Six specialized in what some would call exotic pleasures. Sex, drugs, snuff, nothing was forbidden within the walls of the Triple Six.

The inside of the club was packed to capacity. Goths, gangsters, and business types partied together as DJ Hex played a mix of house, hip-hop, and alternative music. Her ability to rock any party made her one of the most sought-after DJs in the city. Clubs paid Hex a queen's ransom to spin at their events. They'd probably be pissed to know that it wasn't the music she played that rocked the party but the magical undertones she laced it with. DJ Hex was one of the few muses in the United States.

The dance floor was packed with people dancing and drinking and doing whatever the darkness would allow. Tucked into a dark corner Rogue could make out a couple locked in an embrace. The man's face was buried in the woman's neck, while her eyes were lulled back in ecstasy as if she was having the orgasm of her life. Only when he raised his head could you see her blood smeared across his lips. The feedings weren't unusual within the Triple Six. It was a part of the truce between Dutch and the house of Lamia, who were the ruling vampire body in New York City. They could feed from the *willing* patrons so long as no one died; in exchange they provided security for the club against the other supernaturals, sorcerers in particular. The inside of the Triple Six was sanctuary, but outside its walls the war raged on.

Rogue hated clubs. Not because they were hot and overcrowded and smelled like ass but because of the different pulses that ran unchecked through them. Everyone, supernatural and mortal, had a pulse. Supernatural pulses were pronounced and distinct, like body odor, but mortal pulses were much subtler because mortals were unaware of the power they emitted. But when you added the two pulses and threw in a splash of alcohol and a healthy amount of drugs, it could cause sensory overload in someone sensitive to these things. This was what Rogue was trying to fight off at the time.

The nightclub was teeming with mortals, but Rogue could feel the others mixed in with the crowd. Casters, Weres, posers, he picked up on all their magical pulses. Skilled or uninitiated users of magic could pick up on the presence of others like him, even if they didn't know what they were feeling, but Rogue's unique magical bond with the other realm made him supersensitive to it. Whenever Rogue brushed against someone, which seemed like every step he took because of the crowd, his equilibrium felt off.

He hiked the left sleeve of his jacket slightly, exposing the bracelet on his wrist. It was a simple gold link, attached to what looked like a coin in the center of the bracelet. It was a pendent with magical runes of focus and clarity on it, which had been given to him back in Florida. Rubbing a sweaty thumb against the coin to add of himself to the spell, he chanted the words softly. As soon as the last word had left his mouth, he started to feel more focused. The pulses were still pressing against him, but not as forcefully. The power of the bracelet wrapped a thick layer of magic around him, driving the temperature up a few degrees, in the already-hot club, but he'd live. It was a small price to pay in a place like the Triple Six, where not being focused could mean a slow, nasty death.

Normally Rogue would've put off investigating the insurgence of Stalkers until after he had finished the case he was working on, but the fact that he'd almost wrapped his car around a streetlight added urgency to his investigation. He'd been heading up Broadway, on his way back to the office, when a jolt of pain shot through his skull. It was as if someone was trying to boil his eyes out of their sockets. Even their donor seemed to cringe at the sensation. Whatever the force was that had frightened the demon, it was somehow connected to the Stalkers; this he was sure of.

There were several people he could've consulted on the matter, but most either were abroad or wanted him dead, narrowing his choices considerably. He knew there was only one person he could call on for the answers he needed, but to get to him Rogue had to venture into the lion's den, the Triple Six.

Rogue had been to the Triple Six a time or two, but those were because he absolutely had to and they had been by invitation. The warlock king despised mages, as did most witches and warlocks, and with good reason. Though the mages had never officially chosen sides in the Great War between the sorcerers and their servants, the more ambitious of the order had been retained as slave hunters and sometimes executioners of unruly casters. There was more than enough bad blood between the mages and the warlocks, enough to get Rogue killed if his true nature was discovered while he was inside the Triple Six.

With his hands tucked deep inside the pockets of his leather jacket he picked his way through the crowd, trying to keep from making skin-to-skin contact with any of the partygoers. He might've been able to fool some of the young ones, but the older and more seasoned ones would know him, and there were some truly ancient things inside the Triple Six. He swept his shaded eyes through the crowd, trying to pick out the familiar pulse in the darkened club, but couldn't spot it on the main floor. This meant he would have to venture into the VIP area, which he'd hoped he wouldn't have to do.

Rogue kept his head down as he headed for the long corridor that would lead him to the lower levels. The main floor was mostly mortals, but there were some supernaturals scattered throughout the crowd. Through his eyes they looked like a kaleidoscope with magical pulses of all different hues. He was so preoccupied with the swirling colors of the pulses that he walked right into a brick wall dressed in leather. Rogue looked from the man's glowing red eyes to the liquor splashed on his leather vest and knew he had a situation on his hands.

If he had to describe the man in front of him in one word, it would have to be *brute*. He stood a head over six-three with a massive jaw and long brown hair. His shoulders were like two melons connected to arms that stopped just above his knees. Even if those arms hadn't been covered in hair, Rogue would've known he was a Were of some kind.

"Sorry about that, man, let me buy you another drink," Rogue offered.

"To hell with the drink, this vest cost me two hundred bucks!" The brute snarled, giving Rogue a glimpse of canines that were slightly too long.

Definitely a Were.

"Look man, I'm sorry—"

"What are you?" The brute sniffed the air around Rogue. "You smell like one of us, but for some reason I can't figure out what you are. Tell me," he leaned in, "what're you trying to hide?"

"Dig, I don't want a problem in here; I'm just trying to get a drink," Rogue said easily, trying to step around the brute. The brute moved with him.

"I didn't ask you all that, flesh sack. I asked what you were." He jabbed his finger into Rogue's chest.

Rogue looked down at his chest as if something were growing out of it. He looked back up at the brute and in a very calm tone said, "If you put your finger on me again, I'll have to put my finger on you."

The brute snorted. "Little man." He jabbed his finger in Rogue's chest again. "I'd tear out your freaking—" That was as far as he got.

Rogue grabbed the brute's wrist with his right hand and twisted it to the left. It was hardly enough to break the bone of a Were, but it was enough to stun him while Rogue raised his left hand. He stiffened his index and middle fingers, jabbing them into the brute's chest and expelling a wisp of his power. The thread of energy looped around the brute's heart and tightened, stopping it. Before he could sag to the ground, Rogue caught him under the arms and guided him onto a bar stool. The beast's heart would restart in a few seconds and he would be Pissed with a capital *P*, but Rogue had no intentions of being around when it happened. Catching a werewolf by surprise was one thing, but a head-on confrontation would result in a loss of limbs and even that was the best-case scenario. When he was sure no one was watching Rogue allowed the shadows of the club to engulf him. The only sign of his passing at the bar was the twenty-dollar bill he'd left under a glass.

Managing to avoid any more life-threatening skirmishes Rogue navigated the shadows and made his way to the lower levels of the club. The main area was open to any and all, but the lower section was reserved for members of the king's court. If you weren't a witch or warlock of the coven, then you ventured below the club at your own peril, but of course Rogue made his living putting his ass on the line.

"Angel," Rogue greeted the vampire as he approached the entrance of the Black Court.

Angel looked over his shoulder nervously. "Rogue, what're you doing here? You know Dutch is gonna shit a brick if he finds out you're up in his spot uninvited."

"And what makes you think that I haven't been invited?" Rogue challenged.

"Because I work the entrance and I'd know if a murdering, sneaky, blackmailing son of a bitch was on the list, and he ain't!"

"Hey, my mother's got nothing to do with this, errand boy, so let's try to keep the insults personal. Don't worry your pretty undead ass over it, fam; I'll be in and out before Dutch even catches wind that I'm here." Rogue tried to step past, but Angel blocked him.

"Come on, Rogue, you know this'll come down on my head if I let you in here and you start some shit."

"Angel, would I put you in a bind like that?"

"Yes."

Rogue smiled. "Look, all I want to do is see if a buddy of mine is inside. I gotta ask him something and then I'm gone."

"Rogue, you know just as well as I do that you ain't got a friend in this world, let alone Dutch's club. . . . Hell, I can count on one hand how many people in the city actually like you and still have fingers left over. Why don't you do us both a favor and take a hike, huh?"

"Angel." Rogue placed a hand on the vampire's

shoulder. "Why you wanna go and hurt my feelings like that?"

Angel slapped the hand away. "You ain't got no feelings, Rogue. If I were you, I'd make myself scarce before someone saw me and tried to turn me into a goat."

Rogue folded his arms. "Angel, you know I hate to call in markers, but need I remind you who it was that kept Mesh and his boys from carving up that pretty face of yours?"

Angel shivered. A year prior he had gotten himself into a situation where the daughter of a respected mob attorney was murdered and Angel was fingered as the killer. Angel swore he was innocent, but it was discovered that he and the girl had been lovers and he'd been feeding from the girl for several months. Because Angel was a supernatural creature, the lawyer sought justice through one of his special clients, Rupert Croft. Croft was the leader of a syndicate not recognized by the FBI but was respected in the supernatural and mortal underworlds. Croft's favorite killing device was his nephew Gilgamesh.

Gilgamesh was a dark elf who had killed more people than the West Nile virus. His crew, the Black Hand, was worse. Angel knew that it would only be a matter of time before they caught him, so he hired Rogue to find out who had set him up. The Black Hand had captured Angel and nailed him to a cross in the lawyer's greenhouse so he'd have a nice view of the sun when it came up. Just as the first rays began to blister Angel's skin, Rogue turned up the real killer. As it turned out, he was an old boyfriend who couldn't get past the fact that the girl was sleeping with a vamp.

Angel attempted to pay Rogue for his services, but the bounty hunter declined, opting to take his payment in the form of a favor. One thing Rogue had learned in his years of dealing with the unknown was that a favor came in a lot handier than money.

"Rogue, don't do this to me." Angel threw his hands up.

"I'm not doing anything to you, Angel. All I wanna do is go inside and look around for my buddy. I promise I won't even talk to anyone while I'm inside." Rogue held up his hand in a Boy Scout salute.

Angel glared at the man for a minute before stepping aside to let him in.

"Thanks, man." Rogue went to pass and Angel took him by the arm.

"Rogue, if you jam me on this I'm gonna hunt you down and kill you personally," he said seriously.

"You're welcome to try," Rogue said in an equally serious tone. His shadow cast against the wall seemed to grow as threads of darkness snaked about his hands. "But I'd hate to be on either end of that one."

"As long as we understand each other," Angel said.

Rogue didn't even bother to answer; he just kept walking down the corridor. A few seconds later his shadow caught up with him.

Within the walls of the Black Court the magical energy was far more potent than in the main area but also more controlled. Those who frequented the Court ranged from the highest levels of the coven to the lowest, but all knew to exercise control when in the king's domain so as not to become the target of his anger. It wasn't unheard of for Dutch to dispatch swift punishement to those who broke his rules, which Rogue was doing at the moment.

Trying to remain as unassuming as possible, Rogue slid up to the bar. The young lady working it was wearing skintight leather pants and a sheer shirt that left little to the imagination. He was so busy admiring her that she had to ask him for his order twice before he was finally

able to blurt out, "Corona." A few stools down were two
attractive young witches. The blonde had a strong aura,
but it was the brunette who burned brightest. He smiled
at them, and while the brunette returned the gesture, the
blonde snubbed him. "Fuck, snob," he mumbled, and hun-
kered over his beer.

Using the bar mirror, Rogue scanned the room. One
by one he picked the different magical auras apart,
searching for the needle in the haystack. Everyone in the
room had an aura, but the one he was looking for would
stand out amongst them. Rogue's starlit orbs missed it on
the first sweep, but on the second he picked up on it, the
triangle in a room full of squares.

She was a wiry young girl with purple hair and torn
fishnet stockings. To everyone else she appeared to be
little more than a low-level witch who was slumming with
the rest of the anarchists, but Rogue saw through the
mask. As the stars in his eyes began to dance, the layers
of magic began to fall away from the girl like dead leaves.
The image only lasted a second, but it was more than
enough time for Rogue to make a positive ID. Snatching
his beer off the bar, Rogue ambled over to the young lady.

When the girl noticed Rogue coming in her direction
she tried to lose herself in the crowd. Trying to make herself smaller, she skirted to the other side of the room,
sparing a glance over her shoulder as she made for the
door. She'd almost cleared the room when Rogue's frame
cut her off.

Rogue gave her his sexiest smile. "Don't jet off yet,
baby; I haven't bought you a drink yet."

"No thanks." She turned and went back the way she'd
come. She hadn't seen him move, but the mage was again
blocking her path.

"Come on, doll. I think I'd make more interesting com-

pany than these stiffs." He motioned to the other clubgo-
ers, who for some reason didn't seem to notice them.

"I said no thanks," she said a bit more forcefully. When
she tried to walk away, Rogue grabbed her by the arm.

He slid his shades down so she could see the stars shift-
ing in his eyes. The energy he passed through her was so
heady that it caused her form to waver. It was like the reality around her distorted and there was a person within a
person. She forced the illusion back into place and hissed
at Rogue.

"Save the tough shit, because I ain't impressed," he
whispered. "Now, either you can talk to me or I can ex-
pose you to these good folks in here; what's it gonna be?"

Her eyes narrowed to slits. "You'd be just as much up a
creek as me."

Rogue tapped his finger against his chin as if he were
giving it some thought, then smiled. "Yeah, Dutch would
probably be pissed that I came in here without an invitation with me being a mage and all, but," he waved his
hand in front of her, causing the illusion to waver again,
"what do you think he'd do to a demon who violated his
inner sanctum?"

"Filthy darkling puppet, you wouldn't dare," she challenged.

He raised an eyebrow. "Wouldn't I?"

The girl weighed her options. She knew from past ex-
perience that Rogue was a man who didn't play by anyone's rules but his own, so you could never be sure how
far he would go. She could always try running, but with
those blasted eyes of his there was only so long she'd be
able to hide before he tracked her down. With a sigh, she
headed for the exit and motioned for him to follow.

Rogue had just fallen in step behind her when he felt a
familiar magical pulse. Without even thinking, he grabbed

the girl and pulled her into a lover's embrace. She started to protest, but he silenced her with a hand clamped over her mouth. She could feel him working some kind of magic, but before she had a chance to figure out what it was, the lights went out just in the spot where they were standing. Rogue had draped them in shadow, which unnerved the girl, but before she could argue about it, Dutch walked right past them.

CHAPTER SEVENTEEN

As soon as Lucy entered the Black Court she could feel the magic in the stares that came her way. It was such an intense feeling that she stroked her fur collar absently as he moved across the floor. Physically, she was a strikingly beautiful specimen with long black hair and flawless pale skin, but it was the raw power coming from her that drew everyone's attention. Some greeted her with smiles, while others flashed looks of disgust, but none of her enemies were stupid enough to challenge the young witch outright. Lucy carried herself with the air of a princess, because technically she was. At one time her late mother, Wanda, had been the White Queen of the coven, and her power flowed strong within her daughter.

At her usual position at the bar was Sulin, a gifted young healer and one of the few witches Lucy could've called a friend. Sulin was a statuesque young lady with hair the color of cornstarch and striking green eyes. She was leaning against the bar, stroking the head of her Pomeranian and speaking in a hushed tone to a handsome young warlock. She must've felt Lucy's presence, because she looked up from her conversation. Sulin reluctantly excused herself and made her way over to Lucy.

"Trolling for fresh meat?" Lucy greeted her friend with a hug and kissed her on both cheeks. Not wanting to be left out, the Pomeranian licked Lucy's chin. A handsome young man wearing dark sunglasses gave them a flirtatious smile. Lucy smiled back, but Sulin didn't.

"Hardly." Sulin rolled her eyes at the man in shades and turned her back to him. "I'm on call for Angelique tonight and he was just keeping me company." Sulin waved at the warlock dismissively.

"What's Her Highness got you doing tonight?" Lucy sat on the bar stool and ordered two drinks.

"I'd be lying if I said I knew. All she's told me is that something is afoot in New York and she needs me close."

"That explains why everything is so dead. I went to two of my regular spots and there was no one there but mortals; even the Triple Six is looking suspect tonight," Lucy pointed out.

"Maybe the vampires are at it again; you know how ugly their skirmishes can be," Sulin said.

"Tell me about it." Lucy recalled the damage the Gehenna clan had done to the city before the Lamia had gotten things under control. "So what's the action like in here tonight?"

"Other than the Hunt making their usual rounds, nothing special." Sulin shrugged.

"The Hunt, I thought I smelled wet dog," Lucy spat.

"Don't start anything, Lucy." Sulin looked around nervously.

"Give me a break; you guys run around whispering like the Hunt is the bogeyman or something. Asha and her brood aren't so tough."

"We're tough enough to break disrespectful weak little witches," a voice called from behind them. The witch addressing her had been the thorn in Lucy's side since Dutch had adopted her into the coven. With long deadlocks and china doll eyes the color of a smoldering campfire, set in cherrywood skin, she looked like a princess of some forgotten African kingdom. Her shapely hips pressed against her skintight leather pants as she took a wide-legged stance and glared defiantly at Lucy.

The sisters Lisa and Lane rose to stand beside her. From afar you couldn't tell one from the other, but up close you could see the differences. Both had milk chocolate skin and dark eyes, but while Lane was petite, Lisa had more of an athletic build. A large gray wolf spider sat perched on the side of Lisa's head like a flower, while one that was almost transparent crawled across Lane's neck, leaving a trail of silk like a scarf. The witches eyed Lucy from behind their web-like veils, daring her to make a move but not advancing on her. Though they were dangerous killers, they weren't very skilled spell casters, which meant they were no match for Lucy.

"Disrespectful, sure, but broken . . . not in this lifetime, sister," Lucy said as if she couldn't feel the intense power building in Asha. Lucy was skilled, but Asha was brutal in her spell casting.

"Says you," Asha replied, flipping her long auburn dreadlocks behind her. Azuma, a small brownish monkey, danced on the seat beside her, flashing his crooked teeth at Lucy. Asha and her familiar had been together since she was a girl.

"Don't you know when to quit?" Lucy stroked her fur collar. Her eyes warned Asha to stay clear.

"Oh, oh, I think she's getting mad," Lisa taunted.

"Aw, is Angelique's prized pupil having a bad day?" Asha ran her fingers over Azuma's fuzzy head. The monkey rocked back and forth grumbling in anticipation of Asha's command, occasionally slapping his frail chest. When unbound the familiars could wreak all kinds of havoc, but with a power line like the bond he and Asha had going Azuma could complicate things considerably.

Azuma leapt and lashed out with his dirty little claws

at Lucy's left cheek. The motion was so swift that Lucy's eyes never even registered it, but Tiki did. The ferret draped around her neck sprang to life, sinking his needle teeth into the monkey's forearm. Azuma roared and tried to club Tiki with his fist, but the lithe body wouldn't remain still long enough for him to land a blow that would count for anything. With panic setting in, Azuma sank his teeth into the soft skin at the base of Tiki's skull, causing the ferret to let go. Azuma wasted no time darting back to his mistress and glaring at Tiki from behind her leg.

"You'd better control your rat, little Wanda." Asha scooped Azuma up but kept her eyes on Tiki.

"Watch your mouth," Lucy warned, picking Tiki up and draping him back around her neck. "You're not fit to speak my mother's name, the name of a *pure* witch, but I guess you wouldn't know anything about that, mongrel bitch!"

The hurt in Asha's eyes only lasted for a split second before it was replaced by rage. Asha's mother had been a Voundon priestess of a long-dead cult, who had become smitten by one of Dutch's Initiates. She gave herself body and soul to the warlock only to find that he was married, with a family, and she had been little more than sport to him. Shortly after she murdered him she found out that she was pregnant with Asha. As punishment for killing one of their own, the Council took the child and banished her mother to God only knew where. Asha was raised in the circle, but the others always made it clear that she'd never be one of them. The same, however, did not hold true for Lucy. Because of who her mother had been, Lucy was guaranteed a spot at the table whether she wanted it or not. She was the child of royalty and Asha hated her for this.

As if by magic a blade appeared in Asha's hand. "You

white-trash whore, I'm gonna fucking gut you!" She went to move in on Lucy but found that her body would no longer cooperate. When Lucy tried to take advantage she realized that she was also paralyzed. Though neither one of them could as much as turn her head, they heard the clicking of boots on the tiles and knew that they had made a terrible mistake.

CHAPTER EIGHTEEN

"Cool it, ladies," Dutch said, waving a hand over each witch. Their magical auras spilled from them and snaked up his arms like two racing serpents. There were few amongst the covens that could neutralize a witch's power without first preparing the proper ritual and fewer still who could do it to two witches at once. As always, Dutch was dressed in leather pants and a leather vest over his bare arms and chest. Rings of black curls touched the tips of his broad shoulders. He didn't look a day over forty, but it was rumored that he had been around for well over a hundred years.

"I didn't start it, but I'm more than ready to finish it." Lucy struggled against the *immobile* spell Dutch had cast on them. Had she been paying attention during her lessons, she would've known how to break it.

"Dutch, just give me five minutes with this whore; that's all I need." Asha closed her fist and was trying to work her arm forward. The fact that she had even managed to close her hand while under the spell was a testament to her strength. Unlike Lucy, she was familiar with the spell and could break it against an average witch or warlock, but Dutch was a king.

"What part of 'cool it' don't you understand?" Dutch pushed a little more power into the spell. It wasn't enough to hurt Asha, but it was very uncomfortable. "There are battles to be fought, but not amongst each other and not in my house, ever!"

"Sorry." Asha heaved, having spent herself trying to break the spell.

"No need to apologize, Asha. We are all kin here and no one is greater than the circle." With a wave of his hand he returned their magics and freed them from the spell.

"Dutch just saved you from a good ass kicking, mongrel," Lucy said arrogantly.

Asha's hate for Lucy grew so intense that she dug her fingernails so deep into her palms that they started bleeding. Smoke rose from the droplets as they hit the floor. "My king, I would gladly give up my position within the Hunt if you would finally let me shut this bitch up."

"Asha, remember who you are. Personal grievances are second to the strength of the circle. Are you still a part of that strength?" Dutch looked at her.

" 'I am the joint at the elbow of the sword arm and the neck under the executioner's blade if my coven requires it of me.' " Asha recited it exactly as it was written. When she was adopted in the coven she tore into her studies, surpassing most of her peers. It was because of her devotion to the God and Goddess and the laws of the coven that Dutch had initiated a witch so young into the Hunt. The Hunt was not only the judicial system of the coven; it was also its heart.

"Oh, now if that isn't the cutest thing," Lucy taunted Asha.

"Lucille Brisbane." Dutch addressed her by her full name, which she hated. "What trouble do you bring to my doorstep tonight?"

"Nothing much, just out enjoying the scene and trying to help you take out the trash." She glared at Asha.

"Lucy, when are you and Asha gonna let this childhood

grudge go? Both of you are promising young daughters of this coven and will be expected one day to show the younger ones as we are trying to show you."

"My mother taught me all that I need to know about our coven." Lucy looked at Dutch defiantly.

"I find it interesting how you're so quick to make reference to Wanda in your defense, but you continue to drag her name through the mud," Dutch shot back. "Lucy, you are not only one of the most gifted young witches I've ever seen, but you are a child of royalty and I think it's high time you started acting like it."

Lucy took offense at this. "Listen, Dutch, I know this is your place and all, but I really didn't come here for a lecture. I came to get hammered and laid, and not necessarily in that order, so if we're done here?"

You could almost feel the king's power spike as all the air seemed to get sucked out of the room. The wiser ones backed away, but the foolish Initiates moved to get a better view. "If it weren't for my respect for your mother, I would make you show the proper respect for your king."

"If it weren't for my mother, I'm sure there are a few things that you would try and make me do." She looked the king up and down seductively.

"Dutch, you've got to excuse Lucy. You know she can't hold her liquor," Sulin cut in, giving Dutch her million-dollar smile. She knew that Dutch was hot for her and used this to bleed off some of his anger. She tugged Lucy by the arm to let her know that she had gone too far.

"Indeed," Dutch said, barely able to control the anger in his voice. Lucy stared at him for a second or two longer before allowing Sulin to pull her away. Before they reached the exit, Dutch called after her, "You will bend, little witch."

Lucy stopped short and met his stare. "I may bend, but I will never break. My mother saw to that." With that said, Lucy and Sulin departed, leaving Asha and her cronies to endure whatever rage Dutch had left over.

"Dutch—," Asha began but was cut off.

"Save it. Asha, you and Lucy are like two third graders fighting over a boy in the school yard."

"Dutch, if she's disrespecting me every time I see her am I supposed to let it go? I am not my mother, and if I have to kick the ass of every witch and warlock to prove it, then I'm ready for the task," Asha said seriously.

Dutch smiled at her lovingly. Of all the students, Asha was most like him in her ambition. "Asha, you could go down the line and best everyone in the coven, but it wouldn't change how some of them see you. If anything, it would make them think you're more akin to the darkness than the light. If you want to spite them, continue doing what you're doing, which is rising in rank and in power. Even now you find yourself a Captain of the Hunt and you're barely into your twenties."

"Yes, the Hunt recognizes me as somebody, but my authority doesn't go beyond the battlefield. What good is working my way up through the ranks if I'll only be able to go so high? We both know that they'll never let me sit at the table."

Dutch lifted her face so that she was looking at him. "Just because someone is sitting in the driver's seat doesn't mean that they're driving. Come into my office; I need to speak to you about something." Dutch led the way, with Asha close behind him. When he noticed that the twins had tagged along he stopped short. "I don't recall requesting your presence," he told the twins.

"We were here for . . . ah, moral support," Lisa stammered.

"If you want to support Asha's cause, then find me the rogue idiot who is killing mortals in my domain," Dutch said, and left the witches to it.

* * *

"Are you crazy or just stupid?" Sulin snapped once she and Lucy were outside the club.

"What, are you still rattled about what happened with Asha? Don't worry; the Hunt isn't foolish enough to try anything," Lucy said arrogantly.

"I'm not talking about the Hunt, you foolhardy girl. That was stupid of you to show off like that in Court. Dutch could've punished you for challenging his authority in public."

"Fuck Dutch, and fuck those ass kissers at Court. I dance to my own beat." Lucy folded her arms.

"And that's your problem," Sulin hissed. "You think I don't tire of the games Angelique and Dutch play with us? Hell yes, but you'd never hear me say it out loud. See, you're always on someone's shit list because you wear your heart on your sleeve. I will have my day at the table, but I know I can't muscle it, so I'll kill them with kindness and accept the rewards when they come. If you want to rise in the coven, then you need to learn to keep your tongue tied and your teeth showing; trying to kick everyone's ass who you feel is in your way is only gonna get you killed or worse."

"I guess I just don't have the same head for diplomacy as you do, Sulin," Lucy said.

"Which is why the rest of the Initiates are taking bets as to whether you live long enough to collect the trust fund Wanda set up for you," Sulin said seriously. Before she could continue, her BlackBerry went off. "Duty calls," Sulin said, reading the screen. "Do you need to get dropped off somewhere, because going back inside the Triple Six tonight wouldn't be the wisest of moves?"

"I'll find something to get into," Lucy said with a devilish grin

"I'll bet." Sulin looped her arm in Lucy's. "Look, if

you're not doing anything, then why don't you come with me to answer this call?"

"Sulin, I don't wanna get in your way while you're working," Lucy told her.

"Nonsense. Besides, I could use the company for the ride to Brooklyn. I'll take care of the healing and then we can hit this spot that I keep hearing about near Park Slope. I hear it's crawling with delicious young men."

"Sulin, do you ever think about anything besides getting laid?"

Sulin thought on it for a minute. "No, now let's go," she said, and led Lucy around the corner to where her car was parked.

Dutch led Asha to the rear of the room, where an eight-foot mirror dominated most of the wall. He whispered an incantation and stepped through the mirror, causing a ripple in the glass. Asha hesitated. The mirror that served as the door to Dutch's study was empowered by a spell that only he and Angelique really understood. Any who tried to pass through the mirror without being invited by the king or queen would be ripped to pieces. Asha could feel the power coming off the mirror, and from the way Azuma was ranting so could he.

"I don't like it either, but what, am I gonna say no to the king? You stay out here and watch my back," she told the monkey, still staring at the mirror cautiously. She carefully pushed her finger into the glass and found that it gave under her finger. Taking a deep breath, Asha stepped through the mirror and into Dutch's study.

Dutch's office was larger than Asha's entire apartment. It boasted high ceilings and authentic furniture from a bygone era. He had had it remodeled to resemble the receiving area of an eighteenth-century Austrian castle, a tribute to his native home. Each wall was adorned with significant events throughout the country's history, with likenesses of Dutch in place of the actual people who took part in the events. Behind the huge granite desk hung a life-sized portrait of him and Angelique, sitting on thrones. While his was made of onyx, hers was made of ivory.

"Listen, Dutch, if you're pissed about the thing with me and Lucy, I understand," Asha said once they were both seated.

"No, I called you in here on a matter which may be of some importance," Dutch told her.

"Let me know what you need and I'm on it."

"As I knew you would be, which is why I need you to keep what I say to you tonight between us." Dutch's face was serious. Asha nodded. "Something vile has touched the city tonight, and I fear that it may mark the coming of something I dare not mention."

Asha thought back to her dream. "I felt it too. At first I thought it was someone casting some really heavy magic, but it didn't feel right. It was too dark to be a spell."

Dutch studied her for a time and pondered what she'd said. Of all the students in his and Angelique's charge, Asha was a rarity. Because of her mixed lineage she was the best at not only diagnosing different kinds of magic but also neutralizing them. This was the main reason that Dutch wanted to speak with Asha; the brush with Lucy just gave him an excuse to do so. "If this is what I think it is, then you'll be right, and it isn't a spell but something more malevolent. What it is I am not yet sure, which is what I need you to find out."

"So we'll be calling a Hunt?" Asha asked excitedly.

"No, this must be kept as quiet as possible. I don't even want Lisa and Lane totally aware of what's going on until we find out exactly what has surfaced in the city and if we can claim it as our own."

"I am more than willing to get it done for you, Dutch, but tackling this thing on my own could be pretty risky. We don't know what it is, but if it's serious enough to have you send me off on a secret mission, I know it's not something to be taken lightly." Asha gave Dutch a sly look that he knew only too well.

He touched her cheek lovingly. "Asha, you are one of my most promising followers, so it's only right that you are properly rewarded for the courage that you will surely have to show in your mission." Dutch leaned in and kissed her softly on the lips. It was a gentle kiss, but it sent a rough wave of power through Asha. By the time she snapped out of it, she was slumped in the chair, embarrassed at the moisture that had built up between her legs. "That is a sample of the power that you will taste when I make you my Mistress of the Hunt."

Asha was so shocked that she couldn't find her voice. The Council was who everyone respected as elders and leaders of the coven, but it was the Hunt that they feared. To be Mistress of the Hunt would mean a seat at the table. "Dutch, the others would never accept me," Asha said weakly.

"Asha, I am king here and they will accept what I say." Dutch placed a hand on each side of her head and shared more of his power with her. This time it wasn't so intense, but she could still feel the nerves in her body come to life. "Do this for me, and finally be recognized amongst your sisters as a daughter of the God and Goddess."

"Your will be done, my king," Asha said enthusiastically before leaving Dutch's study.

"Of this I'm sure," he said when she was out of earshot. With a wicked grin, Dutch settled back in his chair and waited for the pieces to fall into place. He was so preoccupied with his scheming that he never noticed the transparent spider perched on his ceiling.

CHAPTER NINETEEN

Gabriel staggered through the streets of Harlem, trapped in his own thoughts as well as the thrall of the Nimrod. The relic had been still since he'd left the house, but he could still feel it, raising the hairs on his arms like a cool breeze. He wanted to examine the tattoo to see what he could make of it but didn't want to run the risk of having it let loose another surge of power.

With his head down and his right hand jammed deep into his jacket pocket, Gabriel continued west on 126th Street. From the corner of Eighth Avenue he could see the green globes making the subway station entrance on St. Nicholas. From the corner of his eye he spotted a group of young boys sitting on a stoop, drinking and passing a joint around. Gabriel kept his eyes locked on the ground when he passed, but it hadn't stopped them from accosting him.

"Yo, we got that piff," one of them called to him. Gabriel kept moving. "Yo, son, I know you hear me," the kid said a little more forcefully. His words were slurred by whatever they were drinking, but there was no mistaking the hostility in the words. Gabriel was trying to avoid a confrontation, but hearing the multiple footsteps behind them, he knew that he wouldn't be able to.

"Muthafucka, how you just gonna walk through my

block and not acknowledge me?" the kid who had called Gabriel out said, stepping between him and the train station. The kid was a brown-skinned youth with broad shoulders and a protruding belly. He wasn't fat just yet, but if he kept hitting the bottle he would be soon enough. Gabriel tried to step around him only to find his path blocked by a second youth. This one was thinner, but his glassy eyes said that he would be just as much trouble as the heavy one.

"I don't think my homeboy was finished talking to you," the thin kid said. He was opening and closing his fist like he was spoiling for a fight. It was then that Gabriel felt his tattoo stir.

"Look, he got hair like a bitch. You some kinda faggot or something?" the heavier kid taunted Gabriel.

"He looks like a fag to me and you know homos are always holding," the thinner one added.

"Listen, I don't want any trouble." Gabriel tried to step between them and someone shoved him roughly from behind. He tripped over the front steps of a building and landed hard on his hands. He tried to block the sound out, but there was no mistaking the roll of thunder in his ears.

"We don't give a shit what you want, but we sure know what you got and you're gonna give it to us," the heavier kid said. He was standing over Gabriel holding a small gun. "Run it, pussy," he demanded.

"And let the cleansing begin. My will be done," the Bishop whispered.

Gabriel got to his feet slowly so as not to spook the kid with the gun. It took all of Gabriel's concentration to keep his voice from booming when he spoke. "I don't have any money; I'm just trying to get to the train station." Gabriel raised his hand. The ink from the tattoo seemed to spill from beneath his sleeve, leaving the rough shape of a fork on the back of his right hand.

"If you ain't got no money, then how in the hell are you gonna get on the train?" The heavier kid moved closer. His grip on the gun seemed to tighten.

"I think this cat is trying to play us," a third kid spoke up. He was fat and wearing a dingy baseball cap, pulled over his eyes.

The heavy kid raised the gun and pointed it at Gabriel's face. "You trying to play us, faggot?" The kid never even saw Gabriel move. There was the brief sound of steel against steel and the next thing the kid knew, the barrel of his gun was falling to the ground. He looked at Gabriel and backpedaled when he saw the flashing of lightning dancing in his eyes.

Having been oblivious to what his friend had just witnessed, the thin kid rushed Gabriel, swinging a wild punch. Gabriel caught his fist in his left hand and held it. The kid watched as Gabriel raised his hand, which was now outlined in a crisp silver glow. Gabriel touched his finger to the kid's chest, sending a jolt of electricity into his heart. The kid fell to the ground, twitching and foaming at the mouth. The third kid was long gone, but the heavy one hadn't managed to move from the spot where fear had him rooted.

Gabriel grabbed him about the jaws, burning the flesh of his face where his fingers touched. For a minute the heavy kid could see the brown in Gabriel's eyes and a look similar to regret cross his face. "You don't know how lucky you just got." Gabriel tossed the frightened and burned man to the ground. The kid didn't even check to see if his partner was still alive, just took off running. The Nimrod was again still, but Gabriel could hear the Bishop's voice in his head.

"My will be done."

"So you've said." Gabriel pulled the sleeve of his jacket down and descended the train station stairs.

* * *

Gabriel breathed a sigh of relief when he stepped onto the downtown A train. Of course there were no seats, but he was happy to be away from the mess that was going on in the world above. A few hours ago he was a college student whom no one ever noticed and now it seemed like the whole world was after him. His life and the natural law of things as science dictated were both being dashed to hell in front of his eyes, and there didn't seem to be much he could do about it but ride the wave and hope he didn't drown.

Gabriel tried to busy himself by reading the advertisements that lined the subway car, but the tingle in his arm wouldn't let him be. It was as if being underground in the midst of all the random power fluxes disturbed the Nimrod.

Deciding it was best to keep moving, Gabriel picked his way through the subway car. He was stepping around a woman who was riding with her young son and their hands accidentally brushed. Gabriel was immediately assaulted with flashes of her life. He knew her from the aspiring dancer she had been before getting pregnant and the battered housewife she had become. The feeling of sadness in her heart was so great that it staggered him.

Trying to avoid the battered wife, he bumped into a girl who was standing behind him and her boyfriend. Gabriel immediately saw him working double shifts at his security job to pay for the engagement ring he had presented her with a few hours prior. He had proposed to her in the middle of a crowded street. She had gladly accepted, but now she had to figure out how to tell him that she had stepped out on their relationship and had just found out that she was HIV positive.

Gabriel stumbled clumsily through the car and with each person he touched came their stories and their pains. By the time he leapt off the train at West 4th Street he was almost blinded by tears. Never in his life had he felt such intense hurt. He wanted to reach out to each of the people he had touched on the train and right whatever was wrong in their lives. He wanted to give them a release.

"And when you strike, show them no mercy. Let the Storm wash away their sins and remake the world anew," the Bishop said compassionately.

"I'm not a murderer," Gabriel whispered.

"Cain risked the wrath of God and slew his brother so that history could play out as it was written," the Bishop offered.

Gabriel ran his hands through his hair and tugged at the roots. "Get it together, man; you're talking to your arm," he said more to himself than anyone else. When Gabriel got up to the street level he inhaled, happy to be free of the tunnels. Something familiar tickled the tip of his nose, but he paid it no mind. He had to get his bearings and find the Triple Six.

Gabriel had an idea where the club was but couldn't say for sure, as he had never been there. To his surprise, it didn't take him very long to get pointed in the right direction. As it turned out, everyone except him knew about the exclusive Triple Six nightclub. As soon as Gabriel set foot on the block where the club was located the Nimrod went crazy. The tattoo had almost completely flared to life before Gabriel was able to force it back onto his arm. That he could make it cooperate if he tried was something that would come in handy in the future. From the way the Nimrod had reacted there was obviously someone or something that it recognized inside the club. If he could find Carter and answers to the Nimrod inside the Triple Six, then he was definitely in the right spot.

The line to get inside the club was nearly a block long and growing when Gabriel approached the entrance. The brutish bouncers at the front were turning people away left and right for not being dressed properly or cool enough for the exclusive spot. He was wondering how he was going to go about getting in when the bouncer suddenly gave him a very bold idea.

"Yo, we ain't letting anything but couples in for the next hour. If you ain't with somebody you're gonna have to wait," the brute addressed the crowd.

Gabriel watched himself on the giant screen of his mind as he approached the two disappointed-looking girls. They were two leggy shades of chocolate with faces that were cute but not defined enough to be considered beautiful. But on their worst days they were out of Gabriel's league, so it surprised him more than it did them when he looped his arm in theirs and escorted the ladies to the entrance. The bouncer gave him a funny look about his windbreaker but stepped aside and allowed the trio to enter.

"That was interesting," the thicker of the two girls told Gabriel with a smile.

"I'm sorry. I didn't mean to offend you guys, but I thought . . . ," Gabriel stammered.

"It's cool." The leggier girl took his hand. She flipped his palm over and pressed a business card in his hand. "I'm meeting somebody in here tonight, but give me a call sometime." She walked off.

"Well, I'm not meeting anybody, so if you wanna get a drink we'll be over by the bar. Thanks for helping us get in." The thicker one winked and went to catch up with her friend.

Gabriel stood there momentarily baffled. He looked down at the business card in his hand and saw the tattoo's ink swirling about his wrists. "I guess you do have some uses." He tucked the card in his pocket and went to find Carter.

CHAPTER TWENTY

Rogue felt better when they stepped out the fire door and into a side alley. Granted the air was rank from all the garbage, but at least it didn't reek of magic. He knew he'd been taking a chance coming to the Triple Six, but bumping into Dutch hadn't been something he counted on. There was no doubt in his mind how it would've played out, and he was thankful that he'd been able to get out without incident. His companion wasn't so appreciative.

"You've got a lot of balls dragging me out here like this," the girl said in a not-too-happy tone.

"If that isn't the pot." Rogue raised an eyebrow.

"Anyway, what is it that you want, man?" She shifted her weight from one foot to the other. Rogue could tell that she was nervous. Good.

"First of all, you can drop the face, Marty. I'm starting to feel kind of weird about this." He peered over his shades at her.

Marty sighed. She closed her eyes and her form began to waver. Magic crackled in the air around her as her features became distorted. Her hips and breasts seemed to deflate while her fingers almost doubled in length. The smooth white skin had taken on a bluish tint, similar to that of a drowning victim. The skin on her forehead stretched until Rogue could make out the small horns beneath. No matter how many times he saw it, the trick still fascinated him. Marty went from an unassuming witch to something that was not of this world.

Marty was a shape-shifter, one of the lesser demons who had escaped during the first Dark Storm. They were akin to Weres but had no real power to speak of. Not that they needed it with their unique abilities. Marty's lot could morph into any living thing, making them almost impossible to find when they didn't want to be found, unless you had an edge, and Rogue did.

"Happy now?" Marty said, adjusting his tattered denim jacket.

"Now that's the Marty I know." Rogue slapped him on the back.

"Fuck you, Rogue. Tell me what you want so I can get out of here." Marty swatted at Rogue's hand.

"I need to know about the magical disturbance that hit the city today. It had the stink of hell all over it and I need to know its source."

Marty shrugged. "This is New York City, one of the places of power. Black magic comes through here all the time; it's not unusual."

"It's unusual when it brings Stalkers out in full force," Rogue told him.

"Rogue, I don't know anything." Marty tried to hide the fear that had just crept over him, but it was hard for demons to hide anything from Rogue's eyes, even their true natures.

"Bullshit." Rogue shoved him against the wall. "You shifters slink in and out of more private meetings than I get death threats. Marty, your people see shit before it even happens, so I know you've got something to tell me."

"Listen, I said I don't know anything. Now if you'll excuse me." Marty tried to step past Rogue, but the mage grabbed his arm.

"Marty, you're gonna tell me something or we're gonna have a situation out here," Rogue said seriously.

Marty seemed as if he was weighing it when he suddenly jerked away. Rogue tried to tighten his grip, but Marty's limb had become as thin as a pipe. By the time Rogue realized what was going on, Marty was sprinting down the alley.

"Don't make this harder than it has to be, Marty," Rogue called after him. As soon as Rogue started the summoning, he could feel the owner of his eyes stirring in the back of his mind. He liked to tap into his demonic bond as little as possible because of the lingering effects it sometimes left, but there was no way he was going to catch Marty in a footrace. The shadows lining the alley answered his summons and descended on the fleeing Marty. He tried to leap out of the way, but the first strands had already snaked around his ankles, tripping him up. Marty fought like a caged animal as the tentacles wrapped him from foot to chin. He tried to shrink his body, but the tentacles only tightened to match his decreasing girth.

"Fucking shadow magic!" Marty shrieked. "And they say you shun the dark side, bullshit! This is as black as magic gets!" Marty wiggled around on the floor looking malnourished from all the weight he had shed trying to slip out of the bands. He pushed with everything he had, but the darkness would not give.

"Now why'd you run, Marty?" Rogue asked, slowly raising his hand. The shadows lifted Marty to his feet as if he was a puppet at the end of the dark strings.

"You'd better let me go or I'll—"

"You'll do what?" Rogue jerked his hand upward, lifting Marty from the ground with his shadows. "You gonna call on your brethren to avenge you?" With a wave of Rogue's arm he slammed Marty against a wall and then jerked him violently back. Rogue slowly closed his hand, tightening the bands around Marty as he did so. "Muthafucka, I could turn your freakish ass into a puddle in this alley and no one would miss you. Now, you can talk to me like you got some sense or I can leave a nasty stain out here for sanitation. What's it gonna be, Marty?"

"Okay, okay, just loosen the bands." Marty's eyes were beginning to water. Rogue nodded and opened his hand, giving slack to the bands but not freeing Marty. "Ain't you gonna untie me?"

Rogue smirked, shaking his head. "And risk you doing another hundred-yard dash on me? No thanks. All I need moving is your mouth, so let's hear it. Something really nasty is about to pop off, and I think you know what it is."

Marty gave one last weak push against the bands, but they just tightened. With a sigh he decided to cooperate. "Rogue, you gotta give me your word that you ain't gonna tell nobody where you got this from," Marty pleaded.

"Marty, I'm a lot of things but never a rat. What's going on?"

Marty looked around as if the shadows were listening. "They're saying that someone is trying to bring the storm back."

"Storm?" Rogue asked.

"The Dark Storm; don't you know your history? The big showdown where the Knights of Christ kicked most of our asses back across the dimensional rift."

"Don't be funny, Marty. I know the story of the Seven-Day Siege. They say that all those guys died off and the weapons were lost. The storm was a freak accident and even if someone wanted to try and reopen it, they'd need all the weapons just to create a spark of what that thing was. Last I heard, the weapons and their masters disappeared over the years."

"But they aren't all lost." Marty dropped his voice to a whisper. "The church has snagged a few; some say the Inquisition got lucky. Proof of ownership is hearsay, but the weapons are still out there, waiting for some poor schmuck to wake 'em up. Most people who find 'em can't make much of 'em, but there are some who can and have."

"Marty, I think you're bullshitting me." Rogue raised his hand and Marty with it, a coil of shadow supporting him. "These weapons surfacing at different points in the world wouldn't have caused that riptide."

"Hey, don't shoot the messenger," Marty gasped. "You wanted information and I'm giving it to you; it ain't my fault if you're still too stuck on this side of the line to process it! It's not just the weapons; it's *the* weapon. They're saying the Bishop himself has made a guest appearance in the Apple."

"The Bishop?" Rogue lowered Marty. He knew the stories surrounding the cursed weapon and dreaded the thought of it falling into the wrong hands.

"Mr. Attitude himself, Rogue. I don't know how true it is, but they say it rolled into the city a few weeks ago. Nobody really said anything solid, but I hear the old-timers are spooked. Some are even thinking about going underground. If that thing has popped up, we're all up a fucking creek."

"Where can I find this trident, Marty?"

"That's the question on everyone's lips, but you can't find the trident unless it wants you to," Marty told him. "The last time anybody heard a peep out of it was ages ago, down near Africa I think. The only reason it even made a stink was because it killed the poor sap who woke it up and wiped out his entire village. I can't say for sure if or why it's popped back up, but you can bet your ass it wasn't an accident."

"So the Stalkers were here looking for it?" Rogue asked.

"More than likely, but you'd better be more concerned about who sent them than why they were here."

"There are a few people who can create those abominations," Rogue pointed out.

"But how many of them have a big enough hard-on for the trident where they'd send a pack of Stalkers to tear up Manhattan?"

"Titus." Rogue knew the reputation of the so-called favorite son of Belthon, but he knew Titus' advisor Flag better. Like Rogue, Flag was a mage, but he was of the house of Renoit. It and Thanos were the last official houses. Like Rogue, Flag was an outcast amongst his people. Rogue because he shunned the darkness and Flag because he had dived into it headfirst. Several years prior, Flag had traded the lives of his house's elders in exchange for the favor of the dark lord. As a result, Flag had been marked for death, with the prize being the crown of his slaughtered house and all the secrets that came with it.

"You got it," Marty continued. "As soon as I got the word that Riel and Moses had been spotted around town, I knew it was about to get ugly. Those guys are bad news. Rogue, I know we haven't always seen eye to eye, but leave this one alone, huh?"

Rogue's mind told him that Marty was right and he should abandon the investigation, but his all-damning sense of morality wouldn't let him. Belthon was one of the nine lords of hell, and by far one of the most threatening. He had tasted the sweet chaos of the mortal world and thirsted for more of it. If Titus secured the Nimrod for his master, it would be the beginning of hell on earth.

"Can't do that, Marty." Rogue waved his hand dismissively and the shadows released Marty. "You and I both know what'll happen if Titus gets his hands on that thing. Somebody's gotta piss on his parade, right?"

Marty shook his head. "You're an honorable guy, Rogue. Stupid, but honorable."

"Gee, thanks. Now you got any ideas where I can get a lead on this thing?"

"Can't say for sure, but if you linger around the Triple Six long enough you're bound to get a lead."

"Or killed," Rogue added.

"More than likely, but if you insist on putting your head on the chopping block, the least I can do is send you in with a turtleneck. The kinda magic that's sure to be dripping off the Nimrod, and whoever has it will attract the darkness like a moth to a flame. You might resent those eyes of yours, but they're gonna be your best friend on this."

"Thanks, Marty. Maybe you better lie low until all this blows over."

"Oh, I intend to." Marty's form wavered as he assumed the form of an elderly homeless man. "A buddy of mine has got a boat on the shore that I can crash on. I'm gonna get fall-down drunk and look at the ocean until this blows over," Marty called over his shoulder as he headed down the alley.

"Wise choice," Rogue agreed.

"At least one of us is making them," Marty laughed, disappearing into the shadows.

"The story of my life," Rogue muttered, tucking his hands into his pockets and heading for the main street.

He stepped out of the mouth of the alley to find that the line to get into the club had only gotten longer since he'd arrived. He was about to retrace his steps to the back door when something caught his eye. There was a young man dressed in a windbreaker walking into the club with two attractive girls on his arms. Rogue would've paid them no attention if it weren't for the fact that his demon was going crazy and the boy's aura was lit up brighter than anything Rogue had ever seen.

"I guess Marty was right about these eyes," Rogue said before wrapping himself in darkness and vanishing.

CHAPTER TWENTY-ONE

"What do you see?" Lane asked her sister impatiently. For the last ten minutes Lisa had been sitting motionless on a bar stool staring out into space. Her eyes had gone completely white as she saw what her familiar did. Asha had taught both twins the trick, but Lisa was more adept at it than Lane.

"Shhh, I'm trying to concentrate," Lisa muttered. She squinted her eyes as if whatever she was seeing was right in front of her instead of in the next room. "Shit, I think you messed it up, Lane. I can't see anything now. Let me try to—" Lisa's breath suddenly caught as she grabbed her chest.

"Sister, what is it?" Lane rushed to her side. She watched in panic as her sister slid down the side of the bar gasping for breath.

"How fucking stupid can you two be?" Asha approached them. She had her fist held out in front of her, and every few seconds she would tighten her hand and along with it the stranglehold on Lisa's heart.

"Stop it, Asha; you're killing her!" Lisa pleaded as her sister began to turn blue.

"And I should, because you almost put my head on the chopping block with your little stunt." Asha opened her hand and revealed the spider that Lisa had sent into the meeting on Asha. The spider was crumpled but alive. "You're just lucky I picked up on your little spy instead of Dutch." Asha tossed the spider on Lisa. The crystal arachnid hobbled up the side of Lisa's face and disappeared into her hair.

"We were just trying to make sure you were okay," Lane said while helping her sister back up onto the bar stool. She glared murderously at Asha, but the other witch wasn't moved.

"Bullshit. You were being nosey. Besides, if Dutch was trying to off me, there wouldn't have been much Lisa's bug could've done to help me." Asha held out her arms and Azuma jumped into them.

Lane started to press the issue but decided to leave it for another time. "So?" She looked at Asha inquisitively.

"So what?"

"We didn't get all the details, but we know Dutch is worried about something that's popped up in the city and we're waiting for you to fill in the blanks," Lane said as if she'd figured out some great puzzle.

"Why don't you tell every fucking supernatural in the city what I'm doing?" Asha hissed. She looked around to make sure nobody was listening. "It may be something or it may be nothing, but either way I have to investigate . . . alone."

"What kind of rogue shit is that, Asha? You know we hunt as a pack." Lisa was finally coming around.

"We hunt as a pack when we have an idea of what we're after, not on blind tests of loyalty by the hierarchy," Asha told her. "I can't run the risk of you guys getting hurt while I'm off chasing my tail for Dutch." It was a white lie, but it saved her from hurting their pride by relaying Dutch's orders.

"So we're supposed to sit idle while you rush into Goddess knows what?" Lane asked, sounding less than pleased to be left out of the chase.

"Of course not. While I'm taking care of business you guys will be my eyes and ears around here. Anything peculiar goes down anywhere and I wanna know before it happens." Asha was about to say something else when she suddenly felt finger pricks of ice run down her spine. Her eyes grew wide as she whipped her head back and forth looking for something only she could see.

"What's wrong?" the twins asked in unison.

Asha ignored them as her mind frantically touched different beings in the club, looking for the blot on the page. She whispered something to Azuma and sent him scurrying through the club. Someone had to be either very foolish or very brave to invoke such magic in Dutch's domain, and she intended to find out who or what.

"You wanna tell us what that's all about?" Lane folded her arms.

"Somebody just used shadow magic inside the Triple Six," Asha informed them. Asha was no stranger to shadow magic, because the demons who used it were the same ones her mother's people had worshiped.

"Fucking shadow demons. We need to root them out and bring their heads back for Dutch," Lane said, moving for the exit.

"I'm already on it," Asha said, checking her blades. "You guys hang tight and remember what I said about reporting anything strange," she said over her shoulder, heading towards the exit.

"And where are you going?" Lisa called after her, but Asha didn't respond.

CHAPTER TWENTY-TWO

Gabriel moved with extreme caution as he made his circuit of the Triple Six, trying futilely not to make contact with anyone in the crowded club. The tattoo had been silent, but there was still too much he didn't know about the Nimrod to trust it. Gabriel had circled the main floor twice, and though there was no sign of Carter, he spotted Vince near the bar.

"What's up?" Gabriel startled Vince when he tapped him on the shoulder.

"Don't fucking sneak up on me like that, asshole. I could've knocked your head off for that." Vince tried to hide the fear in his voice. "What're you doing here, nerd?"

"I'm trying to find Carter." Gabriel ignored the insult.

"Do I look like his keeper? He's around here somewhere. Now get the hell away from me before one of these chicks thinks we're friends," Vince slurred. The liquor clearly had a firm hold on him.

Gabriel started to turn and walk away, but he couldn't let it go. "Why do you have to be such a dick?"

"What'd you say?" Vince put his drink down.

"I said that you can be a dick. I've never done anything to you, Vince, but you go out of your way to give me a hard time."

"I give you shit because I can." Vince poked him in the chest.

Gabriel didn't even flinch. "I think you give me shit because you envy me."

Vince scoffed. "Gabriel, you're a noodle-dick faggot who would rather touch a book than a woman; what the fuck could I envy about you?"

"The fact that I'm gonna be something in life and you're just gonna fall in line with the rest of them. Vince, you and I both know that if basketball doesn't work out, you're gonna be out robbing liquor stores for weed money." Gabriel's words were hurtful, so much so that they shocked him, but his shock was nothing compared to the hurt on Vince's face.

"Muthafucka, you must have a death wish." Vince grabbed Gabriel by the front of his shirt and drew his fist back, but Gabriel didn't even flinch.

"What, you gonna hit me?" Gabriel asked defiantly. He heard the storm rolling in his ears but was able to force it back with some effort. "Vince, you can bust me in my mouth in front of all these people and it still won't change anything. So if you wanna throw down, let's be done with it, because I'm tired of you fucking with me."

Vince stared at Gabriel as if he were crazy. Normally Gabriel would've shied away under the threat of violence, but something was different about him that night, something that made Vince nervous. "Man, get away from me before I come to my senses and fuck you up." Vince shoved him.

"You ain't gonna do anything to me, Vince. As a matter of fact, you're gonna stay the fuck outta my way from here on out," Gabriel assured him before spinning on his heels. Everyone who had seen the exchange stared at Gabriel in amazement as he shoved his way back through the crowd.

When he was away from Vince the reality of what Gabriel had just risked finally set in, and it made his legs weak. He knew that if Vince had gotten a mind to, he could've probably mopped the floor with him, but he knew that it wouldn't happen that night. The Nimrod had told him as much, but he wasn't willing to press his luck a second time. His best bet was to find Carter and get out of the crowded club.

As Gabriel passed the hallway he noticed the familiar smell he had picked up on when he came out of the train station. It was stronger inside the club, overpowering the smell of smoke and funk. He followed the sweet scent to the unisex bathroom, where it seemed to be originating. The bathroom was nearly as crowded as the main floor, but Gabriel didn't give the partygoers a second look as he honed in on the sweetness. It invaded his nose and mouth, like water to a drowning man. The more he inhaled, the more familiar the smell was to him. He knew it from somewhere but couldn't think where. With his nose pointed skyward he traced the scent to a half-open stall, where he heard faint moans coming from behind the door. Normally Gabriel would've left whoever was in the stall to their privacy, but something drove him to peek inside. There was Carter, bracing himself against the tops of the stall and moving his waist slowly. He must've felt the presence behind him, because he turned around, and it was then that Gabriel saw the object of his heart's desire sitting on the toilet seat, with her lipstick badly smeared.

Amidst the flashing lights and loud music no one even noticed when the shadows in the corner near the coat check started moving on their own. The darkness snaked and swirled, gradually taking the shape of a man. When the slithering had finally stopped, Rogue stood in place of the darkness.

It took him several moments to compose himself. Being in possession of the demon's eyes allowed Rogue to draw on shadow magic to add to his own, but physical transformation, such as Shadow Walking, caused a great deal of strain on his body. The strain was one of the reasons that Rogue hated to tap into the shadows, but his biggest concerns were the lingering effects the magic caused. With each time he opened himself up to receive the demon's power, he also opened himself up to the demon's whims. It was such carelessness that almost cost his brother his life and had in the end cost Rogue his eyes.

He scanned the club until he found the two girls he'd seen coming in, but their escort was nowhere in sight. Rogue picked his way through, looking for the boy, careful to avoid the werewolf he'd caused to have a heart attack or anyone who would report his presence back to Dutch. Near the bar Rogue spotted a young man nursing a drink and wearing a worried expression. Something was off about him. Rogue peered over his sunglasses and peeled away the layers of the young man. He was mortal but had recently been in contact with the power surrounding the boy Rogue was following. Homing in on the unique aura pattern Rogue searched around until he picked up the trail. It seemed to be getting stronger in the direction of the bathrooms. Rogue was about to investigate further when he was barreled over by two security guards who were heading towards the bathrooms. From the panicked look on their faces it was something ugly, so Rogue decided to wait outside to see what the outcome was.

"Gabriel, what are you doing here?" Carter fumbled with his pants. Katie just looked at the floor and tried to clean herself up as best she could with rough toilet tissue.

"I would ask you the same thing, but it's pretty self-explanatory." Gabriel walked off. He wanted to run as far as he could from the sight, but his legs wouldn't cooperate. Seeing the girl he was so madly in love with going down on his best friend had shattered Gabriel's heart.

"Hold on a minute, man. Let me explain before you run off." Carter caught up to Gabriel and spun him around. He was taken aback at the look in his friend's eyes, as Carter had never known Gabriel to be capable of hate, but there was no mistaking his glare. Katie wasn't his girlfriend, but they all knew he had a crush on her. Carter hadn't even meant to do anything with her, but Katie got wild when she drank.

"There's nothing to explain. You guys are adults, so it's none of my business." Gabriel's voice cracked.

"Gabe, it kinda just happened," Katie offered.

"Oh, his dick just happened to slip into your mouth," Gabriel said scornfully. "I don't even know why I thought I could come to you for help, Carter, when all you think about is your dick." Gabriel tried to leave the bathroom, but Carter cut him off. "Get out of my way," Gabriel said in a low growl. The overhead lights began to flicker. When he heard the thunder rolling, he braced himself in welcoming anticipation.

"Not until we talk." Carter folded his arms as if it wasn't up for discussion.

"Carter, if you don't move I'm not gonna be responsible for what happens." Even though Gabriel didn't want to hurt his friend, he could feel the pull of the Nimrod become stronger. The water in all the toilets began to overflow, soaking the bathroom floor. The mirrors along the wall shattered, spraying everyone in the bathroom with glass.

"What the hell is going on?" Katie asked in a panic-filled voice.

"Just get back," Gabriel warned. He walked backward

towards the front door. Beneath his jacket the Nimrod began to peel away from his skin.

"What the fuck!" one of the bouncers shouted as he charged into the bathroom and slipped in the water. Gabriel moved to leave and the second bouncer grabbed him by the arm.

"Somebody is gonna tell me what's going on," the second bouncer ordered, shaking Gabriel like a rag doll.

When Gabriel looked up at the bouncer the lightning had returned to his eyes. "Let me go," Gabriel ordered him. Seeing the rolling clouds in Gabriel's eyes, the bouncer quickly complied and stepped aside for him to pass. The bouncer wasted no time in doing as he was told and getting out of Gabriel's way.

Gabriel half-stumbled out of the bathroom, giving everyone he touched a good shock. Trying to keep the Nimrod from manifesting was like trying to keep from throwing up when you've had too much to drink, a losing battle. He moved more off instinct than sight and was finally able to find one of the fire exits. He tried to take deep breaths when he got outside, but every time he did Katie's sweetness filled his nostrils. It had been her scent that he was following.

"Gabriel, wait up!" Carter came through the fire door after him. On Carter's heels were Katie and the reluctant Vince.

"The Judas, the whore, and the persecutor. You could be done with all of them in one swoop," the Bishop whispered.

"Shut up!" Gabriel said through clenched teeth, trying to strangle his arm through the jacket. "Carter, just leave me alone." Gabriel stumbled down the alley.

"Carter, if the punk wants to leave, then let him." Vince sucked his teeth in frustration. Carter ignored him and followed Gabriel down the alley.

Gabriel rested on a trash can and took slow, measured breaths. Gradually the pull of the Nimrod subsided, but the tattoo did not go completely still.

"Gabriel, please, man. I just wanna talk," Carter pleaded. His eyes were moist with the realization of how deeply he had wounded his friend.

"I thought that if nothing else, she would be for me," Gabriel confessed.

"I know you were sweet on her, but you never said anything. I didn't mean to hurt you, man; I swear." Gabriel had been there for Carter through some rough times, and a piece of tail wasn't worth their history.

"Oh, this is just so MTV." Katie sighed. "Neither one of you guys has any papers on me, so I really don't appreciate you talking about me like I'm not standing here. Gabriel." She turned his face so that she could see his eyes. Until that moment she had never noticed how beautiful they were. Gabriel's eyes were like looking into the ocean at high tide. "You're a great guy and I'm sure you're gonna make some girl really happy, but don't look for that in me. I'm on the fast track and you're just too much of a sweetheart for that, but we'll always be friends."

"Do you see this?" Vince rubbed his thumb and index finger together. "That's me playing the world's smallest violin. Get on with this stupid shit so I can go back in the club."

Carter had finally had enough and turned on Vince. "Why do you have to be such a fucking dick?" Carter slammed Vince against the wall. He drew his fist back threateningly, but Vince just smiled. "I swear to God I wanna bust you in that shit-eating grin," Carter huffed. Before he could make good on his threat they saw the familiar flash of blue and red lights.

"Oh God, it's the cops," Katie said nervously.

"Cool out, Katie; we're just hanging in back of the

club," Carter told her. He let Vince go and turned towards the headlights that were coming down the alley.

"I've got pot on me; they're gonna take me to prison." She began to pace the alley.

"Katie, don't go fucking Lindsay Lohan on us now. Just be cool and they'll be on their way," Carter said through clenched teeth. He tried to be the cool head amongst them, but he knew what it meant to be a black man trapped in an alley with the police.

The first cop who stepped out of the police van was tall and wiry, with a cropped blond cut that hardly looked up to regulation. His face was as pale as a sheet of paper, but his eyes were deep black. Four more cops spilled from the van and advanced on the group with their weapons at the ready. The blond approached them with an easy smile on his face as he twirled his baton from hand to hand. There was something about his smile that made Gabriel uneasy.

"What've we got here?" the blond asked, eyeing each of them. When he spotted Gabriel he took his time observing him. The blond's eyes lingered on Gabriel's arm as if he could see the Nimrod beneath the jacket.

"Nothing much, Officer, we just came out back to smoke." Vince pulled a pack of cigarettes from his pocket and placed one in his mouth.

"Is that right?" The blond continued to watch him.

"Yes, sir." Vince raised his lighter to the cigarette. His hands were shaking so badly that it took him three tries to get it lit.

"Okay, everybody hug the wall." This was a beefy officer sporting a buzz cut. His hand flexed on the holstered Glock as if he couldn't wait to free it. One by one the youngsters faced the wall, but Gabriel hesitated.

"You hear me talking to you?" Buzz Cut said.

"Get on the fucking wall!" a redheaded officer ordered,

grabbing Gabriel roughly by the collar. He slammed Gabriel face-first into the wall and began to frisk him roughly. "You got any weapons or drugs on you?"

"No," Gabriel said.

The blond walked up behind Gabriel and paused. Gabriel could feel something passing between the officer and his tattoo but didn't know what it was. The blond grabbed him by his neck and applied pressure. "Where is it?" the blond whispered into his ear. The streetlight flickered above them and the alley seemed to get a little darker.

"*Their garments mask their true natures. Comply with the imposters and it will be farewell between us, child of the Hunters*," the Bishop warned.

"I don't know what you're talking about," Gabriel said, trying to ignore the Bishop's rambling.

"Sergeant," the blond said in a commanding voice. The redheaded officer cocked the slide on his weapon and placed it to the back of Carter's head.

"What the fuck is going on here?" Carter asked nervously.

"What's going on is that your friend has until the count of three to give me what I want or I'm going to send you on a grand voyage," the blond replied.

"I told you that I don't know what you're talking about," Gabriel said. In the back of his mind he knew that they had come for the relic, but he hadn't the slightest idea how to give it to them, since it was now embedded in his skin. Gabriel looked around nervously for help, and it was at that moment he realized that he couldn't see anything beyond where the blond cop was standing. Both the club and the mouth of the alley were obscured by darkness. Gabriel thought about running but realized that he couldn't move his legs. When he looked down he noticed the shadows oozing over his sneakers and up his calves.

"I'll not ask you twice, offshoot." The blond's voice was harsher.

"Please, I don't—," Gabriel began but was cut off by the voice in his head.

"The shadows have no patience for your lies, Hunter. Loose the power gifted to you and let both mortals and demons feel your wrath," the Bishop urged.

"One," the blond began his count.

"Gabriel, I don't know what's going on, but if you have whatever these guys want, then please give it to them," Carter begged.

"Two."

"Gabriel, what the hell is wrong with you? Just give it to them!" Katie shouted.

"I don't know how," he said honestly.

"Three."

CHAPTER
TWENTY-THREE

Gabriel didn't hear the shot, but he saw Carter's brains when they jumped from his skull onto the wall. He looked at Gabriel with wide eyes as he dropped to his knees and fell over dead. Katie screamed and was rewarded with a club to the head by one of the officers' guns. Gabriel moved to help, but the shadows wound tightly around his legs. They hurriedly bound themselves around his arms and pulled him down on all fours. He struggled, but the shadows wouldn't give. He looked up helplessly at the blond who was standing over him grinning.

"Is this what has become of the feared Knights of Christ?" the blond laughed. He knelt beside Gabriel and grabbed him by the jaw so that the young boy could look into his eyes, eyes that were swirling pools of darkness. "How desperate the church must've become to entrust the holy weapons to the likes of you. Give me the Nimrod, boy, and I'll kill you quickly."

Gabriel looked from his dead friend to the blond and spat in his face. "Find it your fucking self."

A lone tear of shadow snaked from the blond's eye and wiped the spit away. "You are a brave one, aren't you? Well, let's see if we can have a little fun loosening your tongue." The blond raised his arms and Katie was lifted from the ground by a band of shadow that had wrapped around her neck. The girl whimpered while the blond dragged her over.

"No!" Gabriel tried to get up, but the shadows held him firm.

"Fond of this one, are you? I shall make this most unpleasant." The blond tightened the shadow around Katie's neck.

"Please, God." Katie sobbed.

The blond cocked his head. "God?" A loose strand of shadow slithered up and caressed Katie's cheek. "God has no place in the shadows. This is your last chance." He turned to Gabriel. "Give me the Nimrod or watch your friends die." The shadow band tightened and Katie's face started turning red.

"God damn you, if I knew how to give this thing to you I would." Gabriel was frantic. "Do something, damn you!" he shouted at his arm.

"Well, let's see if we can help you figure it out." The blond closed his fist and broke Katie's neck. Her lifeless body dangled on the band of shadow. Eyes that were once blue and alert were now dead and unseeing.

"I'm gonna kill you!" Gabriel raged.

"That's it; let your hate fuel it. My will be done," the Bishop said anxiously.

With a roar Gabriel managed to free his arm from the shadows and the Nimrod was instantly in his hand. He tapped the shaft against the ground and sent out a burst of light that dissipated the shadows. "Soulless thing, I know your true name, Moses shadow master." Gabriel tapped the shaft on the ground again. "And it is your name that will mark your passing back into the pit."

Gabriel charged Moses wildly, but Moses tripped him up with his shadows. Gabriel made to strike out with the Nimrod, but suddenly he found the weapon and his arm wrapped in shadow. Moses jerked him off his feet and slammed him from wall to wall until Gabriel was dizzy. When his vision cleared, Moses was standing in front of him. Moses had fashioned a piece of shadow into a thin shard and drove it into Gabriel's collar. Gabriel tried to scream, but a patch of shadow covered his mouth.

Moses leaned in close enough to where Gabriel could smell his rank breath. "It is good that you know my true name, Knight. So that when you reach the dead lands you can tell them who sent you." Moses' shadows wrapped Gabriel in a cocoon and began to squeeze so hard that he couldn't breathe. Spots danced before his eyes and he was about to black out when he heard a gunshot.

Rogue almost got knocked over when the boy came charging out of the bathroom. He had a terrified expression on his face and his aura was going nuts. Rogue almost thought he saw the arm of the boy's jacket moving like he had something under it. Three more people followed him out the fire door. They were definitely mortal, but which side of the light they fought on was a question, a question that Rogue intended to get the answer to.

He hadn't even meant to do it when he slipped into the shadows, but sensing his urgency to keep up with the boy, Rogue's powers acted of their own accord. It had happened to him like that a few times over the years and when it did it usually meant his life was about to become more complicated. He just hoped that in his haste to take the proper measures there wasn't someone in the club who might've been adept enough with shadow magic to pick up on what he'd just done. It seemed senseless to worry about it after the fact, though.

He didn't see them when he materialized in the alley, but he could feel the magic crackling all around him. For a minute he heard voices, but they'd suddenly been drowned out. He peered down the alley and realized that he was having trouble seeing the other end. There was nothing wrong with his eyes but the image he was seeing. It was shadow magic, and from the potency of it the barrier wasn't raised by another conduit like him; this was pure shadow magic. Rogue drew his revolvers and went to investigate.

By the time he'd gotten within three feet of the shadow barrier he could feel it calling out the thing lurking inside him. It was said that the entire race of shadow creatures drew their power from one common source; therefore, they all shared a connection. Staring at the wall of darkness, he felt like he wanted to do nothing more than go to it and add of himself to the collective. Luckily, something slamming against the barrier snapped him out of it. He looked down and saw the lifeless body of the girl who had been following his mark. Her neck was bent at an odd angle, but there was no bruising, only the residue the shadows had left. Rogue followed the dissipating shadows to their source and spotted a blond in a police uniform. One look at the cop and Rogue knew what was really hiding inside the mortal shell.

A feral roar brought his attention to the center of the darkness. The young man was now on his feet holding what had to be the Nimrod. When he slammed the shaft against the ground it sent out a flash so bright that it scorched Rogue's face and eyes. The demon screamed so loud that Rogue felt a trickle of blood coming from his eardrum. Through blurry eyes he saw the young man charge the demon, but the shadows didn't let him get far. Rogue watched as the demon effortlessly manipulated the shadows and bound the young man. The boy fought the good fight, but he was too much of a novice at using the Nimrod to stand against the demon. As the demon choked the breath from the young man Rogue decided it was time to react.

With the revolver in his right hand he hit the officer closest to him with two bullets to the back, dropping him. Not breaking his stride, he fired on the demon with the revolver in his left hand. Regular bullets wouldn't have done much other than piss the demon off, which was why Rogue made sure to hit him with the enchanted rounds. As the bullets entered the soft flesh of the demon's host's body, Rogue whispered the words of power and they exploded in a great burst of blue light. The demon howled and the barrier of darkness shattered.

"On your feet." Rogue grabbed the young man and yanked him up by the front of his windbreaker. Through his mass of tangled hair Rogue could see that he was little more than a child, but more important, he knew him. "Gabriel?" He was a little older than the last time Rogue had seen him, but he'd know the offspring of the Red-feather clan anywhere.

Gabriel looked up with dazed eyes. "Rogue? How did—" Gabriel was cut off as Rogue spun him out of the way just as a hail of bullets ripped into the wall. Rogue responded with a few shots of his own.

"We can catch up later, but right now we gotta dip," Rogue told him. "Let's move, kid!" Rogue shouted to Vince, who was in the corner trembling. The shadows were regaining substance and closing in on him. Rogue fired another one of his enchanted bullets at the ground, which slowed the shadows but didn't stop them. "Move it!" Rogue screamed, but it was useless. The shadows washed over Vince like a wave and consumed him.

"Oh, Katie." Gabriel moved towards her, but Rogue grabbed him roughly by the arm.

"Are you crazy? She's dead and we're not, and if you wanna keep it that way, I suggest you get your ass in gear." Rogue half-dragged Gabriel down the alley. He knew that if the shadow demon didn't kill Gabriel, Dutch would. With the shadow barrier broken, all guarantees of secrecy were off. In a matter of seconds that alley was going to be teeming with angry witches and warlocks.

Moses got to his feet slowly, seeming to gain substance as he went. His inky black eyes studied Rogue and a look of recognition crossed his face. "I've heard stories of you, mage. They call you the Stalker with a soul." It was true. Rogue shared his body with a demon but had not had to sacrifice his soul in the bargain.

"And they're gonna call you a fucking ambulance if you don't crawl back to whatever hole you slunk out of. There's nothing here for you, demon; go back to the shadows." Rogue pointed both revolvers at Moses and backed away slowly, keeping Gabriel and the demon in view.

"We are of the same, mage. Don't fight; take your place in glory when darkness consumes the world," Moses offered.

"Eternal darkness?" Rogue pondered out loud. "I think I'll pass." He fired his revolvers. The regular bullets passed right through Moses, and the enchanted ones were swallowed by the shadows before they could do any harm.

"I'm not so easily fooled twice." Moses smirked. The shadows opened up and the enchanted bullets fell harmlessly to the ground. "If you won't stand at my side, then you'll die at my feet." Moses called the shadows to him.

"What the fuck is this?" Angel came barreling out the side door into the alley. He was flanked by Lisa and Lane.

When Moses turned his head in the direction of the new threat, Rogue made his move. He lashed out with a shadow band and grabbed one of the officers. Rogue hurled the officer into Moses as hard as he could, grabbed Gabriel, and hauled ass down the alley.

* * *

"I wouldn't wanna be you pricks when Dutch catches wind of this." Angel looked around at the dead bodies.

"I'll have to ask you people to step back, this being a police matter and all," the cop with the buzz cut said.

"You're a cop and I'm the queen of England." Lisa called up her magic. Both her fists and the spider perched in her hair glowed unnaturally. She watched as the shadows snaked around Moses patching the wounds Rogue's gun had inflicted.

"Fucking shadow demons, I knew it would be shadow demons," Lane said, drawing her buck knife and moving to circle Moses and his fake cops.

"The shadows have no quarrel with the Black King. Stay out of this, little witches," Moses warned.

"Afraid we can't. See, if Dutch finds out that we let you drop these mortals and hightail it, it'll look pretty fucked up on us." Angel drew his guns from beneath his leather blazer. "Let's all go inside and have a little chat with the king."

In response Moses unleashed a flurry of shadow bands. Angel was quick, even by a vampire's standards, but the shadows were quicker. The bands bound his legs and arms and began to pull. Angel howled out in pain as the shadows broke all his arms and legs. Moses turned his attention to the witches and found them moving on him. One of the officers placed himself between Moses and the advancing witches, firing his Glock wildly. With the first swipe of her buck knife Lane erected a shield to deflect the bullets, and with the second swipe she cut the officer's throat.

The remaining officers stood back-to-back, trying to cut down the witches with their guns, but Lisa and Lane moved with amazing speed. They leapt around the officers in what looked like a complex dance, leaving a trail of silky webbing in their wake. By the time the officers had fired off the last of their bullets they found themselves bound in webs that felt like steel and at the mercy of the witches. Moving in a coordinated strike, the witches plunged their knives into the chests of the officers, freeing them from their pact with the shadow master.

Lisa and Lane advanced on Moses, tossing their blades back and forth between each other. "Your turn," Lane snarled.

"Foolish witches. You will rue the day you crossed the Dark Order, but I'm afraid that I will have to wait for another night to take your life, as I have quarry to attend to." Moses melted into a pool of shadow and made his exit.

"I hate fucking shadow demons," Lane said, re-sheathing her blade. "We gotta get hold of Asha and tell her about this."

"I think she already knows." Lisa pointed to a nearby streetlight. Azuma sat perched atop it, watching the scene below. "Let's get back inside and report this to Dutch." Lisa headed back for the side door, with her sister close behind.

"Hey, are you guys just gonna leave me here like this?" Angel called after them. His arms and legs were twisted at impossible angles, but his mouth was still moving at a thousand miles a minute. "At least if you're not gonna help me outside, toss me a warm body so I can fix my fucking legs!"

Asha stared aimlessly through the windshield of her black VW Bug as Azuma transmitted what he was seeing from his hiding spot in the alley. She watched in amazement as the long-haired young man called forth a brilliant trident that seemed to shake the earth. She didn't know what the thing was, but she did know that it was the source of the disturbance she had felt.

For as much power as the young man and his weapon

gave off, it was a one-sided fight against the shadow demon. She knew she'd felt someone cast shadow magic inside the club, but the power coming from the demon felt different. Whereas the demon reeked of malevolent darkness, the caster of the shadow spell hadn't felt so intense. Just then she felt the second pinprick of power manifest. Azuma's focus shifted and another man came into view. Before he'd even cast the magic, she knew that he was the one she had felt.

Through Azuma's eyes she could see the man clearly. Physically she found him breathtakingly handsome, but upon closer inspection she frowned. The shadow caster was without a doubt some type of mage or sorcerer, but there was something else to him. She had Azuma move as close as he dared so that she could try to get a feel for the man's aura, and that's when a pair of soft brown eyes turned to look at her. Rogue was still facing the demon, but the eyes of his other face watched Azuma intently. He stiffened as if he had felt Asha's probing and smiled at the monkey. The next thing Asha knew, pain exploded in her head and the connection was broken.

"What the fuck?" Asha rubbed her eyes with the palms of her hands. When the throbbing in her head subsided she tried to reestablish the connection with Azuma but couldn't. Fearing the worst, she reached out to him with her mind and soul. Azuma was unharmed but frightened almost beyond reasoning. She tried to get him to go back, but the monkey refused. Whatever Azuma had seen must have been horrific if it made him defy Asha.

"That's okay. Where magic fails, science will surely prevail," Asha said to herself, pulling a small laptop from the backseat. Her fingers floated expertly as she entered the information Azuma had transmitted about the magical trident into the WHD database. The WHD, or Witch Hunting Device, was a vast network of information hoarded away by the elders that was said to go as far back as the Great Parting. The system held pertinent information on different supernatural races and events throughout their history, making it easier for the Hunt to study their targets for weaknesses. The loading sign flashed while the bar below it slowly filled up. When the computer had finished its search a name was highlighted in red.

"What the hell is a Nimrod?" She scratched her head.

CHAPTER TWENTY-FOUR

Gabriel stumbled along trying his best not to fall as Rogue pulled him down the alley. The Nimrod had returned to its tattooed state, but he could feel it moving just beneath his skin, ready to be called back to battle. Behind him he could hear gunfire and the sounds of battle, but he was too afraid to turn around. All he kept seeing was the faces of his dead friends and the all-consuming shadows. He and Rogue emerged from the other end of the alley onto a busy street. Gabriel found it odd that no one gave the bloody young man or his gun-wielding partner a second look.

"I've cloaked us in shadow so they can't see us," Rogue answered the question on Gabriel's face.

"Shadows? You're one of them." Gabriel backpedaled, almost breaking their cover. Rogue had to stay within a foot or two of the young man to keep them both masked.

"Gabriel, would you calm down? You know me; I'm just as human as you are," Rogue insisted.

"After what I've seen tonight I'm not sure what I know." Gabriel reared his arm back and with little more than a thought he called the lightning to his hand. It seemed like the longer he stayed in contact with the Nimrod, the easier it was becoming to manifest its power.

Rogue aimed the enchanted gun at Gabriel. "Kid, if I wanted to hurt you I would've let the shadows have you in the alley. Gabriel, I owe your grandfather a great debt. He was a friend to me when I didn't have any, which is why I not only saved your ass but haven't shot you in the face yet. But if you try to use that thing on me, all bets are off," Rogue said in a tone that let Gabriel know he was serious.

"The walking dead is what his people call him behind closed doors. Beware the dark mages and what they represent, young Hunter. You do not want your immortal soul in their hands," the Bishop warned.

Gabriel regarded Rogue. Gabriel had met Rogue when he was fourteen and his grandfather was still teaching at the university. The day Redfeather had first brought Rogue to the house he introduced him as a friend of the family whom they could turn to in times of trouble. He would visit the house every so often to speak with Gabriel's grandfather of whatever secrets they'd kept between them. More than a few times Rogue would spend hours during his visits quizzing Gabriel about school and life. In light of all Gabriel had been through he was distrustful of everyone, but Rogue had been kind to him. Reluctantly Gabriel extinguished the lightning.

"Thank you," Rogue said, putting his gun away. "Are you okay?" He motioned towards the wound Moses had given Gabriel.

Gabriel looked at his collar and expected it to be a mess, but the wound had already begun to heal. "I guess." Gabriel touched the spot tenderly. "Rogue, what's going on?"

"We can play connect the dots once we're away from here. I seriously doubt if two witches and a vampire could've done much other than slow a demon as strong as that one. We need to put as much distance between you and him as possible." Rogue led the way down the street.

"Do you think he'll come after me again?" Gabriel asked nervously.

"He's tasted your blood, so you can count on it. Besides, thanks to your new friend you're the most wanted man in the city." Rogue motioned towards Gabriel's arm.

"Rogue, I don't want any part of this thing. If I knew how to get rid of it I would've already," Gabriel said.

"What you're toting around is not easily lost once it's found you," Rogue said.

"You sound just like my grandfather and everyone else who's been speaking to me in riddles all night."

"Where is Redfeather? Is he okay?" Rogue asked.

"I don't know; he was gone when I came to." Gabriel went on to tell Rogue about how De Mona had brought him the Nimrod and then vanished with his grandfather.

"Demons and a possessed relic, geez, and I thought I had rotten luck." Rogue hit the automatic start on his Viper. The two hopped into the car and Rogue merged with traffic. "Which side is she fighting on?" Rogue asked about the Valkrin.

"Honestly, I don't know. She helped when the Stalkers jumped us near my school, but at this point I don't know who's on whose side. I just know that we need to find my grandfather. If something has happened to him because of this thing . . ." Gabriel got choked up.

"Don't worry; Redfeather is a tough old bird. Wherever he is, we'll find him." Rogue swerved around a slow-moving car and hit the gas. Gabriel watched Rogue steer the car expertly, even though it was in the middle of the night and he was still wearing sunglasses.

"What's with the shades?" Gabriel finally asked.

"These?" Rogue tapped his shades. "The glasses and the car come with the job," he joked.

"I'm serious, Rogue. I've never seen you without those glasses. What're you hiding?"

"I'm not hiding anything, kid," Rogue lied.

"Rogue, if you want me to trust you then you've gotta give me a reason. I saw the way you worked those shadows in the alley, just like the demon. I've already figured you to be some type of magician, but those shadow bands were more than just magic. What are you?" Rogue took his glasses off and turned to Gabriel. Gabriel's mouth dropped open when he saw the stars dancing in the dark pits. "So, you are a demon." Gabriel reached for the door handle.

"Gabriel, chill out." Rogue hit the automatic locks, trapping Gabriel inside. "I'm not a demon; I'm human."

"Rogue, humans don't have outer space in their eyes." Gabriel kept tugging at the door. Rogue could see Gabriel's aura flaring, so he pulled over.

"Gabriel, if you don't calm down you're gonna set off you-know-who. If you give me a minute I can explain it to you." Gabriel stopped fumbling with the door, but he was still eyeing Rogue cautiously. "Look at me and tell me what you think I am."

"How the hell would I know?"

"Because you will. Now, look at me," Rogue urged.

Gabriel stared at Rogue. At first Gabriel couldn't see anything other than the man standing in front of him, but soon the layers began to peel away and he was looking at Rogue with more than his eyes. Rogue's aura was slightly brighter than that of an average man, but there was more to it. Sprinkled throughout the aura were pockmarks of blackness. As Gabriel looked closer, he thought he saw another face staring back at him from behind Rogue's.

"I don't understand. It's almost like you're two people." Gabriel tried to shake the image clear.

"Sometimes it feels like I am. I'm human like you,

but I'm also a mage. My family is from the house of Thanos."

Gabriel looked at Rogue disbelievingly. "From what I've read about mages, you guys are supposed to be humans who can work magic. That still doesn't explain what's going on with your eyes."

"Yes, we can work magic, but there are some of us who seek to do more than work it. Some want to control it, which is how my eyes got like this," Rogue admitted.

"So you tried to work a spell that went wrong?" Gabriel asked. He seemed calmer now, so Rogue kept talking.

"It wasn't my spell, but I ended up catching the worst of it. We managed to send the demon home, but not without a price. With demons there's always a price." The stars in Rogue's eyes danced as he thought back on the bargain. "The eyes I sacrificed saved dozens of lives. But it still didn't stop me from hating them or myself after the fact. When I got these eyes it was your father who helped me get through it."

"My father? How did you know him?" Gabriel was now very interested in Rogue's story.

"Peter and I were college buddies back when I was still doing stuff to piss my dad off. After graduation I went to the police academy and he went back to New York, where he ended up marrying his childhood sweetheart and getting back with the circus. When I had my little situation," he touched his eye, "I turned my back completely on my family and spell casting, so I was on my own with trying to figure out how to adjust to my new handicap. I knew Peter's dad had knowledge of the arcane, so I sought them out. When I showed up in New York I was blind and half-insane, but Redfeather welcomed me with open arms. He and Peter helped me to understand that I was not a part of my eyes; they were a part of me."

"It seems like the deeper I get, the more I'm learning about my father." Gabriel laughed.

"Your father was a good dude, Gabriel. One day we'll get together and I can tell you some stories, but first we gotta find a way to part you and Mr. Happy." Rogue pointed at Gabriel's arm.

"I've been trying, but short of lopping my arm off I can't figure a way." Gabriel rolled his sleeve up and showed Rogue the tattoo.

Rogue studied the tattoo, letting his eyes translate what he was seeing. The clouds rolled over the ocean while the Nimrod stood defiantly on Gabriel's forearm. "That's something you don't see every day. Try to call it again; maybe I can get a better idea of how to get rid of it if it's solid."

Gabriel extended his arm and concentrated. He could hear the thunder rolling and the tattoo moved, but it wouldn't come to him. "*I am still master of the storms, upstart. It will be a while before it recognizes you as my successor,*" the Bishop told him.

"Nothing." Gabriel shrugged.

"That's okay; it'll show its face again sooner or later," Rogue said. He pushed the Viper through the busy streets, occasionally looking in the rearview mirror to make sure they weren't being followed. He knew that they'd had a pretty good lead on the shadow demon, but he also knew that it was still looking.

"Where're we going?" Gabriel asked, noticing the signs leading to the West Side Highway.

"To Brooklyn. I've got a buddy who might be able to help us with your little problem, as well as find your grandfather. I don't know how I feel about him running around with a demon, especially one we know so little about."

"You think she's done something to him?"

Rogue's grip on the wheel tightened. "For her sake I hope not. The Redfeather clan is like family to me, and if she's harmed one hair on his head I'm going to see if I can still remember some of that death magic I was taught as a boy."

CHAPTER TWENTY-FIVE

A shadowy figure sat perched atop a mailbox on the quiet residential block. He was draped in thin body armor that was concealed by a worn-looking leather jacket. He had a pleasant brown face of a young man barely into his twenties, but there was timelessness to his eyes giving away his true nature. By right of blood he belonged to the vampire house of Gehenna, but by trade he was the Hound, the most efficient tracker in their ranks.

A low hissing followed by the screeching caused him to pause his searching and turn. One of the Stalkers who had been following close behind had descended on a cat and was in the process of devouring it. The Hound made a disgusted face and shook his head.

"Can't you control those things?" the Hound addressed Riel.

"They are predators, my friend, just like us." He smiled as if he had said something witty.

"Don't flatter yourself," the Hound said bitterly. "We ain't friends. Your boss is paying for my services in finding this thing that's got you guys chasing your tails."

"Like it or not, the same demonic forces that I serve are the same as the curse that animates your corpse," Riel retorted.

The Hound ignored Riel's comment and continued scanning the block. Sniffing the air, he leapt from the mailbox and stepped out into the middle of the street. "The thing you seek is there." He pointed to the Redfeather brownstone. Dropping to one knee, he sniffed the ground, filtering out the smells of car tires and searching for magical residue. "Or at least it was recently. The scent is strongest here." He tapped the street with a gloved finger.

Riel scanned the brownstone with his own magical sight and confirmed what the tracker had told him. "That must be a handy trick."

"No trick, a gift of the blood," the Hound said proudly.

"If the trident is there, let us claim it for the dark lord." Riel started forward.

"Wait a second." The Hound placed a firm hand, halting Riel.

"Out of my way, bloodsucker. If the Trident of Heaven is in that building I will wrest it for my master."

The Hound spun on Riel with razor-sharp fangs bared. "If you refuse to use your head, at least use your ears."

Riel started to protest until he heard the very thing that the Hound had been referring to. It was a low rumbling that seemed to get louder by the second. Just as the Hound pulled Riel back into the shadows, a modified Hummer turned the corner of the block. It was slightly longer than a regular Hummer and sported two extra wheels in the back to support its extended section. On the side was an insignia of a bleeding cross.

"The Inquisition," Riel hissed. "What are they doing here?"

"The same thing we are," the Hound said as he moved farther back into the shadows. From his position he watched as the Inquisitors spilled from the Hummer and secured the area. Next there was an old man, followed by a young girl wearing oversized jeans. The man was clearly mortal, but the Hound sensed something sinister about the girl. The last to exit the vehicle was mostly covered in light armor, similar to the Hound's own, but you could see the tribal tattoos decorating his arms.

Riel also noticed the tattoos and snarled, "The High Brother."

"The what?" the Hound asked, not quite understanding.

"He is High Brother of Sanctuary; do you know nothing of our world?" Riel asked, clearly annoyed.

The Hound thought briefly on his existence and how he came to be. "*Ours* is a relative term, demon."

Riel started to argue but held his tongue. He watched intently as a large black man directed the Inquisitors to clear a path for Brother Angelo. The Inquisitors placed themselves strategically around the front of the brownstone, weapons ready, while Angelo followed the old man and the girl inside.

The Hound was about to move in closer when something caught his eye. The movement was so faint that a human would've never noticed it, but the Hound hadn't been human for quite some time. At first he thought someone was moving in the shadows, but upon closer inspection he noticed it was the shadows themselves that were moving. Though he strained his eyes to pick out the shape, his vision wouldn't seem to focus. Before he could ponder it further, shouting came from the house.

"A battle?" Riel asked, drawing Poison from its sheath.

"No." The Hound waved him silent. His ears perked up, trying to make out what was being said. "Panic."

"Panic is good." Riel hoisted Poison. "It should make the task of slaying the mortals that much easier. We should move in and claim what is ours."

"*Oui* is French, my man," the Hound said, turning to leave.

"And where are you going?" Riel called after him.

"I was only paid to track the thing. What happens after

that is up to you guys. Good luck, fellas." The Hound's laughter could still be heard after he vanished into the night.

"Coward," Riel snarled. He turned to the Stalkers and raised his blade heavenward. "Let the slaughter commence."

CHAPTER TWENTY-SIX

"What the hell happened in here?" De Mona surveyed the damage to Redfeather's spacious living room. The second-floor banister had been smashed and was hanging halfway down into the living room. The house smelled of burning paper, and several of the overhead track lights were blown out. The most startling thing she noticed was a pale arm hanging between the broken rails.

"Meg!" Redfeather shouted, bounding up the stairs. He knelt beside the old woman's prone body. Lifeless eyes stared out at the room, yet they saw nothing. The floral blouse she was wearing was soaked and torn. Just under the fabric there was the imprint of a broken pitchfork. "What evil have I condemned you to?"

Brother Angelo walked over to where the dead woman lay and examined her body. As he stared down at her he let his natural sight slip back and saw the scene through magical eyes. Both the woman's chest and the room next to where she lay were tainted with the same magical signature, a brilliant gold with splotches of black.

"Dear God, it's already begun," Angelo said, using two fingers to close Meg's eyes.

"Angelo, what aren't you telling me?" Redfeather asked.

Angelo stood. "The Bishop was a power-thirsty man in

life and that thirst has only increased in death. Through the Nimrod he can call back the Dark Storm and free the imprisoned souls of his comrades. With the Knights and all the weapons gathered again, the Bishop could lay claim to the realm of mortals as well as demons."

"But he's trapped within the relic; surely the Nimrod can hold him?" Redfeather said.

"Old friend, the Nimrod was never really a prison but a hiding place. The relic nestled the Bishop tenderly in its bosom until the right elements could be brought together to be prepared for his return. But to cross the plains he needs a willing host."

"Surely Gabriel will not give in to the Bishop's whims." Redfeather sounded surer than he really was.

Akbar moved next to where Brother Angelo was still kneeling over Meg and conducted his own examination. He shook his head sadly but kept his scowl. "I fear that your grandson is already under the sway of the Bishop. The wound was clearly made by the Nimrod."

"No, there has to be an explanation." Redfeather began pacing. "Gabriel!" Redfeather called his grandson's name over and over, but there was no response.

"He's gone," Angelo told Redfeather. The first thing Angelo did was scan the premises telepathically for life signs, and he found none other than those of their group. Angelo looked to Akbar. "Contact the captain and tell him to mobilize the Inquisition. We neutralize the boy before he does any more damage."

Redfeather grabbed Angelo's arm. "Wait; let me try and find him before you send your people into the streets blindly."

"I think we have more to fear from him than him from us," Akbar said, looking around at the damage caused by the trident. "Brother Angelo," he turned to the High Brother, "we mustn't waste any more time here. The longer we dally, the stronger the Bishop's hold will become and the harder it will be to," he glanced at Redfeather, "separate it from the boy."

"Angelo, my grandson is not a malicious child; you know this. The Nimrod is an ancient thing that was never meant for this world; this is its handiwork. My grandson would never—"

"But your grandson has, Redfeather. From the dead witch we know that he is willing and able to kill. We cannot leave safety to chance and risk this happening again. The Nimrod and your grandson must be stopped before more lives are lost." No sooner had Angelo finished his sentence than the sounds of gunfire cut through the night.

One of the guards who had been posted outside the front door came crashing through the window. Clinging to his back was a Stalker that was little more than bones and teeth. The Stalker hungrily tore chunks of flesh from the Inquisitor's shoulder, spraying the carpet with blood. The front door crashed inward and Stalkers of varying stages of decay overran the brownstone.

Akbar was the first to react to the demon invasion. His eyes turned cold blue as he called the power of his bloodline, the Ghelgath demons. Drawing moisture from the air, Akbar proceeded to shape it as it froze and now faced the threat holding a spear and shield made of ice. "Protect the High Brother!" he bellowed, charging the Stalkers. When the first Stalker moved on him he jammed the spear up through its chin and out the top of its head.

This time De Mona welcomed the change when it washed over her. Her eyes hazed over in a film of red as her mother's cursed blood brought forth the predator. A not even remotely human sound came from somewhere in De Mona's chest as talons carved into her first victim. What passed as blood for the Stalker splattered over De Mona's face, snapping the chain that had been keeping the beast at bay. For too long it had been denied, and now it was unbound.

De Mona's claws entered the Stalker with barely a sound. In a swift motion she latched onto its spine and snatched it out through the Stalker's chest. Before the creature could fall she slapped its head off and kicked it away. She barely had time to react when another creature jumped onto her back. This one had been either a child or a midget at death, but it was so rotted that she couldn't tell, nor did she care. Her powerful jaws clamped down on the thing's arm, breaking it. She brought her hands up in a crossing motion, spilling the Stalker's entrails onto the carpet. With a swipe of her claws she knocked the Stalker's head across the living room.

In the center of the chaos, a black wisp of smoke rose from the ground. The blade was visible first, before Riel stepped out of the smoke. "Brothers of the Order of Sanctuary, I bring you the cool release of death." He pointed to Poison for emphasis.

Angelo's throat went dry at the sight of the demon. He had never encountered Riel personally but knew full well what the war demon and his sword were capable of. "I think you'll find that we won't die easily." Angelo advanced on the demon with his own sword upraised.

"Get back, Angelo; I'll take care of this one," Akbar said confidently. Before Angelo could stop Akbar, he'd moved on Riel with the spear. Akbar tried to impale Riel, but the demon sidestepped him as easily as he would've a clumsy child. Akbar spun, with inhuman speed, but the demon was faster. He blocked the second spear strike with the flat end of his blade and aimed a bone-breaking blow at Akbar's chest. Akbar's shield shattered, sending him flying backward, but he kept his feet. When he came out of his daze he saw the scorched edge of Poison speeding for his throat.

Angelo blocked the strike with his own blade and countered with one of his own. He tried to gut the demon, but Riel spun out of the way. "Stand and fight, coward," Angelo demanded.

"Brother Angelo, get back." Akbar pulled himself to his feet with the spear. Even as weakened as he was, he was still trying to protect the High Brother.

"I'll not stand idly by while my men are slaughtered," Angelo protested, trying to move around to Riel's rear. In a fluid motion Angelo decapitated a Stalker that tried to blindside him. It had been ages since he'd seen combat, but his skills were still as sharp as ever.

"Not to worry, priest, there's enough death to go around." Riel spun his blade in a loop and took a defensive stance.

A spray of gunfire shredded what was left of the door as the Inquisitor who had been driving the transport vehicle charged the house, sweeping a compact machine gun back and forth. He'd laid low two of the Stalkers and was turning his gun on the smiling Riel. Akbar tried to warn him back, but it was too late.

Faster than the driver's eyes could follow, Riel dodged the bullets and closed the distance between them. He slapped the gun away from the stunned driver and pressed the blade to his throat. He expected to be decapitated, but to his surprise Riel just nicked the driver on the cheek and stepped back. Everyone looked on in horror as the skin around the cut began to blacken, sending a scab spreading over his face. With the poison racing through his bloodstream the Inquisitor dropped to the ground and began to shake violently. Foam and blood flowed from his mouth as every nerve in his body was killed off by the blade's toxins. In an act of mercy, Akbar plunged his spear into the dying man's heart to put him out of his misery.

Seeing one of his brothers fall sent Angelo into a rage. "Die, hell's spawns!" Angelo bellowed. Riel attempted an overhand strike, which Angelo blocked. The war demon feinted left and struck right, but again Angelo blocked it. Simultaneously the two combatants struck, locking the hilts of their respective swords.

"You fight well for a priest," Riel taunted.

Brother Angelo gave a confident smirk. "I was born to combat your kind." Using all his strength, Angelo pushed off, separating the swords.

Akbar rejoined the fight, blindsiding the demon with his spear. The demon howled in pain as the crystal weapon dug into his side. The host's body sprayed blood like a small fountain, turning the spear a pinkish color. With a grunt Riel snapped the shaft of the blade and examined the wound. Already the head was beginning to melt as power tried to heal the wound. He cast his rage-filled eyes on Akbar. "For this you will pay, Ghelgath."

"Then come and collect the debt," Akbar said defiantly. He opened and closed his fist, trying to will the ice to take shape, but he was too spent. Unarmed, he was sure that he could take Riel, but with that blade between them it tipped the scales in favor of the dark forces. Still, Akbar would protect his brother and his order at all costs. If it meant his life, then he would die for the same thing he had lived for, the order.

Angelo had been Akbar's teacher for over twenty years. He knew the young warrior's spirits as well as he knew those of his own children, and what he read in his student/friend's eyes frightened him. Akbar was fast, but Angelo had to be faster. He reached Riel a split second before Akbar did. Angelo saw Riel tense to sidestep the blow, which was what he expected, so he spun with his momentum to cleave the demon's head. To Angelo's surprise, Riel had been expecting just such a move and caught him at the wrist. Moving with the strike, Riel was able to knock Angelo off balance. When he realized what Riel was doing Angelo tried to pull back, but it was too late.

Akbar's face was peaceful, blue eyes staring dreamily off into space. His lips were curved into a calm smile, oblivious to the clear liquid spilling over them. Akbar looked over at Angelo, and he could see the crystal tears dotting the corners of Akbar's eyes and his cheeks. Trying to keep from choking on the transparent blood of his ancestors, Akbar whispered to Angelo, "Let it be known that I died in service." With the last bit of his strength Akbar pulled himself free of Angelo's blade and lunged at Riel. The demon never even flinched as his blade separated Akbar's head from his body.

Still clutching his bloodied sword, Angelo looked down at the corpse of not only one of his most promising students but also one of the most tortured souls he'd ever encountered. For as long as he'd known the Ghelgath, his sole motivation had been service to the order and righting the wrongs of his people. Of all who had entered the Great Halls, Akbar had to have been one of the most dedicated. Angelo looked up at the grinning face of the war demon.

"Don't look so sad, priest; he died well. Much better than you will, I suspect." Riel flicked the excess blood from his blade onto the corpses of the dead Inquisitors who lay on either side of Angelo. The bodies twitched once before sitting up like marionettes. The previously dead Inquisitors sprang to their feet, guns hanging at awkward angles, facing their former commander. "I had so much fun killing them that I thought I'd give you a go," Riel taunted before setting the freshly made Stalkers on the grief-ridden Angelo.

With his blade raised level with his shoulder, tip poised to strike, Angelo regarded his opponents. "May the Lord have mercy on your souls, brothers, but I must set you free." The fight didn't even last five seconds. Angelo stepped between them without even brushing shoulders and stood in front of Riel. Behind him the heads of the two Inquisitors fell to the ground. Angelo pointed his bloody blade at Riel and said, "Shall we?"

Riel twirled like a helicopter that had gone out of control, destroying everything in his path. Angelo offered a series of weak blocks as he was forced into a corner. He fought the good fight, but the demon was too skilled. With a whirling sweep, Riel sent Angelo's blade soaring into the air. Angelo instinctively reached to catch it, and by the time he realized his mistake Poison had already carved a nasty gash in his forearm. The wound instantly turned a sickly purple just before Angelo felt the first licks of pain. He was able to force enough of his power into the wound to slow the spreading of the poison, but it would only be a matter of time before it overcame him.

Angelo rolled a split second before the cursed blade left a gash in the wall he'd been standing in front of. When he righted himself from the roll he felt dizzy and his limbs seemed heavier. The scar on his forearm had filled with puss and the poison was quickly spreading to his shoulder and hand. With his good arm Angelo tossed whatever he could heave at the demon, but Riel kept coming, savoring the High Brother's death. It was the end and both combatants knew it, but the man in the doorway didn't.

For a man his age, Redfeather moved extremely well. One by one the Stalkers came, only to taste the blade of the enchanted dagger. Though it had never before answered to Redfeather's touch, he wielded it as if it had been made for him.

Redfeather delivered a fatal blow to the eye socket of one of the Stalkers, lodging the blade in its skull. While he was trying to pull it loose a Stalker jumped on his back. As Redfeather struggled with one Stalker, another one latched onto his leg. Together they wrestled him to the ground, while more Stalkers closed in. The thinnest Stalker reached a clawed hand for Redfeather only to have it go up in flames. The Stalker stared at the smoldering nub in shock when the second burst of deadly flames struck it in the side and carried it across the room. The remaining Stalker managed to turn around to snarl only to have its mouth filled with the unforgiving flames. The creature's burning body danced around the living room before another burst sent it flying into the wall.

Jackson stood in the doorway decked out in black leather and clutching an odd-looking shotgun. The weapon was made of polished silver and crafted to look like a striking dragon. Running along the underbelly and extending from the mouth were three barrels. Jackson took a minute to examine what was left of the Stalker before helping Redfeather to his feet.

"You know when Jonas first came up with this thing, I had no idea how much fun I'd having putting it to use." Jackson expelled the shells and loaded fresh ones. His eyes traveled from the smoldering Stalkers to Riel, who was staring at what was left of his creations like a grieving parent. "That your handiwork?" Jackson nodded at the moldering corpses. "Makes for a good show, but the craftsmanship ain't worth shit." Before Riel could respond, Jackson loosed another burst, barely missing the demon who was scrambling for cover.

Brother Angelo knelt, clutching his throbbing limb to

his stomach. "Who are you?" he groaned up at the young-looking black man.

Jackson extended his hand and helped Brother Angelo to his feet. The man looked flushed, but he was able to stand with a little help. "Somebody that doesn't want to see you die tonight." Jackson let Brother Angelo rest his weight on him only to be surprised at how light the man was. Cradling the shotgun in the crook of his right arm, Jackson addressed the few Stalkers that were cautiously closing in on them. "You ugly sons of bitches ready to dance or what?"

The Stalkers moved not only swiftly but en masse as they rushed Jackson and Angelo. Jackson regretted his arrogance as he found himself stumbling backward under the wave of Stalkers. He tried to get a shot off with the shotgun, but it went wild and ignited the silk curtains hanging in the front window.

Seeing the wounded High Brother and the now-unarmed man go down renewed the Stalkers' courage. While they tried to pin Jackson to the floor, the most brazen of the bunch lunged in to take a chunk out of Jackson's arm. It let out a horrible shriek as its teeth struck cold iron and shattered. Before the creature could retreat, Jackson jammed his fist beneath the thing's jaw and flexed his fist. The creature's face went slack when the silver stiletto entered though its lower jaw and came out the top of its head. Bringing his other arm around, Jackson drove a second stiletto through the creature's eye. The prosthetic arms had been Morgan's gift to Jackson during his rehabilitation from the vampire attack. The arms were crafted by Morgan's hands and blessed in the halls of St. Anthony's. Jackson had proven to be a natural with the killing devices, as the Stalkers were learning.

Brother Angelo tried to get his footing but found that

his legs were reluctant to support him. The poison was working faster than he had thought it would. Through his hazy vision he was able to make out Riel standing a few feet away from him. The demon also looked haggard and exhausted, but at least he still had the strength to hold his sword, which at that point seemed impossible for Angelo. The poison had killed all the muscles in one arm and was making short work of the other. Angelo tried to raise his fists, but his limbs felt like they were filled with sand.

Riel's grip on Angelo's jaws was so intense that the bones started to pop. "You and your order are done, priest," Riel said, almost compassionately. "Surrender and acknowledge Belthon as your lord and master and I might be tempted to let you live."

Angelo looked up at Riel. Though the strength had all but left Angelo's body, the fire in his eyes burned with intensity. "Even if I die here tonight, another will take my place and ensure that you and your kind are forced back into the pits of hell."

Riel measured his words. "Possibly, but you won't be around to witness it. I may have failed in capturing the Nimrod, but your death will ensure that I have another chance at it." With a triumphant roar, Riel plunged Poison into Angelo's gut. As the fire from the poison racked his insides, his screams could be heard for blocks.

"No!" Redfeather screamed, drawing everyone's attention. He knew how important the High Brother was to the order, and if he died then all would be undone.

"I'm on it," De Mona snarled, abandoning the Stalkers she'd been fighting. Riel was rearing back to take Angelo's head when De Mona's claws tore into his shoulder, cutting through flesh and muscle. "Get the hell away from him!"

Riel stumbled to the side and took stock of his shoulder. "Sneaky Valkrin bitch," he spat. "I see not all of your wretched line has answered the call. If you surrender now, I'll see to it that Lord Titus shows you mercy."

De Mona smiled, licking his rich demon blood from her claws. "You know, I keep hearing about how badass this Titus dude is, and for some reason I can't bring myself to give a fuck!"

When Riel swung Poison, De Mona ducked under the strike and locked his arm under hers. With a twist, she dislocated it at the shoulder, but it only slowed Riel. He delivered a sharp knee to De Mona's stomach, and when she released her grip on his arm he slammed the hilt of Poison into the side of her head. Before De Mona could recover, Riel kicked her hard in the chest, sending her flying across the room. Almost instantly De Mona was back on her feet, but the war demon had vanished.

Though their master had fled, the Stalkers continued to pour into the brownstone. Jackson tore into the Stalkers with abandon, but it seemed that for every one he slew two more took its place. "This is getting us nowhere, Morgan," he barked into the earpiece he was wearing. "We need a miracle in here!"

"Ask and you shall receive," Morgan replied. A moment passed and there was a brief rumbling just before the eastern wall of the brownstone exploded in a shower of plaster and concrete.

Morgan stepped through the wreckage of the wall, coated in plaster. Beneath his jacket he wore a banged-up iron breastplate bearing a Celtic coat of arms on the chest and tattered jeans. The dust and rubble that was still raining from the damage landed on his skin, only to be absorbed, turning Morgan an off shade of gray. The muscles in his arm bulged as he strangled the handle of his jeweled hammer. "Servants of hell," he began with his hammer upraised. "In the name of my Lord and my family, I cast thee out!"

When the hammer made contact with the ground everything that could break did. The windows exploded, raining glass on everything and everyone. The shock wave from the hammer was so intense that it collapsed what was left of the upstairs banister and the ceiling, burying the Stalkers.

"What in God's name was that?" De Mona asked, sitting in the corner trying to figure out which way was up. Her entire body felt like it'd been dipped in hot water, but she was alive. Unlike her mortal companions, her demon blood had made her invulnerable to the hammer's power.

"Justice," Morgan said, helping her to her feet. "But we've no time to celebrate, so I suggest we leave." He looked at the pile of rubble, which was already beginning to stir. It had slowed the Stalkers, but it wouldn't stop them.

"That cat don't look like he's going anywhere," Jackson said of Brother Angelo. The High Brother rolled on the floor feverishly, muttering to himself.

"I need to examine the wound to determine if it's safe to move him," Redfeather said.

"Man, them things are gonna be back on our asses soon, and angrier than ever. You better pick him up and let's skate," Jackson told Redfeather.

"It burns!" Angelo shouted, clawing at his chest.

"Redfeather's right; we need to check him out." De Mona knelt beside him. She could smell the demonic poison rotting his flesh from the inside.

Morgan sighed. "I'll see if I can buy us a few more minutes then." Morgan walked to the edge of the pile where a decaying arm sprang free of the rubble. Morgan placed his hands flat on the ground and tried to level his breathing. The ground rumbled slightly and the ground split. Everyone watched in amazement as the Sheetrock and brick began to form a wall from the ground up. The end result was a six-foot wall of mismatched pieces, separating them from the Stalkers.

"How on earth did you do that?" Redfeather asked.

"No time for biology lessons, friend. The wall isn't very thick, so I suggest you get on with it before our friends break through." Morgan's voice was tired.

"Angelo." Redfeather knelt beside his old friend. The High Brother's skin was ashen and he was babbling feverishly.

"And God said let there be light . . . it is in the light that we all walk. Where is the light? Why can't I see the light?" he rambled.

"Dude looks bad," Jackson said, standing over the men. Jackson had retrieved his shotgun and was filling it with fresh shells.

Morgan gripped Angelo's breastplate and ripped it down the middle as if it were made of plywood. On the High Brother's chest there was a dark web surrounding the wound and slowly making its way up the length of his body. "It's the work of the cursed blade. I've heard tales of its evil, but sadly I know of no way to treat it."

"The healers will know," a meek voice said, startling everyone. At first they saw nothing but a patch of distorted reality, which began to solidify, revealing a small man. His skin was as pale as an albino, dark curls crowning his round head. Eyes as black as space looked up at the band of warriors nervously.

"You're the thing I saw at Sanctuary." De Mona pointed at the small man.

"I'm not a thing; my name is Finnious, Fin to my friends," he corrected her.

"How did you get here?" Redfeather asked.

Fin paused as if he wasn't sure whether to answer. "I

hitched a ride on the transport when you left to come here."

"Impossible, we would've seen you."

"Not if I didn't want you to." Fin faded into almost nothing, then became solid again.

De Mona sniffed him, trying to figure out what was off about the small man. "You have no scent. Every living thing has a scent, even the vamps."

"It's because I'm not alive. Not dead, but not alive," he told her.

"A wraith?" Redfeather took a step back.

Fin sighed. "Yes and no. It's complicated and I don't have time to explain. We must get Brother Angelo back to Sanctuary so the healers can tend to him."

"Doesn't look like he's going to make it," Jackson pointed out.

"He must," Fin said with such conviction that it surprised everyone. "With the death of the High Brother comes the death of the order."

"What are you talking about?" De Mona asked.

"No time. We have to go," Fin insisted.

"But how—" Redfeather's question was cut off by Angelo's screaming.

"I rebuke thee, Satan!" Angelo howled. His face was slick with sweat and his skin had begun to pale.

"Hold him steady," Redfeather said.

"You have no power over me!" Angelo shouted deliriously. "It burns," he continued, trying to claw at his stomach. Seeing that Redfeather and De Mona were having trouble holding Angelo down, Jackson grabbed his arms and pinned them above his head.

Redfeather examined the wound. The poison had marked its passing with a series of webbed veins snaking across Angelo's chest and arms. Redfeather gently prodded the wound, causing pus to run from it and across

Angelo's heaving chest. "It is even worse than the stories." Redfeather wiped his hands on his pants and crossed himself.

Just then Angelo let out a bloodcurdling scream. His body was contorting at uncomfortable angles and there was blood-laced foam starting to trickle from his mouth and nose.

"We should take him to a hospital," De Mona suggested.

"No, No hospital. Angelique is sending a healer. All we have to do is make it back to Brooklyn," Fin said.

"There's no guarantee that he'll make it without some type of treatment. Isn't there something we can do?" Jackson asked, staring curiously at the traces of the fast-spreading infection.

"Nothing that I know of," Redfeather confessed.

"Maybe I can help," Finnious offered weakly.

"The wraiths have power over death, not life," Redfeather pointed out.

"And as I said, I'm only half wraith. Let me try," Fin almost pleaded. With a nod Redfeather moved to the side so that Fin could kneel beside Angelo. Feeling everyone's eyes on him made Fin nervous, but he tried to shut their stares out so he could concentrate.

Finnious had worked the trick on birds and other small animals but never on a human. As carefully as he could, he laid his hands on Angelo's wound. Angelo bucked, but De Mona and Jackson managed to hold him still enough. Finnious pressed harder against Angelo's wound, sinking his fingertips into the cut. He could feel the poison from the blade working its way through Angelo's body, killing everything it passed. If the poison made it to his heart all would be lost.

"Who's going to look after the children if I go home?" Angelo pleaded.

"Hold tight, Angelo; you'll be fine." Redfeather tried to sound sure of himself.

Finnious visualized the wound in his mind, touching the ruined nerves and muscle. Working backward, he began trying to regenerate the damaged tissue. He first reconnected the muscles and then the flesh, backing to the surface of the wound. Just when it looked like he was making progress, the poison doubled its efforts. The darkness moved from Angelo's gut, snaking its way up Finnious' arm.

"You must break the connection." Redfeather watched in horror as Finnious was engulfed from fingertips to shoulders in darkness.

"I won't," Finnious yelped as the pain in his arms grew more intense. He felt like he was going to black out at any moment, but he couldn't let Angelo down. Even when the darkness had spread to Finnious' face he maintained the connection.

"Too late to call in the cavalry, too late," Angelo gasped. He looked up at Finnious and for a minute his eyes were sane. "You'll carry it for me, won't you, Fin?" Angelo grasped Fin's arm. The priest's grip was surprisingly tight for the condition he was in. "Keep it safe for me, huh?"

"Brother Angelo, please—" Fin's words were cut off when Angelo grabbed him roughly by the back of the neck.

"Promise me you'll keep it safe. Say it!" Angelo demanded in a deranged tone.

Fin had never seen Angelo like this and it scared him so bad that he almost wet his pants. "Okay, whatever you want. I'll keep it safe." He looked at all assembled hoping that someone would help him, but everyone was too shocked to move.

Angelo smiled peacefully. "I knew I could count on

you." In what came as a shock to everyone, Brother Angelo pulled Fin to him and kissed him on the lips. Fin struggled against Angelo, but the High Brother held him there. Angelo coughed, but instead of blood there was a brilliant light. The light spilled from Angelo's mouth and down Fin's throat, turning his insides into molten fire. Fin screamed and thrashed, but Angelo would not release his hold. When the connection was finally broken, Finnious lay panting in the corner, staring at the now-rotted corpse of his mentor.

"Fin, are you okay?" De Mona reached for him, but the boy scrambled away from her.

"No, no, no. If you touch me, I'll die," Fin ranted. He seemed to be afflicted with the same madness that had come over Angelo. Fin tried to pull himself up using one of the dressers, but his hand passed right through. It was as if he could no longer maintain a solid form.

"What the hell is wrong with him?" Jackson asked, backing away from Fin when he staggered next to him.

"It must be an aftereffect of whatever Angelo did to him. We must get both of them back to Sanctuary; they'll be better equipped to handle this."

"He's right, but I don't think we can get everybody there on our bikes." Morgan motioned towards Jackson, then himself. "Do you have a car?" he asked Redfeather.

"No," Redfeather said, wishing he'd listened to his grandson about purchasing a vehicle.

"We can hot-wire the transport," De Mona suggested.

"Good idea, but the front door is on the other side," Redfeather said, pointing to the wall that was beginning to web from the Stalkers' blows. It wouldn't be long before they broke through.

"Then we'll make another," Morgan said, raising his hammer. "Stand clear," he told them. With a grunt he tossed the hammer through the far wall of the living room, destroying it. As gently as he could, he scooped Angelo's decomposing body into his arms. "This way."

"Wait; I lost the dagger in there. It'll—," Redfeather began but was cut off by Jackson.

"Do you no good if you're dead or in prison. Now, you can do what you want, but I wouldn't want to be here if those shitheads get loose or the police show up. I'm outta here." Jackson stepped through the hole in the wall followed by Morgan and Fin, who was having trouble walking. He almost stumbled, but De Mona caught him under his arm.

"Man's got a point, Redfeather." De Mona helped Fin through the hole.

Redfeather looked around at the remains of what had been his home for so many years and thought about how much it reflected his life. The promise he'd made to his son before he died rang in Redfeather's head and his fear of the dark forces was replaced with rage. In his heart he had known that one day this might happen, and he had tried his best to keep Gabriel from his legacy and ignorant of his history. But in trying to shelter him Redfeather had left his grandson vulnerable. Somewhere out there the young man whom Redfeather had sworn to protect was at the mercy of the vile trident and it was his fault. He knew what needed to be done to protect not only his loved ones but also the world from the wrath of the Bishop. But knowing didn't mean that Redfeather would be able to go through with it when and if the time came. Fighting back the tears of a foolish old man, he went after the warriors.

The old man watched from the shadows as the warriors took off mere moments before the police arrived. He smiled at their victory but didn't allow himself too much joy, for he knew the greatest battle was yet to be fought.

The wind shifted, drawing the man's attention overhead. A crow that was almost the size of a falcon was watching the group file out of the ruins of the brownstone. When the Hummer turned the corner the crow flapped its large wings and took off.

"The demon lord has eyes everywhere," the old man said, slinking back into the shadows. "Beware, young Knights, for the gauntlet has been laid down and the war has begun."

CHAPTER
TWENTY-SEVEN

Flag sat in the back of the limo, watching the mirror he held on his lap as the surface began to cloud over. There was a rush of power and then the face of Titus became visible through the smoke.

"Report," the right arm of Belthon ordered. His spies had already sent word to him about the incident, but he wanted to hear it from Flag's mouth.

"The King Maker was undone," Flag said. "The Nimrod was gone from the brownstone by the time the Stalkers arrived, but they did encounter Brother Angelo and his vile Inquisition."

"Damn the High Brother. He's been a thorn in my side for more than a hundred years," Titus fumed.

"Well, you can consider your thorn removed. The High Brother fell to the cursed blade, Poison," Flag said proudly.

"Angelo is dead?" Titus almost couldn't believe it.

"Riel said he saw him fall before he made his escape. Not even one as powerful as Angelo could withstand a strike from Poison; he is technically a mortal."

"And the Core?"

"That I don't know."

"Then you need to find out," Titus told him. The knowledge of his nemesis's demise brought Titus joy, but hardly as much as the sinister plan he was about to put into action. It wasn't enough for Brother Angelo to die; Titus wanted his order broken. "Have you spoken with Orden yet?"

"I'm on my way there now," Flag said, looking out the window. There was a large green sign marking the Bronx Zoo exit. "By tomorrow night all should be in place for the final assault."

"No, there will be no mourning for Brother Angelo and his beloved order. If he's dead, then the order will be vulnerable for the first time in over a hundred years. Tell Orden that Sanctuary falls tonight!"

Flag was shocked by the sudden change of plans. "My lord, it will be morning in a few hours and the goblins must be underground by such time. There's no way they can take down the order before daylight."

"There is a way and you will find it, Flag." The mirror rippled as Titus roared. "You will accompany the goblins to make sure my orders are carried out to the letter."

"Titus, I can carry your orders to the goblins, but there's no way they would allow someone who isn't a warrior to participate in their raid."

"Then let tonight be the first when you actually get your hands dirty. Do not fail me, mage." Titus broke the connection, leaving Flag staring at his own worried expression in the mirror.

A sudden overpowering urge to shatter the mirror on the wall came over Titus, but he managed to suppress it. Realistically speaking, he knew he'd never take the Nimrod by sending anything less than a full troupe of able-bodied warriors, but he held on to the hope that his demon lieutenants would be able to get it done. The fact that the Hunter and the relic had yet to be delivered to him showed him the error of his ways. There was much to think about and even more to do, but it would have to wait. Titus had a visitor, and when you were dealing with beings in the mortal realm who weren't naturally of it time was always a precious thing.

When Titus stepped back into his receiving chamber his guest was in the same spot he'd left her in, standing in the far corner of the room and staring out the window. With her back to him he could appreciate her near-perfect posture and subtle curves. On the back of her neck, just beyond her flowing brown hair, he could make out the tattoos of protection etched into her skin. The words were written in a language that hadn't been used since before Christ, but Titus knew them well.

Feeling his predatory gaze, her body stiffened and she turned to him. Her angular features were sharp, but it took nothing from her natural beauty. Slanted onyx eyes regarded Titus as if she could read every dirty thought on his mind, which she probably could. Tamalla P. Hardy was not only a respected Crime Scene Investigator with the NYPD, she was also a very skilled clairvoyant. She had an uncanny ability to communicate with the dead, which she learned to monopolize at an early age. When there was business to be done between the dead and the living, it was Tamalla who brokered the deal.

"I trust all is well?" Tamalla asked with a raised eyebrow.

"Nothing my people can't handle. So, what brings the voice of the dead lands to me tonight? Does King Morbius have need of my services?" Titus moved closer to Tamalla. He purposely let wisps of his power escape in an attempt to intimidate the shorter woman, but she held firm.

"No, but it has come to my attention that you may be in need of his," Tamalla replied. Titus continued to stare at her like he was ignorant of her meaning, so she continued. "There have been a great many restless souls traveling on the *Jihad* these last few nights."

Titus shrugged his shoulders. "And what business is it of mine who travels between here and there as long as I remain?"

For a moment Titus could see Tamalla's eye twitch with irritation, but she quickly regained her composure. "These aren't average souls; most of them are pretty pissed off for being used as sources for your Stalkers."

"We do what we must to keep our armies strong. Tamalla, for as full as your schedule is, I didn't realize you had time to become an advocate for the rights of human souls," he said sarcastically.

"I could give a shit about what you and your twisted lot do, Titus; it's the stories the spirits are telling in passing. The word is that you're out here fighting some secret holy war with the Knights of Christ over the Nimrod." She laid it on the table. If she was looking to get a rise out of Titus, it didn't work.

"As you so eloquently stated, what we do is our business. What do I care if the dead are complaining to a mortal?"

"Because it isn't just me; Ezrah's caught wind of it too." Tamalla smirked as the color drained from Titus' face.

"Ezrah has no claim to the Nimrod," Titus said.

"Try telling him that. Titus, you should know better than anyone the addictive effect that thing has, so imagine being denied that fix for hundreds of years. It's just hearsay now, but if Ezrah gets it in his mind that there's truth to the rumor that the Nimrod has resurfaced, the Sheut are gonna be all over this thing, and we both know how that would play out."

Indeed he did. Though the *Jihad* and her crew were bound to the service of King Morbius as his ferrymen, it was not unheard of for them to go on bloody rampages amongst the living at the behest of their captain. The lust for power Ezrah had carried in life only became more consuming in death, and his ambition knew no bounds. The captain knew that the same trident that had damned him could be his salvation, and he would spare no effort if he thought he could capture it a second time.

"And why bring this information to me, Tamalla?" Titus asked suspiciously.

"Because until something better comes along you're the lesser of two evils," she said honestly. "With people like you, us mortals have got a fighting chance. If the Sheut get the Nimrod it'll be over before the first shot from our side is fired. I lose enough sleep with wayward spirits pestering me, so I'm really not looking forward to entire cites of them."

"This I can understand, but I still can't see you doing this totally out of your sense of humanitarianism." Titus eyed her.

"Of course not." Tamalla smirked. "For my time and trouble coming up here to deliver the message in person you're gonna wire one-point-five million to my standard business account. And for me not to tell Ezrah that the Nimrod is in New York I'll expect another five million wired to an account whose numbers I've already provided to your secretary." Tamalla headed for the door, but Titus cut her off.

"And what's to stop me from killing you now and burying my secret with your remains?"

Tamalla looked at him seriously. "Because if you kill me, then you'll never see it coming when the Sheut swoop down on this world and make it a ghost planet," Tamalla warned, and left the office.

* * *

When Flag reached the zoo his body stiffened with the thought that the most dangerous part of his mission lay before him. Over the last few centuries the age of magic had died out, giving way to the modern world, but there were still pockets in the fabric of reality where magic and the things spawned of it stirred. These pockets were called places of power. For the most part the wormholes led nowhere, but there were a few that led to the land of Midland and the last kingdoms of magic.

The driver pulled into the service area of the Bronx Zoo and idled outside one of the loading docks. "Wait here," Flag told the driver before sliding out of the limo. The two Stalkers lumbered behind him. The few employees who were still on the grounds acted as if they didn't even see Flag as he entered the main building. At the end of a darkened hallway there was an unmarked door, guarded by a portly man in a security uniform that appeared to be two sizes too small.

"Can I help you?" The security guard looked up from his newspaper and studied Flag. At a glance the security guard appeared quite ordinary, but the trained eye could see smudges of black magic all over his aura.

"I've come seeking an audience with the prince of the Iron Mountains, conqueror of the underworld, and devourer of man-flesh," Flag said in a rehearsed speech.

"All man-things who enterer the bowels of hell do so at their own peril, for the things that dwell here prefer the taste of flesh and blood only second to the screams of battle. The stink of your fear will drive them to frenzy and only the sucking of your bones shall quiet them again. If you value your life, then you'll turn back now."

Flag regarded him. "I fear not for my life, for I come as the voice of Lord Titus, favorite son of the dark lord and earthly vessel of our order." Flag rolled up his sleeve and showed the guard the patch of rotted flesh on his left arm that was roughly the shape of a hand. It was Titus' mark. "Recognize the mark of he who slew the Bishop and for his services was welcomed into the bosom of all things unclean and vile."

The guard's eyes lit up slightly when he studied the mark. When he was satisfied with its authenticity he half-bowed and stepped aside to let Flag pass.

Flag and the two Stalkers passed through the door and found themselves inside a room that was slightly smaller than a linen closet. Flag ran his hands along the wall until he felt the familiar uprising of stone under his palm. He said the words as they had been spoken to him and stepped back. There was a grinding of stone as the wall slid back to reveal a dark stairwell that led farther under the zoo. Before descending the stairs, Flag took a moment to make sure all of the proper protection spells were in place. Titus had a standing alliance with the prince, but there was no telling what Flag might run into between the entrance and Orden's stronghold. Taking a deep breath, Flag proceeded to venture to the levels of the city that weren't on any map, the stronghold of the goblins.

The farther belowground he got, the more he could feel the barriers of science become more frayed and the call of magic stronger. It was subtle, akin to walking into the freezer section of a supermarket. By the time Flag reached the bottom of the stairs he could no longer feel the eerie dullness of science that hindered the powers of all things not belonging to the new world. In Midland it was the magic that held things together and not the theories behind it.

He had been within the bowels of the Iron Mountains before but never on this route and never without Titus or one of the more powerful demons who served them. The entrance beneath the zoo was arguably the quickest but also the most dangerous because of its close proximity to the goblins' fort. Had Flag had it his way, he'd have gone the traditional route, using the Coach, but in the enchanted carriage the journey was at least a day under the best circumstances. Titus didn't have that kind of patience.

Because of the goblins' varying sizes, the tunnels beneath the Iron Mountains were the largest in the new world. The tunnels leading to the Iron Mountains were probably the largest of any built under the city. The beasts ranged between six feet and nine feet, but no matter the size, they were the fiercest race of creatures in all of Midland.

The walls in the tunnel were slick with moss and other vegetation, none of which was native to the United States, but it grew freely in Midland. Flag could feel the temperature rising, no doubt from the wild pockets of lava that ran freely within the mountains. In the shadowed hollows he could feel the eyes of the creatures that dwelled in the bowels on him. Even with the two powerfully built Stalkers guarding him, Flag still felt uneasy. It was not unlike the flesh-loving goblins to descend on intruders and make feasts of them, regardless of which side of the light they fought on. Within the Iron Mountains the strong ruled and the weak were food. The carcasses that crunched under his feet were a testament to that.

A few yards ahead the tunnel opened up to a larger chamber, where something stirred that he couldn't quite see. Only God knew what refugees of the fairy lands dwelled within the tunnels, and Flag wasn't sure he wanted to find out. The Stalkers grumbled uncomfortably, but Flag settled them with a raised hand. He cast a light spell, more to avoid startling whatever was waiting for them at the end of the tunnel than to see his way, and motioned for one of the Stalkers to lead the way. As soon as the Stalker cleared the tunnel a massive hand grabbed it and lifted it off its feet. The second Stalker moved to help its comrade but was pinned to the ground beneath a clawed foot. The goblin centurion was almost ten feet tall and his body was easily the width of a bus. His head was completely shaved with the exception of a long braid that snaked from the back of his skull to his waist. The skin that coated the goblin was an off shade of green and covered with pus-filled sores. The Stalker hissed and squirmed, but it did nothing to stop the thing that held it from clamping his massive jaws around its head, removing it. Pale yellow eyes turned to Flag as if to say, "You're next."

"All man-things that enter the Iron Mountains are meat for the strong," the thing hissed, raining bile and saliva onto Flag's suit. The goblin's massive jaws opened unnaturally wide as he leaned down so that he was eye level with Flag. His instincts bid him to run, but he knew he would never make it out of the tunnel before the centurion devoured him. Instead he raised his hand.

"I bear the mark of Lord Titus," Flag said as calmly as he could, showing the rot mark on his arm. "Harm me and risk his wrath." The goblin examined the mark carefully, as if he was weighing his options. After a brief sniff of the mage the goblin determined that Flag was telling the truth and withdrew.

"What business do you have here, ass wiper of the dark lord?" the goblin demanded. His voice sounded like two worn brake pads rubbing together.

"I have urgent business with Prince Orden; I must speak with him immediately," Flag said.

"If my prince wishes it, you must do nothing but die!" the goblin said.

Fearing that his life could possibly be in danger, Flag called on his magic. As he waved his hands in a mystic symbol the air around his hands ignited. The air in the room seemed to almost boil at the magical energy that was suddenly gathered within the chamber. Flag pointed a glowing hand at the goblin but did not release the energy. He knew that killing one of Orden's men would come at a heavy price, so he was hesitant, but if it came down to a choice between his life and that of the goblin, Flag would destroy him. Luckily the door to the inner chamber flew open, saving Flag from having to make the choice.

"Silly things who interrupt Orden's council not value their lives!" The speaker was a goblin, but one far smaller than the centurion. He was about the size of a small child, with coal black eyes and yellowing fangs. Small wings flapped about wildly, but he seemed to hop rather than fly. The tip of one of his ringed ears had been bitten or chopped off. Flag never bothered to ask which. Though the goblin was small, the centurion lowered his head and backed away. All the goblins knew better than to harm Gilchrest, brother of Prince Orden.

"Alford, you know the rules about disturbing Orden when he holds court," Gilchrest said, leaping onto the larger goblin's shoulder. "Taken leave of your senses, have you? Or tired of living, you must be?"

"Forgive me, Prince Gilchrest," Alford said, trying his best to hide his loathing of the smaller goblin. "The man-thing entered the goblin lair uninvited. No outsider may cross our threshold without invitation."

Gilchrest slapped Alford on the back of his shaved head. "Silly beast, who gives you power to say who comes and goes into the Iron Mountains? Only sons of the royal family have that power here. You're just a stupid guard!" Alford growled as if he were about to attack, but Gilchrest held up the royal crest that hung around his neck, halting Alford. "You know the price for hurting a royal. You ready to give your life over rage?"

Alford fought to bring himself under control and knelt before Gilchrest. "No, my prince."

"Good." Gilchrest kicked Alford in the rear with his tiny clawed foot. "Go guard tunnel while I take the mage to Orden."

If looks could kill, the one Alford was giving Gilchrest would've caused him to drop dead on the spot. Most of the goblins in Midland hated Gilchrest because of the way he abused his princely power, but none would dare touch him for fear of what Prince Orden might do. The poor fool who had bitten the tiny goblin's ear off was still hanging in the dining hall, where he had been for the last half century. Every so often Orden or one of his guards would bite away a chunk of the offender's flesh, but they refused to let him die. He would serve as a warning to all those who dared lay hands on one of the royal family. Alford slunk away into the main tunnel, but he vowed that he would have his revenge against the little prince one day.

After making sure Alford was gone, so he wouldn't have to turn his back on the centurion, Gilchrest addressed Flag. "You play a dangerous game, wizard. Alford bring death to him who offends. You need learn goblin protocol."

"I should tell you the same," Flag said, dousing the magic he had called.

"I not outsider. Only fools try to hurt prince of goblins. Now, what you want here, Gilchrest missing trial?"

"Trust that if I had it my way I wouldn't have come to this hovel that you goblins claim, but Titus has sent me to speak with Orden," Flag said, looking around the chamber in disgust.

Gilchrest looked at Flag suspiciously. "And what the dark lord want with goblins now?"

"That is between Titus and Orden. Now, take me to him."

"Gilchrest not take orders from you, wizard. You are murderer of your own, like the Halfling, Titus. The mages say Flag a dead man." The small goblin snickered mockingly.

Flag's hand shot out faster than Gilchrest could dodge and gripped him about the throat. He released enough power to make the small goblin uncomfortable but not enough to hurt him. "Make no mistake, you animated footstool, I do not fear the likes of your or the decomposing circle of half-ass conjurers. I would gladly risk the wrath of my lord, as well as the goblin prince, if it would silence your insufferable ranting. You will take me to Orden, immediately."

Gilchrest mustered a weak smile. "No need we fight, friend Flag. I shall take you to my brother." Flag released Gilchrest, allowing him to drop to the ground. The tiny goblin gave Flag a wicked look before leading him through the gates of the goblins' keep.

Inside the goblins' lair the air was twice as bad as in the tunnel. The smell of rotting flesh was more pronounced here and the screams of the tortured souls louder. Crossing the rickety bridge, Flag was allowed a better view of the kingdom. Below him fires raged and whips cracked across the backs of the dwarfs who served the goblins. What was left of a once-proud race now toiled beneath what was once their home, making weapons and armor for the goblins who now ruled the Iron Mountains.

"No pity for the slaves, wizard. It's better to live as a servant than to die as a meal," Gilchrest said after having read the look on Flag's face.

At the far end of the bridge was a door embedded in the mountain. The door was at least twelve feet tall and made from a finely hammered bronze. On either side stood a goblin guard, armed with a heavy spear and shield. Through the door Flag could hear shouting and the clashing of steel. He hoped that Titus hadn't made the mistake of sending him into the bowels during one of the goblins' notorious feedings. When truly caught up in the bloodlust the more primal of the species had a hard time controlling it and were known to turn on friend and foe.

The armored centurion bowed from the neck at Prince Gilchrest before pushing the massive door open. Beyond the door was a sea of goblins of different shapes and sizes. They exchanged snarls and pats on the back while focusing on something in the center of the room that Flag couldn't see just yet. Several heads turned hungrily towards Flag when they recognized the smell of the magic in his blood. Had it not been for Gilchrest leading Flag through there was no doubt in his mind that the goblins would've descended on him. Regardless of what Titus needed, Flag vowed that this would be his last trip to the Iron Mountains.

"Move aside; move aside. Make way for your prince." Gilchrest swatted and nicked the goblins blocking his and Flag's way. There were more than a few murderous glares sent their way, but the goblins parted like the Red Sea for the little prince.

In the center of the room a brutish-looking goblin was pacing back and forth, naked from the waist up. The beast wasn't quite as tall as Alford but was still quite imposing, sporting three battle-scarred arms. Jutting from his left side was the stump where the fourth had once been. His massive head lolled from side to side as he moved, but his deformed red eyes never left the goblin standing opposite him, Prince Orden.

Orden resembled a shaved gorilla with his squat legs and arms that almost brushed the ground without him bending. Fangs jutted from behind his bottom lip and tickled his top lip like short tusks. A spearhead was woven into the blood-dyed braid on his head, which swung freely every time Orden rolled his thick neck. Physically he was just as imposing as his kin, but his blue eyes held an intelligence that was rare amongst the cannibals.

Standing between them was a third goblin, who was only slightly taller than Flag. The goblin had an angular face that was obscured by stringy purple hair that hung almost to his knees. His skin was a sun-blasted yellow and smooth, unlike that of his deformed brethren. The only imperfection he seemed to have was his right arm, which was as black as night from fingertip to elbow. Had it not been for the reptilian eyes staring at the two combatants, he could've almost passed for human. In his hands the purple-haired goblin held two five-foot curved blades, which he handled as easily as if they were pocket-knives. When he addressed the crowd, Flag was thoroughly surprised at the clarity of the goblin's speech.

"Look well, brothers and sisters of the Iron Mountains, and bear witness as two of our fiercest brothers have come to settle a dispute. The offender," he pointed to the three-armed goblin, "has laid challenge for the ax that has led our people into battle for the last ten thousand years. And in so challenging for the weapon, he so challenges for the throne now held by Prince Orden." He pointed at the smiling prince. "As it has been since the beginning of us, blood will settle this dispute." The crowd roared at the proclamation. "Are the two combatants ready?" He addressed both of the goblins, who nodded. "Good. Die well, brothers." The purple-haired goblin tossed both the blades into the air, signaling the beginning of the contest.

The three-armed goblin moved incredibly fast for a creature his size. Two of his hands seized one of the blades and he immediately moved to gut Orden, but to his surprise the prince hadn't jumped for the other blade. Instead the prince caught the three-armed goblin when he was coming down and slammed his fists into his opponent's side. He flew to the other side of the room and crashed against the wooden table that had been turned over to act as a barrier between the combatants and the crowd. Orden tried to put his fist through his opponent's head, but he moved just as the fist made contact with the wooden table. The three-armed goblin swung the blade in an arc that would've splayed Orden had he not already moved to the other side of the room. He too was incredibly quick for a goblin.

The three-armed goblin howled and rushed Orden. Orden managed to avoid the blade's wild swing but not the crushing blow landed by the goblin's third arm. Orden stumbled and the three-armed goblin slashed him across the chest. Blood sprayed the combatants and the crowd, adding to their frenzy. A small pocket of goblins had broken out into a fight, which resulted in one of them losing an eye before the attention was turned back to the contest. The three-armed goblin tried to take Orden's head, but he rolled out of the way and came to a crouch on the other side of the circle, holding the second blade.

This time it was Orden who took the offensive, attacking his opponent with a series of thought-out strikes that opened up several gashes on his arms and legs. He was a warrior, but Orden was a skilled swordsman. Orden took his time with his opponent, opening a cut on his back before creating an identical one on his chest. The three-armed goblin tried to attack with his third arm again, before Orden hacked it off. Next went his opponent's ear, followed by his left arm. By the time Orden had finished his circuit of the three-armed goblin, he was on his knees with one arm left and defenseless.

"Mercy," the now-one-armed goblin croaked.

Orden laid the blade at the base of his opponent's neck. "Under the Iron Mountains, death is the only mercy."

Orden soundlessly removed the goblin's head and addressed the crowd. "Look well, brothers and sisters of the Iron Mountains." He held the head up for all to see. "The challenge has been met, and as it has been since the beginning of us, the debt is settled in blood." With his free hand he picked the three-armed goblin's body up and held it above his head. "Under the Iron Mountains, only the strong rule, and he who rules provides his people with strength and flesh!" Orden tossed the body to the crowd. The goblins wasted no time in swarming over the corpse, devouring it.

"Save some for Gilchrest." The little goblin hopped around, trying to get to the corpse. He was roughly snatched up by his wings just before being trampled by a goblin who was just smaller than an elephant.

"Quiet your babbling, little brother." Orden sat Gilchrest on the edge of the table. "I've not left you out of the feast." He handed Gilchrest the severed head.

"Many thanks, my prince," Gilchrest said happily before sinking his teeth into the head. Flag had to turn away from the spectacle.

"What's the matter, wizard? No stomach for the feeding?" Orden taunted Flag. A bloodied goblin tore himself from the feeding long enough to present Orden with the heart of his enemy. The heart was always saved for the leader.

"I think this is the most disgusting thing I have ever seen," Flag said, rubbing at a spot of blood that had landed on his shirt.

"And that is why you are weak, man-thing," Orden said, licking the blood off his hands. "Tell me, what brings you into the bowels of Midland this night?"

"I have come on behalf of my lord Titus," Flag said.

"And what does the murderer of his brother need of the goblins now?" Orden asked, amused.

"Something of great power has been loosed topside and the mighty goblin army may be needed to help us retrieve it for the Dark Order."

"And what does he offer for our services?" Orden rubbed his blood-caked hands together greedily.

Flag smiled. "The flesh of holy men."

Orden's laugh sounded like rocks crashing together in a cardboard box. "Illini!" Orden bellowed.

"My prince." The purple-haired goblin knelt before him, with his blackened hand planted in a puddle of blood. The liquid seemed to sizzle under his touch.

"Ready the Adder and a battalion of our hungriest. Tonight we dine topside."

CHAPTER
TWENTY-EIGHT

Rogue brought the Viper to a stop on an isolated block off Flushing Avenue. Aside from a large warehouse that dominated one side of the block and the gas station at the corner, the block was abandoned. On the buildings and posted on street signs was an eight-hundred-number for anyone who wanted to get in on the ground floor of a prime real estate deal. Rogue got out of the car and started without waiting to see whether Gabriel was following.

"Where are you taking me, Rogue?" Gabriel got out of the car and followed him.

"I told you that I was taking you to see a friend of mine."

"Your friend lives in a warehouse?" Gabriel studied the building across the street.

"No," Rogue said, and kept walking. The building he stopped in front of reminded him of a school that had seen its prime come and go. Removing his glasses, Rogue scanned the building. "He's home," he told Gabriel before pulling one of the planks off the entrance. "Stick close to me while we're inside. You make a wrong turn in here and there's no guarantee that I'll be able to save you," Rogue warned him before stepping inside. Gabriel pondered it for a minute, but he eventually followed Rogue inside the abandoned structure.

The first thing Gabriel noticed when he got inside was the smell. The stench of rotted flesh pushed up into his nose, almost causing him to vomit, but he was able to hold it down. It reminded Gabriel of when his history teacher had played the movie *Glory* in class for them one afternoon. Gabriel figured that the corpses of the Union soldiers they dumped on the beach had to smell as bad as the abandoned building, if not worse. He was so preoccupied with trying to keep from throwing up that he didn't notice Rogue stop and walked into him.

"Sorry, Rogue. If we had a flashlight or something, then—," Gabriel began but was cut off.

"Trust me; you don't wanna see what's in here." Rogue scanned the room with his eyes. He could feel several life-forms moving around him but wasn't sure which was the one he had come in search of. "Father Time!" Rogue called out. The wind picked up, scattering trash in the darkness. There was the loud rattling of chains followed by a ghostly wailing.

"I don't like this, Rogue," Gabriel told him. There was a light rush of wind and what sounded like metal grinding against metal. The Nimrod empowered him, but the trident didn't manifest. Something within the building made the relic uneasy, and it conveyed this to Gabriel.

Rogue felt the pinpricks of power coming from Gabriel. When Rogue looked at Gabriel he noticed the faint glow that had come over him. "Gabriel, I need you to stay calm. Father Time is a bit of a recluse and I really don't wanna spook him."

"Spook him? That's a riot." Gabriel jumped as something scampered across his face. A low howling seemed to come from everywhere at once and something that felt like burlap brushed across his face. Of his own accord his hands began to flare with power.

"Gabriel, I need you to relax." Rogue touched his arm and got a painful shock. Gabriel's body began to burn so bright that Rogue had to turn away. "Father Time, if I were you I'd cut the shit before this gets too far gone." He whipped his head back and forth, but all he could see was the darkness moving. From the way lightning was shooting from Gabriel he knew he had to do something. "Fuck this." Rogue pulled the revolver from the right holster. He took his time, anticipating where the darkness would shift next, and fired two shots. There was a thump of something hitting the ground and suddenly the wind and howling stopped. "It's okay, kid," he told Gabriel while re-holstering his gun.

Gabriel tried his best to calm down to keep the magic raging in him from going wild. The feeling was akin to having a great gas bubble in his stomach that refused to pass. He was able to bring about some measure of control, but the Nimrod was still agitated. Gabriel watched as Rogue pulled something from his pocket and tossed it into the air. He shouted something and the room was suddenly illuminated. Gabriel took one look at his surroundings and wished it was dark again.

The floor was littered with the corpses of rats, cats, dogs, and birds. There was even the half-mummified body of what looked like a pig lying at the bottom of the stairs. A grunt of pain brought Gabriel's eyes to the center of a room, where Rogue was attending to what was in the shape of a man, but he looked anything but human.

"Damn you, mage!" the vampire known as Father Time cursed Rogue while attending to the hole in his shoulder. Pinkish pus oozed from the hole and down his worn topcoat.

"I asked you to stop, but you wouldn't listen. Now shut up and let me see that shoulder." Rogue knelt beside him and examined the hole. Most vampires would've recovered from such a wound in a matter of minutes or less, especially one as old as Father Time, but those were vampires who were well fed. Rogue could tell by the animal corpses and Father Time's withered body that it had been a while since he'd fed properly.

"Get away from me; I can heal the wound myself." Father Time swatted at Rogue with his good arm, which looked like it didn't have the strength to rise on its own, let alone do any real damage.

"Not if you keep starving yourself like this." Rogue pressed his hand against the wound and whispered the words. When he removed his hand the wound had closed. "When is the last time you've had something that was capable of speech?" Rogue motioned towards the carcasses littering the ground.

"I will not drink of the sheep. My thirst keeps me focused while I wait for the end of us to come to pass," Father Time said wearily.

"You'd better get it in your mind to drink from something or you ain't gonna be around to see it, buddy."

"Is that a vampire?" Gabriel stood over them and studied Father Time curiously. He'd always thought of vampires as beautiful and magical, but the man lying on the ground before him looked like something out of a horror movie. The man was little more than a corpse with a dirty nest of white hair covering his face and head. His withered lips were drawn back into a sneer, showing yellow fangs jutting from rotted gums. Bloodred eyes stared up at Gabriel maliciously from their sunken sockets.

"He used to be, before he went nuts," Rogue said, wiping his hands on his jeans.

"It is you who are insane, mage. For even with your demon's eyes you do not see the writing on the wall. The descendant of Usiri and his mistress walks the earth in search of his place at the table."

"What's he talking about?" Gabriel asked.

"Father Time here thinks that some supervamp is gonna come through and wipe out the vampire race. It's a far-fetched story, but it's kept him hiding and living off the blood of animals for the last few years."

"Your story is my truth, mage. When the greatest mistake of us draws first blood he shall be filled with our knowledge, strength, and all-consuming thirst. The thirst will burn his insides and drive him to the point of madness and the blood of one hundred sheep shall not sate him, for he hungers for the blood of the wolf. What was done will be undone."

"And the cow jumped over the moon." Rogue waved him silent. "Listen: while you're in here waiting to be eaten I need a favor from you."

"As it always is with your lot. I've no desire to barter with you tonight, mage. Take your hellish eyes and this befouled boy and leave this place before you bring the agents of hell to my doorstep," Father Time snarled.

"So you know there's something wrong with the boy?" Rogue asked.

Father Time looked over Gabriel slowly. "All who can see will know what this boy is. A mortal who walks with the power of a god is not an easy thing to miss."

"I need you to tell me what's going on with him, Father Time," Rogue said.

"What is to pass will pass. There's nothing that you or the boy can do about it." Father Time grabbed a passing rat and tore into it. In a matter of seconds he'd drained the rat and discarded it amongst the others.

"I need to tell exactly what it is that's supposed to go down," Rogue told him.

For a minute Father Time looked almost sane. "Rogue, to get involved in this will draw attention that I don't want or need right now. Already you've tainted my lair by bringing him here. If you've ever valued our strange friendship you'll take him away from here and trouble me no more with this."

"Father Time, I know you value your privacy and I'd have never come to you if I felt I had another choice, but you're our best bet at solving this riddle. This boy can mean life or death for all humanity, including the vampires. I need you, Father Time, most gifted of the Seers," Rogue pleaded.

Hearing the name of his vampire coven struck a chord in Father Time. Since the vision he'd seen during the last war of the vampire covens, he'd been in hiding, waiting for the end as he had seen it. But it hadn't always been like that for Father Time. He was once a proud warrior and powerful psychic.

Father Time looked at Rogue. "After I do this thing for you, our business is concluded."

"I understand." Rogue nodded. "Gabriel, give him your hands."

Gabriel looked hesitant, but when Rogue assured him that it was safe he stepped forward and extended his hands. Father Time skittered back so fast that he crashed into a pile of rubble, sending a dust cloud up.

"No, no. I dare not touch this one directly. Something personal to him will work just fine," Father Time explained.

Gabriel was patting himself in search of something to give the strange vampire when his fingers brushed against his necklace. It was a simple wooden fang at the end of a leather cord, but it was one of his most prized possessions. It had been his father's when he was a boy and Redfeather had passed it on to Gabriel when he came to stay with him. Gabriel took the necklace off and placed it into Father Time's withered hand.

Rogue and Gabriel watched the vampire as he crouched

over the carving and studied it like a child would an in-
sect trapped under a glass. He rolled the carving back and
forth on the ground, muttering to himself and scratching
at whatever had made a nest in his beard. Rogue was beginning to wonder if Father Time was even seeing anything when the vampire suddenly went stiff. Father Time's
eyes went wild and he began to shout.

"You foolhardy boy, what have you brought into the
world?" Father Time moved so fast that Rogue didn't
even realize the vampire had gotten off the floor until he
bumped past him to get to Gabriel. The two went crashing to the ground, with Father Time landing on top of the
struggling Gabriel. "You've damned us all!" Father Time
rained spittle on Gabriel.

Rogue grabbed the vampire roughly by the collar and
slung him across the room. "You really must've taken
leave of your senses to attack someone who is under my
protection." Rogue pulled both revolvers and placed them
to Father Time's eyes. "I know your eyes would eventually regenerate, but it might be kinda fun watching you
try to catch rats blind." He pulled the hammers back with
his thumbs.

"Do what you will, Rogue. The boy has already en-
sured that we will all burn in the flame for what he has
awakened. Tonight I heard the screams of God's faithful
as the walls of their mighty house shook under steel and
magic. The blood of the Hunter is the prize and the servants of the underworld are quite thirsty," Father Time
told them.

"You'd better start making some sense, Father Time."
Rogue pushed the barrels into Father Time's eyes, causing them to tear. Trails of crimson rolled down his face
and dotted his beard.

"Use your eyes, Rogue, and see him for who he really
is." Father Time pointed a gnarled finger at Gabriel. "The

boy is twice damned for falling into the favor of the Nimrod and its one true master. Through him, the Bishop will have his revenge and all humanity is expendable."

"How do we stop the Bishop?" Rogue put his guns away.

"You can't. Even now I look at him and see the Bishop's mocking sneer. The end is coming and it is he who will bring it about." Father Time's head suddenly whipped up. "Even now darkness swallows the moon."

Rogue thought that the statement was another one of Father Time's riddles until he looked out one of the boarded windows and realized that he couldn't see the moon. Not only had the moon vanished, but so had the sky and everything else outside. The entire building was wrapped in darkness. "Talk about fucking persistence." Rogue whipped his revolvers back and forth, looking for a target.

CHAPTER TWENTY-NINE

When they pulled off the FDR it started drizzling, blanketing the ground in a light mist. The Hummer rumbled through the quiet streets, with the occupants of the car equally as quiet. De Mona sat in the second row with Jackson, pondering all that had happened that night. Ever since the trident had come into her life people had been dying: her father, Akbar, Angelo, and possibly Gabriel. She felt bad that she'd brought the thing to him instead of just burying it in the deepest hole she could dig. It wouldn't have brought her father back, but it might've saved the lives of those people. De Mona vowed that she would do whatever it took to help them find the trident and then she would see it destroyed.

Redfeather sat alone in the third row, peering at Finnious and the body of Brother Angelo. The High Brother looked more like a mummified corpse than the intelligent and powerful spirit whom Redfeather had traded words with just a few hours prior. With the spark gone, Angelo's body had succumbed to its natural aging process. The young wraith looked rattled, occasionally casting a sad glance at Angelo's body. Finnious had managed to keep his body solid enough to keep from falling out of the Hummer, but his color was still faint. In the center of his ghostly form a tiny spark burned.

The others were confused about what had transpired between the High Brother and the wraith, but only Redfeather had an idea of what the exchange had been about. The wraith being in possession of the Core didn't bode well for the current situation or the Order of Sanctuary.

"I hate the rain," De Mona said, staring out the window absently.

Jackson shrugged. "Could be worse; we could all be dead."

"True." She smiled. "That reminds me: we never got a chance to thank you guys for saving us. How'd you even know what was going down?"

"Because we've been following you," Morgan said from behind the wheel. He looked in the rearview mirror and saw the look of distrust in De Mona's eyes, so he clarified. "We've been keeping tabs on the shithead uprisings in the city over the last week or so, trying to figure out what they were up to. The ones you slew near the college led us to you."

"At first we didn't know which side you were on, which is why we didn't butt in until the attack at the brownstone," Jackson added. "What did those things want with you?" De Mona wouldn't meet his gaze. Jackson leaned forward so that she could see the seriousness in his eyes. "Don't clam up on me now, sis; we almost got our asses tore out in there, so I think it's only fair that you tell us why?"

"They were looking for my grandson and the vile thing that is trying to gain a hold over his soul, the Nimrod," Redfeather said heatedly.

This got Morgan's attention. "I always thought that was just a myth?" Morgan said over his shoulder.

"Myths don't generally get people killed," De Mona said.

Jackson unsheathed and retracted one of his blades. "That all depends on who you ask."

"No, my friend, it's real. Real and loose somewhere in New York City," Redfeather said.

"You getting this, Jonas?" Morgan asked into his earpiece.

"*Yeah, and cross-searching it against the database,*" the static-filled response came through.

"Who the hell is Jonas?" De Mona questioned.

"A friend," Jackson said, not bothering to elaborate. They still didn't know how far they could trust the demon or her mortal companion.

"Being that we're sharing information, what are your stories?" She looked from Morgan to Jackson.

"Me, I was a victim of the ghetto," Jackson joked.

Morgan was more serious with his reply: "Like the rest of you, we have been touched by the forces of hell one way or another. Jackson," he nodded at his companion, "was carved up and left to die, by some nasty little bastards that are no longer amongst us."

De Mona leaned forward and rested her arms on the backrests of the front seats. Morgan's eyes twitched uncomfortably, so she leaned in closer. "And you, what's your story?"

"I don't have one," he said, trying to focus on the road. His fist gripped the wheel so tight that his knuckles were starting to turn white.

"Bullshit." De Mona took in his tangy odor. "Even if it weren't for the fancy hammer, I'd know one of my own."

"I'm not one of yours, girlie. There are no more of my kind; the war saw to that," he said with his voice laced with emotion.

"Morgan's people are descendants of the elementals." Jackson picked up for his friend. "When the nine lords decided to cut up again they reached out to the elementals.

Some threw in with their lot, but the ones that didn't were hunted and destroyed."

"Cassie was the last of us." Morgan took over the story. "My sweet little Cassie, who had never harmed a soul in her life, butchered like cattle just before her mother was cut down. I lay there, helpless, while my family was punished for the blood in my veins and the thing in my possession." He picked up the hammer and tested its weight. "It had been in my family since its creation, a gift for our services and faith. The dark forces came looking for it, and I gave it to them over and over," he said, recalling the bloody rampage he had gone on in the name of his family.

"I'm sorry," De Mona said, feeling a bit ashamed for prying.

"It's not your fault, child. There were no Valkrin present during the slaughter, and the things responsible . . . I would not even do them the service of speaking their cursed names aloud. I thought killing those things would help to fill the void my wife and child left, but it hasn't; all it does is make me angrier. So I continue, casting those I encounter back to the pit, and their mortal servants," he tossed the hammer up and caught it easily, "they find not so pleasant ends."

"Then your ancestors fought during the siege?" Redfeather asked.

"Maybe they did, or maybe one of my drunken great-kin stole it. The story of my people has been so stretched over the years I don't think any of us could tell you accurately. I just know that it has always been the job of the eldest son to keep the hammer."

Redfeather absently stroked his beard as a theory began to develop in his head. "The Nimrod and the hammer appearing in the same city in the midst of a demon uprising is a little too convenient to be a coincidence."

"What are you on about, old-timer?" Jackson asked.

"A gathering," Redfeather said. He unfolded a sheet of paper that he'd placed in his pocket before making the first trip to Sanctuary. "It's said that before the first siege a gathering was called. The cardinals went to all the provinces in the world to gather the pure-of-heart souls who would be the Knights."

"Man, I can't buy into all this shit. I ain't never been no savior of anybody but myself, and my heart sure as hell ain't pure," Jackson said.

"And correct me if I'm wrong, but didn't the Knights fight against the demons, not with them?" De Mona pointed out.

"Not true." Redfeather scanned the page before flipping it over and reading from the other side. "The Ghelgath came, the Weres, and even some of the elementals."

"We aren't demons," Morgan challenged.

"Nor are you human, my friend. For the weapons to have stayed parted all this time only to come together in the wake of a demon uprising . . . it's too perfect of a fit to ignore."

"So, say we are these mythic warriors from yesteryear, where's this great general who will unite our powers?" De Mona questioned. "No disrespect, man, but Gabriel didn't strike me as much of a hero."

"There's a little hero hiding in the most unlikely of us." Morgan patted Jackson on the shoulder.

"Sanctuary," Fin whispered from the back. He was still kneeling at Brother Angelo's side but appeared to be gaining substance. Just ahead of them was Sanctuary.

The building was as it had been when they'd left, but it looked to be losing its luster. The rain was coming down heavier now, and the front steps were almost covered in mist. Standing in front of the structure were members of the Inquisition. The brothers were dressed in full armor and carrying automatic weapons. Lydia stood in the doorway whispering frantically into the ear of a man dressed in priest's robes. He looked to be slightly older than Gabriel, and there was a worried expression on his face.

"I'll get the body," Morgan offered, after putting the Hummer in park.

"No, the brothers will attend to him. It's their right," Fin said, sliding from the SUV. No sooner had his tattered sneakers hit the pavement than Lydia was down the steps and at his side.

"Oh, Fin, what were you thinking, running off like that?" She ran her hands over his body and then his face to see if he'd been harmed. Lydia's face slacked and she held him at arm's length. Though she couldn't see the radiant glow about him, she could feel the power creeping up his arms. "What's happened to you?"

Fin gave her a lazy smile. "He asked me to keep it, Lydia. I didn't want it, but he made me promise." With that he collapsed into her arms.

"Fin?" She shook him, but he didn't stir. "What's happened to him?"

"I fear it's the spark." Redfeather stepped up. "Just before he died, Brother Angelo passed something to Finnious, and if I'm right he now carries the Core of this Great House."

"What do you mean, the High Brother has entrusted the spark to a wraith? The soulless creature can't even carry it," the man in the priest's robes said, disregarding whether Fin could hear him or not.

Lydia's head whipped back and forth, trying to pick up signs of her surrogate family. "Where are Angelo and Akbar?"

"We lost them in the battle," Morgan said.

"Who are you? What's happened to our people?" the brown-haired man in the priest's robes questioned them.

"It's like the man said: we lost them in the scuffle." Jackson stepped up. He didn't like how the priest was coming at them, and made no secret of it. "We can explain all of that once we get off the streets. There are still some things out there looking to finish what they started, so why don't you cut the bullshit and let us in."

Anger flashed across the priest's eyes. He drew the short sword that he carried on his belt and faced Jackson. "How dare you speak to a brother of the order in such a way? I could have you disciplined for this!"

"If you don't put that knife away you ain't gonna do shit but bleed." De Mona stood beside Jackson. Her claws hadn't extended yet but were ready at a moment's notice. She and Jackson made brief eye contact and there was an unspoken agreement. "We've been through a lot tonight, probably more than most could handle in a lifetime." She glanced at the Hummer, where the Inquisitors were collecting Angelo's remains. "There's been enough bloodshed."

"Please, Brother David," Lydia pleaded as one of the Inquisitors took Fin's limp body from her.

Brother David scowled at the tired bunch for a moment before bidding them to follow him. "We will speak of this more inside." He stormed up the stairs with the group in tow. Everyone was so preoccupied with the death of Brother Angelo and the transformation of Fin that no one seemed to notice how thick the fog had gotten.

CHAPTER THIRTY

"God, I hate the rain," Sulin said, turning off the Prospect Park Loop. The sky had been clear when they set out, but by the time they'd exited the Brooklyn Bridge it had started storming. "Where did this damn monsoon come from?"

Lucy stuck her hand out the window and let the raindrops fill her hand. The rain was surprisingly chilly, far colder than it was outside. "Flash flood?"

Sulin looked over at her. "In a perfect world, yes, but you and I know that neither of the worlds we live in is perfect."

"You think it's rogue magic?" Lucy asked.

Sulin looked up through her soaked windshield. "I don't think so; there's no source to it. It's like it's coming from everywhere and nowhere, typical of Mother Nature."

Lucy flinched as lightning cracked overhead. She stroked Tiki's head. "I don't like it, Sulin. It doesn't feel right."

"Goddess, I didn't realize you were so paranoid, Lucy." Sulin laughed. "The freakish rain is probably because we're getting close to Sanctuary. I didn't recognize it from the address Angelique sent me, but I'd know this area anywhere."

Lucy tried to muster a smile to spite her mounting

dread. "Who would've thought that the Ellis Island of the demon world would have a park-side view?" Lucy examined her surroundings as Sulin pulled up in front of the building. She couldn't help but think how odd it was that the fog seemed to be concentrated on that block.

"Prime real estate," Sulin said, sliding from the car and retrieving her dog. The Pom squirmed in Sulin's arms, agitated by something about the building. "What's the matter, boy? The haunted house got you spooked?" Sulin kissed the top of his fuzzy head. "Don't worry; we'll be in and out in no time."

"I don't blame him for being spooked; this place stinks of black magic." Lucy put her hand over her nose. "I don't know how long I wanna be here, Sulin."

"Quit your bitching, Lucy; this isn't going to take that long. Angelique didn't say what was going on, but she seemed sure that I could handle it until she got here."

"Wait; you didn't tell me that Angelique was coming here." Lucy stopped in her tracks.

"Lucy, stop being so catty. By the time Angelique gets here I'll have fixed whatever is wrong and you can take credit for helping me. Goddess knows you need to score as many points with the White Queen as possible."

"Sulin, remind me never to come on a call with you again." Lucy followed Sulin up the walkway to Sanctuary. The moment Lucy's foot touched the sacred grounds she felt a chill. "Couldn't they have called a priest to perform the exorcism?"

"It's not an exorcism, silly ass. They needed a healer, so naturally they had Angelique send her best," Sulin boasted.

"Whatever." Lucy folded her arms. "Just do what you came to do so we can get out of here." Lucy stood off to the side while Sulin knocked on the door. While they waited for someone to answer, Lucy busied herself watching the slow-rolling fog. From where they were standing at the top of the steps she had lost sight of the street below as well as the car. Lucy turned to mention it to Sulin when something wet splashed on her face.

Sulin's perfectly bowed lips curled back into a sneer while the Pom wiggled in her unyielding clutch. A thick red line appeared at the base of her pale throat. The blood came slowly at first, but as she sank to her knees it began to flow steadily. Sulin's body disappeared into the fog, leaving nothing but the yapping dog to mark her passing.

Lucy's magic shields went up without her having to call on them as the fog began to thicken. She backed up against the building, whipping her head back and forth, trying to see who or what had killed Sulin, but it was too thick. Lucy's eyes picked out a blur of motion, but before she could figure out what it was everything went black.

Flag stood dressed in a red robe, marked with the symbols of his house. Flanking him were two young witches of blond and brunette hair. Unlike Flag, they couldn't hide their fear of being so deep within the Iron Mountains. Had he had more time he'd have sought more experienced assistants for the spell, but it was roughly three hours to sunrise, so time was not a luxury they could afford. It would take three casters to work the spell, so they would have to do.

"Move you, dog. Put your back into it!" Orden barked as he made his way up the hill, followed by a troupe of goblins, armed with everything from swords to clubs. His muscular arms cracked a leather whip against a goblin who was just a hair shorter than a one-story house. "If you want your pound of flesh then you'll move your worthless hide!" Orden continued his abuse.

The goblin howled and pulled harder on the chains that were harnessed to his back. At the end of the chains there was a cannon on a wooden cart. The cannon was the size of a missile launcher and painted to resemble a striking serpent.

"Ready the gateway, mage, we have feasting to do," Orden ordered Flag.

Instead of answering Orden, Flag turned towards the witches who had already started the spell. The large circle painted against the brick began to glow faintly. The crossing spell they were about to cast was one of the most dangerous and most complex of the travel spells, and it became more so when you tried to use it to cross between realms, which was why it was outlawed by all circles of magic. The ban meant nothing to Titus, though, when it came to pleasing his master, so he ordered Flag to perform it.

Already the witches looked worn and one was even bleeding from her ears, but they couldn't break the connection, which was why Flag had them start the spell. The more of your power you added for the spell to feed on, the more likely you were to be consumed by it. Flag wanted to add as little of himself as possible, but he knew his magic would be needed to complete it. When Flag added his own magic to the mix the circle grew brighter and a fog appeared out of nowhere, which spilled into the circle. Through the fog they could see what looked like a building, bearing two crosses at the entrance. On the steps stood two young women.

"The tender flesh of witches will be even sweeter than that of the Inquisition." Orden drew a large curved blade from the skimmer on his back. "Illini, let the first taste be yours," he told his captain.

"It will be a pleasure." Illini charged through the circle and disappeared in the fog.

Orden turned to the rest of his troops. "To arms, my brothers, and let the blood of our enemies taste like the sweetest wine as we gnaw at their bones in the Great Hall." Orden led his goblins through the portal.

The spell had drained the witches to the point where they looked like old hags, kneeling in the thrall of power. They looked at Flag with pleading eyes, but he ignored them while he addressed the goblins who remained: "Wait until I'm through the portal and then you're welcome to them." Flag motioned to the helpless witches. Before he'd even stepped out the other side he could hear the screams of the witches and the tearing of flesh.

CHAPTER THIRTY-ONE

"Poor Angelo." Lydia sobbed over the High Brother's body, which was laid out in the chapel of Sanctuary. "He was so good to us, him and Akbar."

"They died well." Morgan placed a consoling hand on her shoulder. "Tonight I watched these men stare down the forces of hell and spit in their faces. It was an honor to fight beside them."

"Honor?" This was a young man wearing the robes of the Inquisition but carrying a sword, which he couldn't seem to stop fumbling with. His long, colorless hair blew in the breeze as he paced the chapel, occasionally turning his blue eyes on the strangers. "The honor of everyone here, except those who are a part of this house, is in question. There is still much to discuss, including the fate of two men whom I've known all my life."

"They're gone, Julius," Lydia said over her shoulder.

"So I keep hearing. But what I'm not hearing is what happened." Julius stepped closer to the body. His trained eyes were already searching for signs of the magic he knew Angelo carried within him. When there was no sign of it in the body, Julius studied everyone in the room. When he got to Fin, Julius' eyes suddenly widened as he noticed the tiny spark flashing in Fin's gut.

"Brother Angelo and Akbar left here with a team to

retrieve the Nimrod and were ambushed by a troop of Stalkers." Lydia recounted what she knew of the mission, in addition to what Fin had told her.

"Is this true? Has the Nimrod responded to your grandson?" Julius addressed Redfeather.

Redfeather nodded. "Yes, the Nimrod had bound itself to my grandson and stirred the forces of hell. We fought as best we could against the demons but were overrun. Had it not been for these two brave souls, we'd have become victims of the dark lord." He pointed at Morgan and Jackson.

"Yes, you two." Julius approached them. His hand rested on the hilt of his blade when he spoke. "How is it that you happened upon all this so conveniently?"

"As I've already explained, we've been following De Mona and Gabriel since the Nimrod first manifested in Manhattan. Until the demons attacked them we weren't sure which side they were fighting on," Morgan said. Though he seemed unmoved by Julius, Jackson fidgeted.

Julius looked to Brother David. "And what do you make of their story, priest?"

Brother David looked up, the worried expression still on his face. "The wraith confirms what they've told us, and so have our people on the street." He placed his head in his hands. "I can't believe Angelo is gone."

Julius took David by the jaw and raised his head so that they were eye to eye. The black irises of Julius' eyes seemed to expand when he spoke. "Save your tears for when we celebrate the execution of Angelo's murderer, and all his accomplices." He gave the guest a quick glance, then turned back to David, who was trying his best to keep from becoming hysterical. He knew that he was technically the next in line for the position of High Brother and didn't look forward to holding the position if they were approaching a time of war.

"And the spark?" Julius asked, already knowing the answer to the question but not quite sure how to change it.

"He gave it to the Halfling." Brother David pointed at Fin, who had paused his sipping at the sound of him being drawn into the conversation.

Julius released David's face and started towards Fin. His sword clanged against his leg as he closed the distance. He knelt before the wraith and spoke in a voice that was colder than an Arctic winter. "Is it true, Finnious? Has Angelo entrusted the spark to you?"

Fin's eyes got wide and he crept back in the cushioned chair. "I don't know what happened in there; I just know that I didn't ask for it."

"But how can this be? One without a soul cannot carry the life force of our order." A little of the authority had returned to Brother David's voice.

Julius gave Brother David a look of disgust before turning back to the nervous little man. When Julius spoke, his words were directed at David, but his eyes remained on Finnious. "Have you been so far removed by your ambitions of becoming High Brother that you've forgotten the story of one our closest childhood friends?" He touched Fin's cheek and his fingers were like ice against his skin. There was love in Julius' voice, but his eyes were scornful. "Fin is the oddity amongst oddities, aren't you?" The wraith got off the couch and went to stand beside Lydia.

"Even in adulthood you still carry the cruel qualities of a child, Julius." Lydia hugged Fin to her. "Fin," she turned to where she knew their guests were standing, "is no oddity or abomination, regardless of the feelings your curiosities may have created. He is a blessing to the order and the world, a miracle of life and death."

"More aptly put, Finnious is a mutation. The child of a life-giving forest nymph and the scourge of the dead lands," Julius said.

"Morbius," Redfeather gasped. "Impossible, a spirit cannot procreate with a living being; genetically it can't happen."

"But Finnious is proof that it can," Julius pointed out. "Though his mother never spoke of what happened to her, the traits are apparent in the little one and only Morbius is powerful enough to dominate both flesh and spirit."

"Lies," Finnious hissed at Julius. Finnious' mixed lineage was known amongst the order, but his mother never spoke of his father's identity, only that he was one of the spirits. Some speculated that only Morbius was powerful enough to accomplish such a thing, but it was never proven.

"Regardless of who your parents were, it doesn't change the fact of what you are, little brother," Julius said. "The question we are faced with now is how to part the spark from you."

"The only way for the spark and its host to be parted is death," Brother David said, with an edge to his voice that didn't carry over well with the others.

"Don't touch him." Lydia shielded Fin with her body. She pointed her staff in the direction of Brother David. "You won't be experimenting on Finnious, spark or not."

"What's the deal with this spark?" Jackson asked.

"The spark and the High Brother who held it were the foundation of this very house. Without the spark, the magic will fade and this chapter of the order will be undone," Redfeather answered.

"So you mean that thing that Angelo put inside Fin is the only thing holding this place together?" De Mona looked around nervously, as if the house would collapse on her.

"Not just the building, Valkrin, but the very magic that protects us," Julius said. "Even now the light from our Great Hall dims." He motioned towards the flickering candles that lit the house.

There was a soft knock on the door.

"That should be the witch healer. She can assist us with the removal of the spark from the wraith," Brother David said.

"You'll do no such thing. Finnious will die if the spark has bound itself too closely to him," Lydia said.

Brother David's eyes were serious now. "The death of one for the life of millions is more than an even exchange."

"What kind of animals are you people? He is a living creature." Redfeather looked from the priest to the captain pleadingly.

"He is a member of this Great House, and like the rest of us has taken the oath to put this order before all, even his own life," Julius said sternly.

"It is decided: the wraith will relinquish the spark," Brother David said finally, heading for the door. Two of the Inquisitors followed, while the rest stayed behind with Julius and the guests.

"Man, this shit is beyond greasy." Jackson got to his feet. One of the Inquisitors moved with him, training his gun on Jackson. "Y'all keep pointing those things at me and I might take it the wrong way."

Julius waved the Inquisitor back, easing some of the tension but not much. "Good people, we are beyond thankful for what you've done so far in helping us to further our efforts, but if you really want to help I suggest you do not interfere. This is the business of the order."

"What kind of order slaughters its own?" Morgan asked.

"Man, I ain't buying into this shit." Jackson unsheathed his blades. The Inquisitors moved to surround him, but he didn't back down. "We tore ass through a small army of shitheads to watch you wax this little dude. I can't sit by for it."

"You don't have a choice." Julius drew his sword.

"I think he does." Morgan stepped up. The tension in the air was so thick that you could barely breathe. The newly formed Knights faced off against an order that had been around longer than any of them had been alive. Magical energy crackled through the air as the threat of violence lingered, but it was all brought to an abrupt halt when the second floor exploded in a ball of flame.

CHAPTER THIRTY-TWO

"Surely you didn't think you could evade me that easily, especially after I'd tasted the young one." Moses descended from the ceiling, supported by webs of shadow. More uniformed officers came in through all entrances of the building, holding automatic weapons.

Rogue stood between Gabriel and the demon, with his guns ready. "What, did the NYPD have a fire sale on these guys or something?"

"The dark lord has many allies." Moses touched the ground soundlessly. The web of shadows snaked throughout the room, sealing all possible exits. This time there would be no escape. Father Time tried to bolt, but a shadow caught up about his ankles and held him upside down. The shadows carried Father Time to Moses and held the struggling vampire in front of him. "So, even the vampires defy the dark lord these nights, do they?"

Father Time gave Moses a very sane smile. "What is to pass will pass."

"Indeed," Moses said before commanding the shadows to rip Father Time's head off. The thousand-year-old vampire was dust before he hit the ground.

"He wasn't a part of this!" Rogue shouted, watching the wind take away what was left of his old friend.

"It matters not what he was, mage. Now he's a passenger on the *Jihad*, and unless you wish to join him, I suggest you stand aside while I claim my prize," Moses told Rogue.

"I got your prize, demon!" Rogue blasted away with the two revolvers. The first bullet struck Moses in the stomach, but he had melted into shadow before the rest could connect. An officer tried to play hero and was rewarded by being shot in the face. His body sailed backward and crashed into the other officers.

The officers returned fire, barely missing Rogue as he darted across the room. He managed to lay low two of the officers in his passing, but they were still coming. He knew that in such closed quarters he didn't have much of a chance against the shadows, so he needed to take the fight outside. As if in answer to his prayers, one of the shadows grabbed him by the head and hurled him through one of the boarded-up windows.

Gabriel dove behind some boxes just as the police officers cut loose with a barrage of bullets. He tried to move to a better cover position but was tripped up by shadows. Gabriel raised his arm to call the Nimrod to him, but a band of shadow bound his wrists above his head and lifted him off the ground. He watched helplessly as Moses oozed up from the shadows and closed in on him.

"Unlike Riel, I came prepared for the Bishop's trickery." Moses thrust his hand out, slammed Gabriel into a wall and then bounced him roughly off the ground and into a corner. Moses called the shadows back, dragging Gabriel with them. His face was bloody and he looked out of it. "Tonight, I present your head and your weapon to the favorite son."

"Sorry, this one is already spoken for," Asha said from her perch on the catwalk. The air around her crackled with magic as her hands began to glow.

Moses immediately recognized the signature black and gold threads tainting her magical energy. "As I told your sisters, this is no business of yours."

"I'm afraid it is. The dark forces aren't the only ones with an interest in the young man you're trying to kill." She bounded gracefully down from her perch and stood a safe distance from the shadow master. She'd seen enough of his tricks to not risk getting too close.

Moses looked at her with an amused grin. "Very well then." He turned to one of his officers, who was carrying a shotgun. "Kill this bitch and then come help me with what's left of the Knight."

"With pleasure." The officer raised the shotgun and pulled the trigger.

Asha's nimble hands traced a symbol in the air and raised an invisible barrier just as the shotgun pellets reached her. The ball bearings smacked against the barrier and dropped harmlessly to the ground. She produced a sharp silver disc from a compartment of her leather vest and hurled it at the officer. It spun in a wide arch, opening up a gash in his shoulder, before returning to Asha.

The officer examined the cut on his arm and frowned at her. "It's gonna take more than a little to save your little ass, sweetheart," he told her.

Asha raised the disc above her head and let the officer's blood run freely down her wrist and arm. "Sometimes a little bit goes a long way." She invoked her power and her bloody hand began to glow. "Come on, big daddy. Bleed for Mama."

At first there was nothing, but then the officer felt the tingling in his arm. The tingling increased to a throb and eventually an intense burning. To his surprise the blood began to flow freely down his arm. He tried to place a hand over it to stop the blood, but it only increased the flow. Soon he had lost so much blood that he couldn't stand. Blood pooled at the feet of the other officers as their partner bled to death before their eyes.

"If you get out now, this won't have to get ugly," Asha warned.

An officer holding a small black machine gun stepped out. "You little black bitch, I'm gonna air you out for what you did to Sarg!"

Asha frowned at his racist comment. She rubbed the remaining blood together in her palms until both her hands were red and slick. She could feel the dead officer's energy seeping into her hands, and she savored it. The blood on her hands glowed brilliantly. "I gave you a chance to leave, but now you can't." Her voice was heavy with power.

The officers tried to raise their guns, but she was already on them. Asha gracefully dodged their kicks and punches, laying a bloody palm on each of them as she passed. By the time the officers were able to get a handle on things, Asha was standing on the other side of the room. There was something about the unnatural sparkle in her eyes that made them afraid, and they were right to fear the young orphan.

Using the blood, she traced a rune on the floor and laid her hand over it to give it power. "As it was with the people of my mother, and her mother's mother, the blood is the essence of life and death. Gentlemen, I give you the latter: die!" The word struck each officer like a massive heart attack as the blood magic of Asha's ancestors did its work. One by one they fell over, bleeding from every hole in their bodies, dying slowly and painfully. Asha could've ended it quickly, but she wanted them to suffer.

"Pitiful," Moses said as he approached the dazed Gabriel. Moses could feel the power coming from the young man and it made him giddy. He had been ordered to capture the boy for the dark forces, but Moses had his own plans. A tendril detached itself from the band holding Gabriel and gently raised the arm of Gabriel's overcoat.

When Moses saw the living tattoo his eyes grew wide. "What trickery is this?" Moses demanded. When Gabriel didn't answer, Moses slammed him violently against the wall. Moses leaned in so close that their noses were almost touching. "You wear the mark, but you are no vessel. Riel is a liar and a fool."

A small sound escaped Gabriel. At first Moses thought Gabriel was sobbing, but as it got louder Moses realized it was laughter. He tried to snap the young man's neck with the shadow, only to have it dissolve in a crackle of lightning. "It is you who are the fool," Gabriel said in an all-too-calm voice. As if by magic the trident appeared in his hand, pulsing violently.

Moses recoiled in horror when he saw the storm cloud in Gabriel's eyes. "The Bishop has returned?" Moses backpedaled.

"And with him comes the Storm." Gabriel pointed the trident and unleashed its fury.

Asha barely avoided Moses' body when it went sailing across the warehouse and smacked into a wall. One side of his face was badly burned, and there was a gaping hole in his chest. Tendrils of shadow flailed wildly from the demon's wounds. Gabriel stepped through the wreckage, gripping the Nimrod. An officer who wasn't quite dead clutched at Gabriel's pant leg. He gave the officer an emotionless stare before crushing his jaw with the heel of his sneaker.

"All I wanted to do was find my grandfather." He blasted the demon's writhing form with a bolt of lightning from the head of the trident. "I didn't ask for this thing to come to me." He hit the demon again, knocking him into another wall. "I didn't ask for any of this!" Gabriel threw the trident with everything he had. The twin points barely missed Moses' jaw as they lodged themselves in the wall, pinning him around the throat.

"Kid, we gotta get outta here." Asha grabbed Gabriel by the arm. He turned to her and just stared as if she were speaking a foreign language. "Man, are you hearing me?" Something rolled against Asha's foot, drawing her attention. It was a black tubular object, with a flashing red light on top of it. She looked over at the pile of officers, and the one who had called her a black bitch was smiling. When he gave her the middle finger she saw the small silver ring dangling from the object and realized what it was.

"Fuck!" was all she was able to blurt out just before the room was engulfed in flames.

CHAPTER THIRTY-THREE

Rogue found himself lying facedown on the concrete, across the street from the boarded-up building. When he tried to get up, he felt something shift at his side that stole his breath. He looked down and saw a shard of wood jutting from his ribs. Moving to a sitting position, he removed the wood and examined the wound. The wood had pierced his skin, just below his body armor. The wound was small, but it was deep. It would need medical attention, but he had bigger problems.

Rogue patched the wound with a bit of shadow and headed back for the warehouse. From the inside he could hear the cries of battle and gunfire. When Rogue got within three feet of the building he heard the sound of thunder and a bloodcurdling scream. He smiled, knowing that Gabriel was holding his own against the shadow demon, but the smile was wiped from Rogue's face when an explosion rocked the building.

The night sky was lit up like a summer afternoon, with glass and flaming embers raining all over the block. Rogue managed to dive out of the way just as something heavy slammed into the ground. It landed so hard that he thought it was a kitchen appliance, but when he looked it was a person . . . two people actually.

Asha had managed to erect another magical barrier

just before the grenade went off. It absorbed most of the blast but still didn't save her and Gabriel from being sent flying through the side of the wall. She was knocked senseless, but he was already getting back to his feet, holding the Nimrod.

"Are you okay?" Rogue asked Gabriel.

Gabriel checked himself. His clothes were scorched and he had a massive headache coming on, but he was otherwise unharmed. "I don't think anything is broken."

"Speak for yourself." Asha groaned. She tried to stand but found it difficult. Rogue helped her to her feet but kept his gun trained on her. "Is this how you treat everybody who saves your ass?"

"It's not often I find my ass in need of saving. Who are you and what are you doing here?" Rogue eyed her suspiciously.

Asha batted her eyes at him. "My name is Asha. I like long walks in the park and candlelit dinners," she said sarcastically. "Dude, we've got a building full of dead cops and a pissed-off shadow demon on our hands. How about we save the questions for when we're out of here, huh?"

A ghostly wail pierced the night, drawing all their attention back to the warehouse. A massive blob of shadow oozed from the side of the ruined building. The blob detached itself and went airborne, reshaping itself into a bird of prey made completely from shadow. The only signs of its host were the blue eyes staring maliciously at the trio.

"That is not good," Asha said, looking up at the shadow creature.

"I think a spell would be more useful coming out of your mouth than stating the obvious, kid." Rogue drew the revolver from the left and opened fire on the shadow creature. The enchanted bullets tore holes in its frame, but the shadows quickly filled them. The creature roared something at Rogue before striking with its talons. Rogue dove to one side and countered with a hard right to the side of the creature's head, but his gloved hand passed right through the shadowy form. A massive wing slammed into Rogue's back, sending him flying. Before he could right himself, the shadow's claws tore through his coat and struck his body armor. Rogue slipped a small vial from his pocket and spun on the creature, chanting a spell as he did so. The vial shattered on the shadow and the liquid inside exploded in a bright blue burst.

With the Nimrod flaring, Gabriel charged the shadow creature. The Nimrod ripped a hole in the beast's chest, spraying shadow all over the street. The shadow creature howled and took to the air, circling back for Gabriel with its talons bared. Gabriel dodged the strike and lopped off one of its wings. The shadow beast crashed awkwardly into a parked car, setting off the alarm. Its eyes flashed rage as it charged full speed at the young man.

Asha had composed herself enough to work another barrier spell. The creature crashed into it headfirst, shattering the barrier but throwing itself off balance. Asha quickly slashed the palms of her hands with her thumb rings, spilling blood down her palms and wrists. She flicked the blood onto the creature and stepped back. With her bloodied hands raised she uttered a single word: "Burn." The shadow beast's body was engulfed in crimson flames, sending it into a panic.

"Run!" Rogue shouted to Asha and Gabriel. With their combined powers they could slow the creature, but Rogue knew they weren't properly armed to destroy it.

Asha and Gabriel took off after Rogue, with the screams of the shadow beast in their ears. The voice in the back of Gabriel's mind urged him to stand and fight, but he wasn't listening. He saw Asha sprint out to his right and Rogue sprint to the left. They'd almost reached the corner when Rogue was lifted off his feet. Gabriel turned around and saw that the beast had grown another wing and was making off with his only chance at finding his grandfather.

"Wait," Gabriel called after Asha.

"Wait my ass; we gotta get outta here before that thing comes in for seconds," Asha said.

"Asha, I can't just leave him like that."

Asha looked at him to see if he was serious, and as she feared, he was. She could've left the young hero to it and saved her own ass, but she still needed to bring him and the Nimrod back to Dutch. Her mind told her to come back and retrieve the thing from Gabriel's corpse, but there was no guarantee that it would still be there. Grudgingly she agreed and they ran off after the creature.

Rogue felt like his ribs were being crushed as the creature tightened its grip. He tried to bring the enchanted revolver around, but a strand of shadow knocked the gun away. With a screech, the creature bit into Rogue's collar. The pain was so intense that he couldn't even compose himself enough to think of a spell that might help him. There was only one thing for him to do if there was going to be even a remote chance of survival, but he wouldn't do it unless he absolutely had to, and from the way things were looking, he did. Rogue was just about to call the change when something slammed into the shadow beast. The beast howled and released Rogue, drawing a sigh of both relief and dread from the mage. One the one hand, he was free, but on the other, the beast had released him five stories above the ground.

Rogue tried to use his own shadow tendrils to stop his fall, but he was weak from the loss of blood, so his descent was only slowed. Rogue bounced off the hood of a minivan and crashed into the street. Most of his body was numb, and the parts of him that weren't numb were in

intense pain. Through blurred vision he saw the boy and
the young witch attack the shadow beast. They were a
powerful duo, but Rogue knew they didn't stand a chance
against the demon. Seeing no other option, Rogue called
to the demon within him.

Gabriel welcomed the trident when it reappeared in his
hand. The shadow beast was now flying in an awkward
pattern, wounded from the trident. The smell of death in
the air spurred Gabriel to action as he took off to engage
the wounded demon. He was about to plunge the trident
into the wounded creature's underbelly when bands of
shadow slithered from the ground and bound his legs. He
raised the trident to cut himself free, and it too was
wrapped in shadow. The shadow ripped the trident from
Gabriel's hand and slammed him to the ground. Before
he could even scream he was mummified in shadow.

Asha cursed the overzealous young man as she
watched him get wrapped up in shadow. The relic had
probably been their best bet of making it out alive, but
he'd lost it to his heroic heart. The creature whipped tendrils of shadow out, tossing debris at Asha, which she
was able to dodge. It was badly wounded, but that didn't
make it any less dangerous. She circled the creature at
a distance with its hateful eyes watching her the whole
time. With the proper spell poised on her lips, Asha
closed in on the shadow beast.

The beast roared and rose to meet the attacking witch,
but to its surprise she split into three. The creature slashed
the duplicates, only to have those multiply. By the time
the shadow beast was able to determine which the real
Asha was, she was perched on its back holding a black
dagger. The dagger's blade was dark and smooth, reflect-
ing no light. The handle had been carved from the arm of
a mortal infant and cured in its blood. The sacrificial dagger

was the only thing Asha had left to remember her mother by and the most powerful physical weapon she had.

"Back to the shadows with you." She infused power into her words before plunging the knife into the beast's spine. The beast thrashed, knocking Asha off its back. She hit the ground in a roll, crashing into a pile of trash. She righted herself, expecting the dagger to have dissipated the black magic, only to find the creature still standing and tendrils of shadow rushing her. She raised her hands to counter, only to have them bound in shadow. The shadows pulled her roughly to the ground and dragged her towards the awaiting jaws of the winged beast.

A flash of black darted across her line of vision, and she was suddenly free from the shadow bands. The creature howled as gashes began to open up at different points on its body. When she was finally able to scramble to safety she got a glimpse of the creature's tormentor. From the shape of it she knew it was the other shadow caster, but he no longer looked human. A patch of midnight sprinkled with brilliant stars that were roughly the shape of a man stood defiantly between Asha and the shadow demon.

Rogue lunged into the air and tore into the beast with shadow claws. Pools of blackness dotted buildings and cars as Rogue slashed the shadow beast. The beast countered with fang and fury, tearing a chunk out of Rogue's shoulder. The mage expelled a wave of shadow, knocking the creature backward, and took a minute to examine the wound. At the rate the shadows were spilling from the wound he knew that he wouldn't be able to hold the form long. He had to finish it quick.

Rogue launched his shadow form into the air, turning his fists into large shadow blades. Pieces of his form were knocked away as he closed on the beast, but he would not be denied. In a double-crossing motion, Rogue severed the beast's head. The great beast reared up once, before falling to the ground, dissipating as it went. When he finally connected, it was little more than dozens of shadow splotches on the ground.

Rogue's shadow form staggered backward and came to rest on the bumper of a car. The darkness began to drip from him, exposing the haggard man beneath. His glasses and his ribs had been broken in the fight with Moses. With the protective shadow gone, blood now flowed freely from his shoulder and torso. When he tried to take a step he fell to his knees.

"Are you okay?" Gabriel rushed to his side.

"No, but I'm alive." Rogue coughed. Blood and shadow spilled from his lips when he spoke.

"Rogue, we've got to get you to a hospital." Gabriel helped him to his feet.

"I think we've got bigger problems." Asha pointed at the pools of shadow that were inching back together.

"Let him come." Gabriel powered up the Nimrod and pointed it at the pools.

"No, we might not be able to beat it again. We gotta get to the car," Rogue insisted. Gabriel and Asha were able to help him to the car. Rogue didn't look like he was in any condition to drive, but he didn't trust anybody with his baby, so he made do. The headlights landed on the shadow that was starting to take the shape of a man again. Rogue managed to muster a weak smile, just before he gunned the Viper and smashed the shadows.

"So, what's your stake in all this?" Gabriel asked Asha once they were away from the warehouse.

"What makes you think I have a stake in anything?" Asha asked as if she didn't know what he meant.

"Don't bullshit me, Asha. I didn't realize it at first, but I know you were at the Triple Six. I felt your magic." Gabriel recalled the confrontation in the alley outside the club.

"What you felt was Azuma. He's my familiar," she admitted.

"Your what?" Gabriel was confused.

"A conduit. The witches can channel power through the familiars, and vice versa," Rogue explained.

"You're awful versed in witch etiquette, mage." Asha looked directly at Rogue, letting him know that he wasn't the only one who knew things.

"Listen: let's not stray off the subject. Why are you following me, Asha?" Gabriel demanded.

"I wasn't following you, Gabriel. I was investigating the disturbance in the city and just happened to come across you in the process," Asha told him.

"So, the king and queen sent the Hunt to sniff out the Nimrod?" Rogue asked.

"Not exactly. I'm kind of conducting my own investigation. Look, the important thing is that we may be able to help each other here. Maybe the coven can come up with some clues as to what's going on. I can take the Nimrod to Dutch and—"

"Girl, I was born *at* night, not *last* night. There's no way in hell that I'm gonna let Dutch get his hands on the Nimrod. For all that, I might as well deliver it to Titus myself," Rogue said.

"And the mages would be better suited to handle it?" Asha shot back.

"Wait a second; why are you guys sitting here arguing over me like I'm a lawn tool?" Gabriel looked from Asha to Rogue. "Nobody is gonna handle anything. All I wanna do is find my grandfather and be rid of this thing. Now, if you wanna help me, I'll gladly take the help, but if not, let me off on the next corner and stay out of my way."

Rogue and Asha looked at each other knowingly. If Gabriel wanted to take the Nimrod and leave, there wasn't much either of them would be able to do about it. "Okay, Gabe. We can go back to—"

"Fuck!" Asha's scream cut off Rogue's statement. She was in the backseat clutching her head as if she was in great pain.

"Are you okay?" Gabriel reached to touch her, but she moved away.

"No, stay back. I don't want to risk losing the vision." She tried to focus on what Azuma was seeing. There was so much going on that she couldn't make heads or tails of it, but there was blood and shouting coming from everywhere. She heard a loud explosion just before the connection was broken.

"What did you see?" Rogue asked anxiously.

"An army . . . blood . . . They're all being slaughtered, the Great House is falling!" Asha's words were clipped from the intensity of the vision.

"I don't understand." Gabriel looked to Rogue, who obviously knew something from the worried expression on his face. He threw the car into a U-turn so unexpectedly that Asha and Gabriel were thrown to one side.

"What the hell is with you, buddy?" Asha was shaking her head clear.

"The Great House. I don't know why I didn't think of it before; I'm so freaking stupid." Rogue punched the steering wheel. He redlined the car up Flushing, praying that he would get there in time.

"What is it, Rogue?" Gabriel asked.

"I think I know where your grandfather is."

CHAPTER THIRTY-FOUR

"Where did this fog come from?" Morgan wondered aloud when he stepped out of the burning house. Both the Knights and the Inquisitors were on his heels. The entire block was covered in a fog so thick that he couldn't see his hand in front of his face, but Jackson could see just fine and he didn't like what he saw.

"I think we've got bigger problems than the weather." Jackson's blades slid out. There were shapes moving throughout the fog. He didn't know what they were, but he knew they weren't human. He was about to say something when he spotted a shape darting from the fog. He intercepted Illini's spear right before it made contact with Morgan's skull. "My, but you're an ugly son of a bitch," Jackson taunted the goblin.

"Die, human!" Illini pushed Jackson away and attacked. The goblin moved inhumanly fast, but Jackson matched him strike for strike. Illini tried to come at Jackson with an overhand strike, which Jackson dodged and countered by slicing him across the stomach. Before Jackson could follow up, a massive fist slammed into his jaw, knocking him to the ground. Before he could figure out which way was up he was snatched to his feet by what could only be described as a monster. The creature holding Jackson was a pale shade of green, with a head that was almost twice the size of a pumpkin. Oversized teeth sat back in his massive jaws while a bone jutted through his lower lip.

"You don't know who you're fucking with." Jackson rained blows on the creature's massive head with his steel fists, which only seemed to amuse him.

"You have spirit for a mortal, and I'm sure you'll make a fine snack." The goblin sneered.

"You'll find Jackson's hide pretty tough to chew, especially with no teeth," a voice called from behind the goblin. When he turned his head in the direction of the voice, Morgan smashed Illini's face in with the hammer.

"I owe you one," Jackson said, picking himself up off the ground.

"You owe me several, but we'll settle up another time, old friend." Morgan swung the hammer in an arc. "We've evil to banish."

Goblins and wayward Stalkers dashed through the fog cutting down anything in their paths with teeth and steel. In the center of the carnage stood the large goblin that had dragged the cannon through the portal. His massive arms laid down friend and foe, and he devoured those he was quick enough to catch. When Jackson saw the broad smile spread across Morgan's lips he had a bad feeling.

"Come on, Red," Jackson pleaded, but Morgan was already moving towards the goblin.

"Foul creature, from that which is unclean," Morgan addressed the goblin. "In the name of my Lord and my family, I cast thee back!" Morgan hurled himself and the hammer at the goblin. The creature let out a mighty roar when Morgan's hammer connected with his jaw. He staggered backward, falling on the cannon and setting himself and everything around him on fire. Morgan thought that would be the end of the creature, but he came back at him as if he hadn't even noticed the flames.

"Oh, damn," Morgan blurted out as the creature swung for his head. Morgan dodged the blow and delivered a strike with his hammer to the creature's ribs. He tried to land another blow, but the creature snatched Morgan off the ground, pinning his arm and the hammer at his side. The creature roared triumphantly as he clamped his teeth onto Morgan's head. When the creature's teeth shattered against Morgan's skin he dropped him back to the ground.

Morgan's skin was now covered in a stone layer and his eyes ghostly white. "The Dark Order will have no more of my blood in this lifetime." Morgan hefted the hammer and lunged. This time he put everything he had into the swing. The hammer landed square in the middle of the creature's forehead, shattering his skull. The goblin huffed and fell over dead at Morgan's feet. He thought that the worse was over but realized that he had been wrong when Orden stepped from the fog.

"Usar was one of my most faithful," Orden said, adjusting his grip on his blade.

"And now he's your most dead," Morgan shot back.

The two combatants circled each other.

"You will learn that to slay one of my subjects is an offense that I don't take lightly," Orden warned him.

"And you will learn that we don't fight fair!" Jackson lunged through the mist with his blades drawn.

Three fierce-looking goblins leapt from the fog and landed on the front steps of Sanctuary, where De Mona and the others were huddled trying to make sense of what was going on. Brother David tried to scramble back inside, only to be cut down by the goblin's blade.

"Brother David!" Julius drew his sword and attacked the goblins. Julius and the two goblins went flying off the steps and disappeared into the fog, leaving De Mona to deal with the other one.

With a roar the goblin attacked with a spiked club, but De Mona was ready for him. With a slash of her claws she reduced the club to splinters. Before the creature could recover, De Mona opened him from his chest to his neck. The goblin fell down the stairs choking on his blood.

"If it ain't one thing it's another." De Mona took a defensive stance, alert for more attackers.

"What's going on?" Lydia asked, recognizing De Mona's voice. Fin was at her side, trembling. Unlike the rest of them, he could see perfectly clear in the fog.

"Goblins!" he belted out before bolting through the fog.

"Fin," Lydia called after him.

"Leave him; we've gotta get outta this fog." De Mona pulled Lydia along.

"Pity, I thought it was rather romantic," a familiar voice called from behind De Mona.

She sighed, knowing who she would see when she turned around. "You can't be serious."

"It will take more than the petty efforts of your ragtag bunch to defeat me." Riel banged his blade to his chest. He looked like shit from the beating he'd taken earlier, but there was still plenty of fight left in him.

"Friend of yours?" Lydia asked, backing up, holding her staff defensively.

"More like a rash that won't go away," De Mona told her. "I kicked his ass once; I can do it again." De Mona rushed Riel, claws bared. A brutish goblin stepped out of the mist between De Mona and her prey and was rewarded by having half his face torn off. De Mona bounded over him in search of Riel, but the demon had disappeared back into the fog. Riel reappeared behind her and caught De Mona with a crushing right hook. De Mona spun and landed awkwardly, banging her head on the ground.

Lydia honed in on the sound of battle and caught Riel

in the jaw with her staff. The demon winced and looked at her as if she were a peon. "First a High Brother, and now a whore of the church, how many will the order have to lose before they realize they are undone?"

"We will never surrender to the likes of you," Lydia told him. She recognized the scent of his cursed blade from Angelo's body. "For what you've done to the High Brother, I'll be sure to make your death a miserable one."

"So you say, but how can you kill what you cannot see?" He stepped farther into the fog.

To his surprise, Lydia followed and tore a nasty gash in his face with the tip of her staff. "I'm blind, asshole, so all I have to do is follow your stink to know where you are."

Lydia was as quick as lightning with her strikes, but the war demon was quicker. He effortlessly knocked aside her strikes and countered with a lazy one of his own, which Lydia blocked, but she fell victim to a leg sweep. Riel brought his blade around with all his might, and when it connected with Lydia's staff there was a great explosion of light.

Riel shrieked as the celestial light blinded him and singed his face. Swinging the blade wildly, he backed himself into a corner and tried to clear his vision. When his focus returned, his eyes widened at what he saw. Lydia stood calmly in the center of the mist of the fog, surrounded by a soft glow. The ivory shell that had been her walking stick began to fall away, exposing the double-pronged spear that had been hiding within. Next to the hammer and the trident itself, the Spear of Truth was one of the most famed of the anointed weapons.

"Who are you?" the demon snarled.

Moving off instinct, Lydia waved the spear in a series of complex designs, leaving glowing runes in the fog. "I am Lydia Osheda, descendant of Sinjin Osheda, known to your kind as the demon slayer. Now, come so I can spill your blood as my ancestor did!" Moving as if the spear were a part of her, Lydia tore into Riel.

The war demon found himself flustered at the intensity with which Lydia attacked him. The spear was like a kaleidoscope of color, striking the demon over and over. For every blow Riel threw, Lydia countered with two. He came high and she went low, plunging the spear into his gut. For a moment she could see the demon within try to separate from the host body, but Riel was able to pull himself free of the spear before he completely lost hold of the body. His body had taken too much damage that night to continue, so he called in help.

"Attend me!" he shouted. From out of the mist came the shambling Stalkers who had managed to survive the fight at the brownstone. Lydia tried her best to fight off both the Stalkers and the demon, but she was being overwhelmed. The Stalkers finally managed to wrestle Lydia to the ground and take the spear from her, which Riel picked up.

Riel twirled the spear expertly with one hand and brought the point to rest against Lydia's throat. "It may not be the Nimrod, but I think this will please my master."

"And this is gonna please me!" De Mona tackled Riel, jarring the spear loose. Riel tried to raise Poison, but she knocked it away from him. "Not this time. I'm gonna down you once and for all." She raised her hand for the killing blow but was denied when a Stalker pulled her off Riel. She dispatched the corpse in less than ten seconds, but when she turned back to Riel he was gone. "I fucking hate it when he does that!" De Mona cursed before moving back into the fog to find another target.

Redfeather crawled on his hands and knees, trying to stay as low as possible. Around him he could hear the screams of both friends and enemies mingled with the clashing of steel and gunfire. To his rear, the Great House of Sanctuary burned. Redfeather's hand brushed against something smooth. He looked up and found a blond man dressed in mage's robes standing over him.

"I would've thought more of the descendant of the mighty Hunter." Flag smirked. Two goblins appeared from the fog and snatched Redfeather to his feet. Flag examined him and frowned. "You are definitely one of the Hunter's kin but not the wielder of the Nimrod. Where is he?"

"Far away from the likes of you, and if you were smart you would let him be," Redfeather said defiantly, and was rewarded with a slap across his face.

"I've no time for your games, old man. Either you can give me the information I need or I can have my associates pry it out of you." Flag motioned towards the salivating goblins.

"Not if I have a say in it," Lydia said defiantly. Her form was obscured by the fog, but the spear burned bright. Flag recognized the spear and wisely stepped back.

"Get away, child," Redfeather called to her.

"There will be no more innocent blood spilled tonight." Lydia ignored Redfeather and walked calmly towards Flag.

"Of course not, because there won't be that much left of you when I'm done." Flag lashed out with a beam of energy from his hands, trying to incinerate the girl.

Lydia leapt out of the way just before the beam scorched the ground. She got low and raced towards Flag with the spear folded against her body. Lydia moved more off the impulses of the spear than conscious thought as she dodged Flag's attack. Like all the other weapons, it was adding to her natural abilities. She flung herself into the air above Flag, and with a whoosh of power she split the spear in half and zeroed in on Flag with the two blades. Flag didn't even have time to think of a spell, so he did what came naturally and threw himself on the ground. Screaming for help and on all fours, he scrambled across the floor trying to escape Lydia's wrath.

"Don't run, coward," Lydia said, cleaving through Stalkers with the two blades as she moved after Flag. She managed to back him into a corner and laid the blades crossways over his throat. "If it were up to me I would kill you for what your people have done tonight," she said with tears streaming down her face. "But it's not for me to judge you, that is the work of the order. I'm no murderer."

"Well, it's too bad that I am." Flag laid his hands on her stomach and pushed out with his power. Lydia flapped around on the ground like a wounded fish as Flag tried to fry her.

"No!" Redfeather cried as he charged Flag. The old man hit Flag in the jaw, causing him to break his connection to Lydia. Redfeather gave him two more good licks before he was knocked out by a goblin. The creature knelt over Redfeather and was about to take a bite of the old man when Flag stopped him.

"No, we'll need this one to find the boy. Take him back to the mountain while I retrieve the spear," Flag ordered the goblin. The goblin grudgingly did as he was told, leaving Lydia to Flag. "Foolish child." Flag stood over Lydia, who was trying to get back to her feet. He was about to finish her when the sound of screeching tires drew his attention. He turned around just in time to see a pair of headlights barreling down on him.

CHAPTER THIRTY-FIVE

The fog was so thick that neither Gabriel nor Asha could see what was going on, but Rogue could. He'd heard stories about the goblin hordes but never thought he'd ever encounter them, especially topside. The Inquisitors and their allies fought valiantly, but they were no match for the ferocity of the goblins.

"What do you see?" Gabriel asked. All he could make out in the fog was shadows and the screams of the dying.

"It's bad," Rogue said, drawing his remaining revolver.

Asha stopped using her physical eyes and let her magical senses roam. "Looks like the shit is getting thick," Asha said, drawing her knife and smearing leftover blood on the blade.

"*Thick* ain't the word." Rogue mowed down an unsuspecting goblin with the Viper.

"What the hell was that?" Asha craned her neck to try to see what they had hit.

"You don't wanna know," Rogue told her.

"My grandfather is in there, isn't he?" Gabriel was getting agitated.

"Gabriel, just be calm," Rogue tried to soothe him.

"I'm tired of being calm; being calm has gotten me nothing but my ass kicked all night." The Nimrod appeared in his hand. Gabriel reached for the door handle.

"What the hell are you doing?" Rogue spared a glance over his shoulder.

"Finally taking responsibility for the mess I created." Gabriel pushed the door open and threw himself out of the speeding car. His body never made a sound when it hit the ground and disappeared into the fog.

"Damn that kid!" Rogue swerved the Viper. He was so busy scanning the fog for Gabriel that he didn't see the two bodies directly in front of him.

"Rogue, look out!" Asha grabbed the wheel and yanked it to one side. The Viper fishtailed and slammed into a parked car.

"Are you crazy? I should blow your head off for that." Rogue aimed the gun at her.

"If you shoot me, then I won't be able to save you from him." Asha pointed out the window. Rogue turned in time to avoid Illini's spear that was crashing through the window. While Rogue and the goblin struggled for the spear, Asha climbed out the window and stood on the hood of the car. She raised her hands to the heavens and shouted, "Azuma, be my strength!" From the monkey's hiding place on an adjacent rooftop he answered his mistress's call, adding his power to her own as she rushed Illini.

The goblin abandoned his spear and turned his attention to the hurling witch. He deflected her blade's strike and placed his palm on her stomach. Pain shot through her body as he burned a print of his hand into her gut. Asha hit the ground and looked up at the goblin in shock. In all that she had learned about the warrior race, she'd never known them to have a hand of power.

Illini flexed his smoldering hand and answered the question in Asha's eyes: "It was a gift from one of the fire elementals. I took it as my own after I ate him. I wonder what I'll be able to salvage from you when you're reduced to bones."

"You won't be finding out anytime soon." Rogue appeared behind Illini, holding his spear. Rogue drove the spear through the goblin's stomach and tossed him into the fog.

"On your feet, girl; that little nick won't keep him out of our hair for long." Rogue helped Asha up.

"You drove a spear through his stomach. I don't think he'll be a problem for anyone anytime soon," Asha said, gently prodding the handprint on her stomach. The skin was blistered and raised, but she would live.

"That's because you don't know jack shit about goblin anatomy. Now, let's go find Gabriel." Rogue pulled her deeper into the fog. Rogue did his best to avoid being stabbed, shot, or bitten as he navigated the mist. He spotted a girl lying prone on the ground, aglow with magic . . . mage magic. His eyes whipped back and forth in search of the mage who had cast the spell, and Rogue's blood went cold when he laid eyes on Flag. Asha took a step forward, but Rogue held her back. "Tend to the girl. I'll handle this." He moved to meet Flag in the center of the fog.

Asha carefully approached Lydia, as she knelt with her blades gasping for breath. "Are you okay?" Asha called to her.

"Who's there?" Lydia raised one of the blades and turned in the direction of Asha's voice. She didn't look like she had the strength to swing it, but Asha wasn't taking any chances.

"My name is Asha and I'm on your side, so can you put away the blades so I can see how badly you're hurt?" Asha said. Lydia hesitated for a minute, but she let Asha examine her. The girl was still crackling with mage magic, but she would be okay. "How many of them are there?"

"I don't know; it seems like they're coming from everywhere," Lydia told her. Lydia felt around for the second blade and put the two back together again. "I have to go; they've got Redfeather." She used the spear to pull herself to her feet.

"Sister, you gotta let that magic bleed off before you do anything." Asha touched Lydia's shoulder. Flag's magic felt vile when it touched Asha's, but she let it seep into her from the girl. "Who's got him and where did they take him?"

"The goblins. I heard the mage say something about taking him to a mountain," Lydia recalled.

Asha didn't know what Lydia meant by the mountain, but she knew what goblins were. The elders would tell them horror stories about the tunnel dwellers when she was a girl. If they were what were lurking in the fog, then Asha knew that it was the last place she wanted to be. "Come on; we're getting the hell outta this fog." Asha grabbed Lydia by the hand and led her off.

"You know, I knew if I looked hard enough I'd find a murdering sack of shit like you tied up in this. There's a king's ransom on your head." Rogue raised his gun.

Flag waved his hands through the air and called up his power. "You're welcome to try and collect the bounty, freak. Rogue, if you try to stop me, Lord Titus will make sure that the demon who pulls your strings suffers for it. I'd like to see what would happen if he decided to take more than your eyes this time."

"To keep the likes of you from bringing about hell on earth it's a risk I'm willing to take." Rogue fired his weapon at the same time Flag released his power. Rogue managed to raise a magical barrier, but it only slowed the blast. For the third time that night he found himself airborne. Rogue righted himself just in time to see Flag rushing him with one of the goblin's discarded swords. Against his better judgment Rogue again called on the shadows and sent a pillar of darkness swirling at Flag. It staggered the mage, but Rogue didn't have the strength to make the blow a fatal one

In a fair fight, taking down Flag wouldn't have been easy, but as injured as Rogue was it was almost suicide. He dropped to one knee and with shaky hands tried to re-load his revolver, but Flag was on him. Rogue was barely able to duck out of the way of the swinging blade. Using the empty revolver, he backhanded the blade away and punched Flag in the nose, breaking it. Rogue followed with a spin-ning kick that put Flag on his back. Before he could get up, Rogue hog-tied him in shadow. Flag opened his mouth to work a spell, but Rogue gagged it with another shadow patch.

Rogue leaned over Flag and smiled. "It ain't no fun when the rabbit got the gun, is it?" Rogue had barely had time to savor his victory when pain shot through his skull. A hulking goblin lifted him from the ground by his dreads and shook him violently before tossing him to the ground like a piece of trash. The goblin raised his battle-ax over Rogue's head for the killing blow and suddenly found his leathery hide pierced with dozens of needle-thin shad-ows. "I've spent more time on the ground tonight than a homeless person." The shadows lifted the goblin from the ground. "And frankly, I'm tired of it." At Rogue's com-mand the shadows tore the goblin to pieces. Unfortunately, the distraction had allowed Flag time to escape.

Gabriel hit the ground in a roll and was back on his feet before he had come to a complete stop. In the dense fog he couldn't see his hand in front of him, but all he needed was his ears to know what was going on. People were dy-ing left and right and it was all because of him. He wanted to curl up into a ball and pity himself, but the Bishop wouldn't let him.

"Licking your wounds in the dark will do nothing to help them, Hunter," the Bishop whispered.

"But what can I do?" Gabriel asked in a defeated tone.

"What you have been chosen to do. Stop fighting your destiny, Hunter. Take up your weapon and bathe your enemies in the cleansing light."

Gabriel looked at the relic in his hands, which was glowing in anticipation. Images of what he was hearing flashed through his mind like a movie reel. One by one he watched them fall, the elemental, the thug, the demon. The goblins overtook them all. *"My will be done,"* the Bishop said before going silent again.

"Show me what to do," Gabriel said to the Nimrod. In response the relic flared to life and turned night into day.

Jackson had long been knocked out of the fight, leaving Morgan alone to face off against the goblin prince. The Irishman was bloodied and he felt like he could no longer lift his arms, but he would not let the evil win.

"You are a brave soul, elemental, but your bravery will not save your kin. Lay down and die like the rest of your miserable race." Orden lashed out with his sword, only to have it blocked by Morgan's hammer.

"For as long as there is breath in my body I will fight, goblin." Morgan launched a two-handed strike that Orden easily swatted away. Morgan was so preoccupied with keeping Orden in front of him that he didn't notice Gilchrest sneak up behind him. The smaller goblin tripped Morgan, making him vulnerable to Orden. The goblin prince made to dispatch Morgan was suddenly blinded by light.

"The sun, impossible!" Orden shrieked, shielding his eyes from the blinding light. Sunlight was the greatest enemy of the goblins, for its rays could turn them to stone.

"Not the sun, goblin, but its rays burn just as bright."

Gabriel walked towards them, dissipating the fog as he went.

Orden tried to take a step towards Gabriel, but the light was too much to bear. "Back, my brothers, back to the tunnels." Orden slammed his swords against the ground, splitting it open. The goblins reluctantly abandoned their feeding frenzy and heeded their prince as they escaped into the sewers. Orden looked at Gabriel and warned him, "We will meet again, man-thing."

"And when that day comes, all who serve the dark lord will feel my wrath." Gabriel fired a blast of lightning, but Orden had already disappeared down the hole.

"No, not leave Gilchrest!" The smaller goblin pounded his fist against the rubble.

"Not so fast." Asha worked a binding spell on the goblin. Her clothes were torn and she looked tired, but she had enough strength left to bind the goblin.

"Filthy witch, I'll eat your eyes!" Gilchrest squirmed.

"I'm sure you'll try, but not before I pry what I need from you." She tightened the bands.

"Granddad!" Gabriel called out. He frantically searched the bodies looking for his grandfather. "Has anyone seen Redfeather?"

"They took him," Lydia said. The girl was still shaken up, but the magical stain had faded.

"What do you mean, 'took him'? Took him where?" Gabriel asked frantically. He took a step towards Lydia, but Asha stepped between them.

"Calm down, Gabriel. From what she's told me the goblins took him to someplace called the mountains," Asha said.

"If he's a prisoner of the goblins, then my guess is the Iron Mountains," Rogue offered. He was limping and bloody, but he would heal and when he did he was going to hunt Flag down.

"Fine, then let's go get him," Gabriel said.

"You don't just rush into the mouth of hell half-assed, young man." Morgan came over. "But rest assured you'll have another crack at them."

"I'm sorry, who the hell are you again?" Gabriel snapped.

"They saved our asses when the Stalkers rushed the house looking for you," De Mona added.

"And had you not dumped this thing in my lap they wouldn't have been looking for me and my grandfather would still be here!" Gabriel shot back.

"Hey, don't act like you're the only one who's lost something because of the Nimrod. Your grandfather might be missing, but my father is dead thanks to the Nimrod. Had I known what that thing was capable of, I'd have gotten rid of it the moment I laid eyes on it," she said emotionally. Her eyes welled with tears, but she wouldn't allow herself to cry in front of the strangers.

"The both of you need to shut up." Rogue stepped in between them before things could get more heated. He was hurt, tired, dirty, and overall pissed off at the night's turn of events. "Arguing like two kids isn't going to find your grandfather, Gabriel. Or bring your father's killers to justice. We've all got a reason to want to be rid of the Nimrod and see Titus' efforts fail. I think our best bet is to work together to sort this mess out."

"I agree." Morgan stepped forward. "The dark agents have taken everything and everyone I've ever loved. If for nothing else I will fight in the name of my family." He put his hand out and looked at the others.

"For my father." De Mona added her hand.

Gabriel stepped forward and placed his hand on top of hers. The two looked at each other and there was an unspoken truce established. "For my grandfather."

Asha thought of Dutch and his promise. The mission they were about to undertake would be dangerous, but for what Dutch had promised it would be worth it. "For my coven." She placed her hand over theirs.

"For Angelo," Lydia and Fin said simultaneously, adding their hands to the pact.

"For the hell of it." Jackson placed his hand in.

This left just Rogue. The mage stood with his arms folded. He had never been a team player, but in light of everything going on, everyone would have to make allowances if they wanted to stop Titus. His eyes lingered on what was left of his Viper for a few moments before adding his hand to the pile. "For my car."

EPILOGUE

Dutch's attention was yanked away from the book he was reading when the mirror that served as the entrance to his office exploded. He covered his eyes to protect them from the spray of glass but felt nothing. He peered from behind his arm to find hundreds of tiny shards suspended all around him. He reached for his desk drawer only to have one of the shards embed itself in the wood just above his hand.

"Who dares to violate my inner sanctum?" Dutch snarled.

"I dare," a voice called from the other side of the broken mirror. The woman who stepped through stood almost six foot three in her white stiletto boots. Beneath her full-length white fur coat, a pale leather bodysuit hugged her slender frame. The woman's blond locks were done up in tight curls that crowned her face. Eyes the color of the Pacific Ocean glared at Dutch as the White Queen stood before him.

"Angelique, you have no right to—," Dutch began but was cut off.

"Stay your tongue, snake." Angelique waved her hand and the shards moved closer to Dutch. "I have all rights when it comes to protecting the lives of my students and the integrity of this coven."

"Angelique, I have no idea what you're talking about," Dutch said nervously. He was a powerful warlock, but Angelique was an equally powerful witch.

"Oh, I doubt that." She perched herself on the edge of his desk. "I've had less than two hours of sleep, so I really don't have time for your bullshit, Dutch. Tonight I lost two of my most promising students, and I have it on good authority that it's your fault."

"Two of your girls are dead?" Dutch asked, genuinely surprised.

"As you've probably already heard, Sanctuary fell this morning," Angelique told him, watching for telltale signs that he was lying. Dutch knew this, so he told the truth, or as much of it as he had to.

"I'd heard as much. Does anyone know what happened?" Dutch asked. He had heard varying stories but wasn't sure which one to go with just yet.

"Some say it was the Stalker, led by that troublemaker Riel. Others say that the goblins had a hand in it. Neither theory matters to me at this point. What does matter to me is that Sulin and Lucy left here together, now Sulin is dead, and I can't find a sign of Lucy anywhere. From the way things look, she's likely dead, too. The healer fell victim to a blade; this much I was sure of. But I have reason to believe Lucy fell to magic, blood magic." Angelique studied Dutch and saw the telltale twitch in his eyes. "From the expression on your face I take it that you know something?"

"Both Lucy and Sulin were here last night, but I cannot account for their whereabouts after they left." Dutch folded his hands in front of him on the desk and tried to remain as calm as possible, but he had an idea that he knew where Angelique was going with it. He was trying to be calm, but a very ugly scenario was unfolding in his head.

"Liar!" Angelique sent several shards to perforate the

curtain behind Dutch. "We found the body of her familiar, but he's in some sort of coma and can tell us nothing. Dutch, you've known me long enough to know that I am hardly a fool and I will not be played. You sent Asha on some secret errand tonight, what it was I can only speculate, but that's second on my list of concerns. What I want to know is what happened between Lucy and Asha before the murders?"

"Angelique, you know as well as I do that Lucy and Asha have been at odds since they were children. What's so unusual about that?" Dutch asked, not really understanding where Angelique was going with this.

"What's unusual is that my people have found traces of both Lucy's and Asha's magic auras at the scene of the crime. Lucy's was faint, but someone invoked some heavy blood magic," Angelique informed him. "Only Goddess knows what happened out there, but what you can be sure of is that the deaths of my students will not go unpunished."

"Agreed. I will mobilize the Hunt to launch a full investigation," Dutch assured her.

"How convenient; send the perpetrators to cover the crime," Angelique spat.

"What are you trying to say, Angelique?"

The shards of glass moved when she got up from the desk. "I'm not *trying* to say anything. What I am telling you is that I made a promise to Wanda that I would watch over her daughter and now she may be dead or worse. When we revive her familiar, it will tell us what really happened." Angelique walked back towards the broken mirror. "Only one of two things can come of this, Dutch."

"And they are?" he asked defiantly.

"Either you will turn Asha over to me so that we can get to the bottom of this or I will formally bring the Black Court up on charges of treason."

"My followers will not stand by while you try to have me convicted for something I have nothing to do with," he threatened.

"Then we stand on the verge of a second parting of the magics. Bring me the killers of my children or prepare yourself for war, good king." Angelique executed a sarcastic bow before stepping back through the broken mirror. Only when she had exited the Triple Six did the shards of glass fall harmlessly to the ground.

Julius gasped as he woke up from what felt like a bad dream. As the fog lifted from his mind he recalled the events that had unfolded. He was in the fog battling the goblin invaders who were laying siege to Sanctuary. He fought as hard as he could, but there were too many of them. Eventually the goblins had overrun him and the remaining members of the Inquisition, with their blades cutting down the holy men.

Julius went to check the wound he remembered receiving to the gut but found his arm chained. He looked around expecting to see the block where he had watched his friends and enemies slain, but instead there was only the cool darkness of the confined space he was in. Julius jerked frantically at the chain, but it wouldn't give.

"Those chains were crafted to hold stronger things than you," a voice called from the darkness.

"Who's there?" Julius called out.

The darkness opened up and a man stood before Julius. The speaker was dressed in black leather armor, with sandals of the same sturdy material covering his bronze feet to the toes. His head was completely bald, save for a thick black braid that rested on his shoulder. Ghostly white eyes, lined in black paint, studied Julius before the man answered him in a ghostly voice.

"I am called Ezrah, ferryman of the dead, and you are on my ship, the *Jihad*," Ezrah told him.

"Am I dead?" Julius asked. He had heard stories of the ferryman and his ghost ship.

"You almost were. I sent my shades to retrieve you just before your last breaths," Ezrah told him.

"So you've rescued me to be a part of your pirate crew?" Julius asked.

Ezrah regarded him. "Only those who died as members of this crew may have the run of my ship. I have other uses for you, mage."

Julius' face went slack at the mention of his true nature. Since he had first come to the order his lineage had been a secret to all but Brothers Angelo and David. "Then if not service, what do you want from me?"

Ezrah cast his ghostly eyes on Julius. "The chance to be flesh again."

The first thing Lucy noticed was that her head felt like it was going to explode. As painful as it was, she was grateful for it. If she could feel the headache, then that meant she wasn't dead, but from the smell of wherever she was it may as well have been a grave. The last thing Lucy remembered was the horrible expression on Sulin's face before somebody knocked the snot out of her. Lucy had always imagined that it would be her who fell to a violent death, but not Sulin. She would have her revenge against who- or whatever had killed Sulin, but first Lucy had to figure out where the hell she was.

Slowly she raised her head and took stock of her surroundings. The enclosure smelled heavily of animal musk and feces, like a barn or zoo. All around her were cold steel bars that glowed faintly. Upon closer inspection she could see the faint runes etched into them. She tried to work a spell, but as she expected, nothing happened.

Whoever had built the cage obviously knew something of magic. Lucy tried to call to Tiki with her mind but got nothing. At first she feared the worst but she'd have felt if he were dead. He had to be badly ruined, but the cage kept her from detecting how bad.

"Out of the frying pan and into the fire," Lucy thought aloud.

"Very well put," a voice said behind her.

Lucy spun around and found that she wasn't alone. In the far corner of the cage there was a silver-haired old man. He was a mess of cuts and bruises, but from the way her body ached she imagined she looked pretty much the same.

"Who are you and where the hell are we?" Lucy approached the old man.

"My name is Redfeather and we are prisoners of the goblins. They brought us here after they destroyed Sanctuary." Redfeather struggled to his feet.

"Destroyed?" Lucy sounded shocked.

Redfeather nodded. "I'm afraid so. The Dark Order intends to make slaves out of humanity."

"Sorry, I'm not real big on manual labor. I think I'll pass on becoming a goblin slave." To Lucy's surprise, Redfeather laughed at her. "And what the hell is so funny?"

"The goblins do not take prisoners, dear child. That would be far too merciful for that lot."

"Then what do they plan to do with us?" Lucy asked worriedly. There was an inhuman scream somewhere at the other end of the corridor, followed by the smell of burning flesh.

Redfeather looked at her sadly. "They intend to eat us."

THE BEGINNING

Read on for an excerpt from Kris Greene's next book

DEMON
HUNT

Coming soon from St. Martin's Paperbacks

"Redfeather, are you still with us?" Asha snapped him out of his daze. He had been sitting completely motionless for the last ten minutes and it unnerved her.

Gabriel blinked and looked around as if he was seeing the faces surrounding him for the first time. "Yeah, I'm good," he lied. He had been receiving images from the Nimrod ever since he'd come into possession of it, but they were usually through the eyes of the Bishop. What he'd just seen was different. Even before he heard the dark-haired man speak, he knew who he was. The question was, why was he seeing it?

The fuel light on the dashboard blinked, but they dared not stop until they were out of Manhattan or the sun had fully risen. It was sheer luck that they had survived the initial onslaught of the dark forces, and in their present condition, not even luck would save them from a second attack. The stretched Hummer drew more than the occasional glance as it rumbled down the FDR en route to the Queens Borough Bridge. It wasn't every day that you saw a modified Hummer with a religious emblem etched into the hood and doors. The cross sat in the center of three rings, which represented man, demon, and spirit. The ancient symbol once struck fear into the hearts of the enemies of the order, but that morning it served as a grim reminder of all that had been lost.

Each passenger's face bore a different expression, but their eyes all held the same weariness. In what felt like the blink of an eye, several totally different people from different walks of life had found themselves thrown together by one common object: the Nimrod. The Nimrod was a thing of pure magic which was neither good nor evil and empowered by the imprisoned spirit of a man known as the Bishop. During the Seven Day Siege, it was the Bishop whom the Nimrod had called master. It was the warped love affair between wielder and weapon that had kept the Bishop from passing into the afterlife when his comrade Titus slew him. The Bishop's displaced soul lay nestled in the bosom of the thing he had loved most in life, waiting for the moment he would have his revenge on the betrayer and lead his Knights once again. With the Nimrod and a willing vessel, the Bishop would be able to breach the planes of flesh and spirit. And it was through Gabriel that he sought to accomplish this. But one thing none of them had counted on was the strength of Gabriel's will.

With his tattered clothes and mussed hair, you'd have hardly taken Gabriel as someone who a few hours prior had been living a bland life. He was a bookish-looking young man whose biggest thrills came from deciphering ancient languages and Thursday night Chess Club. He and his grandfather had lived a quiet life in a brownstone in Harlem until the day he met De Mona Sanchez and lost everything he had, including his free will. To everyone's, especially Gabriel's, surprise, the Nimrod responded to his touch and stirred the spirit within it. The Nimrod had bound itself to his flesh while the Bishop invaded his heart, constantly threatening to corrupt him. For the most part, Gabriel was still in control, but there was no denying the strength in the Bishop's words. He looked over at De Mona and cursed her for the hundredth time for coming into his life.

De Mona rested her head against the window and stared out aimlessly at the pinkish sky. The bubble-gum effect of the increasing light playing on the clouds took her back to when her mother and father would buy her cotton candy at the carnival. That was before she'd found out that she was the real freak. De Mona walked in two worlds, those of men and demons. Her father had been a retired professor turned antique dealer who fell head over heels for a demon. Her mother Mercy was a Valkrin, a race of demons whose sole purpose was to wage war. Next to the goblins, the Valkrin were the most feared creatures in service to the dark lord, but that all changed shortly before De Mona was born.

Mercy had been the first of the Valkrin to cross over to the light and she wasn't the last. Soon others came seeking peace from the war which had been raging since the beginning of time. And they found that peace within the walls of Sanctuary, but it wasn't to last. Not long before the anointed weapons began resurfacing, the Valkrin and some of the others began disappearing. No one knew what caused the withdrawal, but when a Valkrin was connected with the mass murder of a missionary village in Guam, the reason had become clear. The dark lord had put out the call to arms and the Valkrin had answered.

De Mona ran her fingers through her hair and winced when she nicked her scalp. She held her hands in front of her face, almost expecting to see the smooth knuckles and frail digits she'd known for the first eleven years of her life, but she didn't. She hadn't called the change, but her hands were deformed. Her fingers were gnarled and about a half inch too long, with spear-like nails hanging from the ends. She tried to force the change back, but the best she could do was smooth out the skin over her talons. Since coming in contact with the Nimrod, she had been having difficulty controlling her changes. It was as if the beast inside her was becoming stronger and she didn't like it.

What felt like a soft whisper of wind touched her cheek and she immediately knew what it was . . . magic. She turned her hooded eyes towards the rear of the transport where the mage and the witch sat whispering with each other. Occasionally they would look over at De Mona, but neither of them would hold her gaze. For this she was glad because there was something about the starry flakes in the mage's eyes that made her uneasy.

"Why don't you take a picture or something?" De Mona snapped.

"Somebody woke up on the wrong side of the bed," Asha said with a crooked grin. Azuma bristled on her lap, but he dared not go near the demon. Whereas her form was hidden to human eyes, Azuma could see her for just what she was.

"You'd be in a pissy mood too if you'd been getting sucker-punched by demons all night," De Mona said.

Asha rolled her eyes and folded her arms. "Try getting blown out of a third-story window. You ain't the only one who's had a trying night."

"I think we've all been through a lot over the last few hours so why don't the both of you cool it?" Rogue interjected. His ribs were still busted to hell, but at least he had gotten the bleeding to stop. He hadn't heard a peep from the demon he shared his soul with since he'd taken shadowform. Normally the demon encouraged Rogue to tap further into his shadow magic, but never to attack one of its own species. Using his shadow form, Rogue had managed to defeat Moses, who the shadows referred to as "Shadow Master." Rogue had managed to destroy his host's body and compromise his magic, but he wasn't foolish enough to think that it was the end of Moses, for you couldn't destroy a real shadow, only hold it back.

"You're one to talk. I don't even know you like that to be giving me orders, dude. So please tell me why your opinion should count for a damn thing?" De Mona asked defiantly. She hadn't known Rogue more than a few hours and still wasn't sure where he fit into the mystery.

"Because if it hadn't been for him, we'd all be dead," Gabriel spoke up unexpectedly, drawing the attention of everyone in the Hummer. De Mona hadn't noticed it before but there was something different about him. He seemed somehow older. "Rogue saved my life so I could be around to save yours, even though I don't know why I bothered since you caused all this."

"I don't think pointing fingers is going to help us much," Jackson said from the passenger seat. His leather jacket was ripped, but other than that, he seemed in better shape than the rest of them.

"Let me be the judge of what's helpful and what isn't since I'm the one with a centuries-old relic bound to his arm." Gabriel flashed the tattoo on his arm which was pulsing slightly.

"And how did you manage such a trick?" Morgan asked from behind the wheel. "My hammer has been with me since I was a boy and it's never done more than open the overripe skulls of demons and vampires. I fancy myself somewhat of an authority on these weapons, but I've never heard tales of the trident merging with flesh."

"As soon as I figure it out, you'll be the first to know," Gabriel said sarcastically.

Morgan had asked the sixty-four-thousand-dollar question. Ever since he had come into possession of the Nimrod, he had learned a great many things, but its darkest secrets were still kept from him by its true master, the

Bishop. When it suited him, the Bishop allowed Gabriel to taste undreamed-of power, but the more powerful he became, the more of himself he seemed to lose to the addictive properties of the magic he now wielded. The rational side of him said that he should get rid of the trident and the vengeful spirit as soon as possible, but there was a little piece of him that craved the old magic, the same piece that seemed to be steadily growing.

"Vile creature," Gilchrest hissed from the corner. Until he'd spoken, they'd forgotten about the lone goblin they'd been able to capture. His small body was still paralyzed from Asha's binding spell, but his mouth worked just fine. Gilchrest's voice was somewhere between fear and hate when he spoke to Gabriel. "Most man-thing carry magic like second skin, in your soul this evil is." He swept his reptilian eyes over everyone in the Hummer. "Shadow of death follows this one. Bound for the Jihad are we all for keep with him."

Jackson snatched Gilchrest off the floor and pressed his face against the blackened window of the hummer. Slowly he started to roll it down, sending a swift breeze through the vehicle. "Now I've read a thing or two about what direct sunlight can do to you suckas, so unless you shut your damn mouth, you're gonna get a real good view of this sunrise."

"Destroy me and risk the wrath of the entire goblin empire!" Gilchrest threatened nervously. He could see the pinkish sky begin to turn blue in certain patches.

Jackson flicked one of his blades out and nicked Gilchrest's cheek. "Bullshit, what would make me think that those nasty sons of bitches would give a rat's ass if a toad like you went missing?"

"Law say any who murder royal family meet slow death. Prince Orden not take kind baby brother killed by man-things. Eat you I think he will, after boil you alive."

"That is a goblin prince?" Asha poked him mockingly, which caused Gilchrest to snap at her hand. "Keep that up and I'm gonna show you some of my nastier spells." Asha's eyes sparkled as the small gash on Gilchrest's cheek began to bleed more freely.

"Filthy witch!" Gilchrest shook his head from side to side in an attempt to stop the pain spreading across his face.

Rogue placed a soothing hand on Asha's shoulder and the bleeding stopped. "If this thing is a goblin prince, we may be able to use him as a bargaining chip to get Red-feather back."

"Goblin never barter with topsiders, especially demons posing as humans." He glared from Rogue to De Mona. Something about the way the goblin looked at her made De Mona uncomfortable. "Why you hide your true face, bitch?"

De Mona snarled, "That's it, I'm offing this fucker!" In a flash De Mona was across the Hummer with her claws fully extended. Even if Gilchrest hadn't been bound, there would've been no way he could've moved faster than De Mona. Just before her claws tore into his pocked flesh, De Mona found herself wrapped from fingertip to elbow in shadow.

"Enough," Rogue said evenly. "He's worth more to us alive than dead, so why don't you cool it, or would you rather have to worry about every goblin within a hundred miles gunning for a piece of your hide?"

De Mona bared her fangs. "I can handle myself."

"That remains the question," Rogue told her. "I don't know if you noticed it or not, girlie, but we're in the *shit* here. This ain't about egos anymore, it's about survival, because you can bet that as sure as my ass is black, we're all on the short list of who Titus wants whacked. You're free to play the tough ass loner if you want, but I'm of the thinking that there is strength in numbers. We've gotta stick together if any of us plan to make it out of it alive."

"I agree," Lydia spoke up. She stroked Fin's head affectionately with one hand and ran her thumb over the runes on her spear with the other. "We are all that is left of the great house and we must uphold what it stood. Whether we are five hundred or five we must keep the darkness at bay."

Jackson stared at Lydia quizzically. Even though she was blind, she still displayed more courage than most when it came to tackling the dark forces. The gesture brought a smirk to his face. "For as much of a fool as I feel like for saying so, I'm with the young lady. Look, each of us has been fighting our own battles; be it with the dark forces or our own souls." He glanced at De Mona when he said this. "The point is that going at it solo ain't working so maybe it is time that we clicked up and put an end to this."

Gilchrest scoffed. "Impossible, put an end to something older than you or I. This war go since first blood shed in Eden. This war go on forever, or until goblin rule all."

"Now that's a world I could do without," Asha said.

"Then we're all agreed. We regroup and put a plan together to get our people back," Rogue said.

Gilchrest laughed. It sounded like a sick wheezing when it belched from his chest. "Man-thing, no need plan for death, only hold on to prince and it come find you soon enough."

"Goddess, why don't you shut up already?" Asha waved her hand and an invisible strip clamped over Gilchrest's mouth.

"Plan? Why do we need a plan when we've got his highness?" Gabriel pulled up his sleeve and exposed the pulsing tattoo. "If this thing is so powerful, then why don't we just use it to find my grandfather and go get him?"

"Did we just establish the fact that we didn't wanna die?" Asha asked sarcastically.

Jackson placed a hand on Gabriel's forearm. "Dawg, I know you're hot right now, but we need a game plan to go off into the Iron Mountains."

Gabriel slapped his hand away and manifested the trident. "I've got a game plan right here."

"Gabriel, cool it with that thing before you give away our position," Rogue warned. Gabriel gave him a defiant look but did as he was told. "Gabriel, you know no one wants to help you get Redfeather back more than me, but I have to agree with Jackson on this one. Even on holy ground, we barely made it out with our skins so charging into the bowels of Midland is suicide at best."

"What's Midland?" Asha asked curiously.

"The last place of true magic," Fin murmured before he went back to staring aimlessly at the blacked-out window from Lydia's lap. Ever since Angelo had forced the spark into him, he had been drifting in and out.

Seeing the confused expression on their faces through the rearview, Morgan chose to explain. "Keep in mind that what I am about to tell you is supposed to be a myth, but in light of some of the things my brothers and I have come across, I have to believe the truth isn't too far off. Centuries ago, when magical things walked the earth, this was all Midland. When the science forced the magic out, Midland began to die. To protect itself the land separated from this plane and retreated to a realm between the worlds of men and demons, where magic still flourishes. But like a tree, Midland's roots are still in this world. When the land separated, it caused small tears in the fabric of the realities called rips. These rips act as access points between this world and the forgotten."

"So you mean to say that both worlds occupy the same place, but on different levels?" De Mona asked. Her father had spoken of Midland, but he'd always made it seem like it no longer existed.

"In a way," Morgan confirmed. "The earth is one world of many, but it has different layers."

"Kinda like those Grams biscuits at the supermarket," Jackson offered.

Morgan shook his head. "Not quite, but my leather-clad friend isn't far off with his assessment. Midland is everywhere, yet nowhere all at the same time. It hovers between the two planes like a layer of protective skin, keeping the realms of men and demons from colliding. As a boy, my father used to tell me tales of great magicians who could walk between both worlds as simply as walking through a door, but days of magic that potent have long passed. The most conventional way to cross into Midland now is through the rips."

"So why don't we just roll up on one of these rips and cross into Midland?" De Mona asked.

"If only it were that simple," Morgan said. "With the passing of time and the evolution of technology, there are fewer and fewer rips. The only ones that have withstood the changing of the world are the ones which lead to the last Kingdoms of Midland, and even those are fraught with danger unless you are a member of that particular court. One such rip is the gateway to the Iron Mountain."

"Then why don't we have him lead us to the rip to find my grandfather?" Gabriel suggested, pointing at Gilchrest. The goblin tried to mumble something that sounded less than friendly.

"The little one would surely be helpful in gaining access to the Iron Mountains, but it's navigating the bloody place and the things that dwell there that chill my blood," Morgan said honestly.

"What if we went in through one of the other pockets?" Rogue suggested.

"What are you getting at, Rogue?" Lydia asked. Until then, she had just been listening and trying to comfort Finnious.

"We need to get to the Iron Mountain, but we may not have to use that pocket to cross into Midland. I've got a buddy I can reach out to who owes me a favor."

Asha tossed him her cell phone. "Be my guest." To her surprise Rogue wrapped her phone in shadow and crushed it. "Hey, do you know how much I paid for that thing?"

"It's a small price to pay for your life. Titus has got everybody from street dealers to politicians on his payroll. If somebody's tracking the cell phone signal, then using it is like painting a bull's-eye on your forehead," he said, brushing the rubble from his hands. "Besides, the person I plan to contact won't talk over the phone and I can't reach him until after sundown."

"Rogue, I know you ain't about to call in no vamps for help," Jackson said in disgust. He had a special hatred for vampires because of what they'd done to him.

Rogue smiled at him. "Vampires aren't the only things that go bump in the night."